ZANE PRESENTS

W9-CDM-868

J. LEON
PRIDGEN II

A NOVEL

HIDDEN SECRETS, HIDDEN LIVES

Dear Reader:

Thank you for picking up *Hidden Secrets, Hidden Lives* by J. Leon Pridgen. After years of acting on both the stage and screen, Leon has launched his writing career with his debut novel, set in his home base of Charlotte, N.C. We follow Travis Moore as he returns home from college with a degree and a position as an internal auditor. However, your past often will catch up with you as his "hidden" secrets eventually come to light.

Travis is now married with a child and his dark past haunts him. Shady characters and old buddies from a former lifestyle appear to the surface. He volunteers at a drug and alcohol rehab center for young men. Travis bonds with one particular teen, Baby Jar, and it becomes his mission to rescue him from a troubling environment. Meanwhile, a longtime hustler, Kwame "Bone" Brown, seeks vengeance against Travis.

Leon cleverly weaves the tale of both mainstream and urban storytelling, showing both sides of the spectrum: the corporate world and the gritty streets. The novel keeps you turning pages until the ultimate ending when all worlds collide.

I hope that you enjoy this inspirational story which shows a man—a husband, father and mentor—who emerges as a hero despite the odds.

As always, thanks for supporting the authors that I publish under my imprint, Strebor Books. All of us truly appreciate your support. If you would like to contact me, please email me at Zane@eroticanoir.com.

Blessings,

Zane

Zane
Publisher
Strebor Books International
www.simonandschuster.com/streborbooks

J. LEON PRIDGEN II

A NOVEL

HIDDEN SECRETS, HIDDEN LIVES

SBI

STREBOR BOOKS

NEW YORK LONDON TORONTO SYDNEY

Strebor Books
P.O. Box 6505
Largo, MD 20792
http://www.streborbooks.com

This book is a work of fiction. Names, characters, places and incidents are products of the author's imagination or are used fictitiously. Any resemblance to actual events or locales or persons, living or dead, is entirely coincidental.

© 2010 by J. Leon Pridgen II

All rights reserved. No part of this book may be reproduced in any form or by any means whatsoever. For information address Strebor Books, P.O. Box 6505, Largo, MD 20792.

ISBN 978-1-59309-323-5
ISBN 978-1-4391-9884-1 (ebook)
LCCN 2010940490

First Strebor Books trade paperback edition February 2011

Cover design: www.mariondesigns.com
Cover photograph: © Keith Saunders/Marion Designs

10 9 8 7 6 5 4 3 2 1

Manufactured in the United States of America

For information regarding special discounts for bulk purchases, please contact Simon & Schuster Special Sales at 1-866-506-1949 or business@simonandschuster.com

The Simon & Schuster Speakers Bureau can bring authors to your live event. For more information or to book an event, contact the Simon & Schuster Speakers Bureau at 1-866-248-3049 or visit our website at www.simonspeakers.com.

For every man, woman and child,
young or old,
everywhere,
who has made the wrong choice
for the right reasons
and
the right choice
for the wrong reasons.

ACKNOWLEDGMENTS

Hidden Secrets, Hidden Lives is a work of fiction. The characters and incidents that transpire are of the author's imagination. Any references to real people or locations are used to give the novel a sense of reality.

I would like to thank a number of young men that I have had the honor of knowing. They have helped inspire this particular work of fiction. This is your "look in the mirror" and know that there is more there than just the reflection. Sometimes, the ends do justify the means. In all of us, there is a destiny of greatness if we choose to pursue it.

To my literary agent, Sara Camilli, thank you for your continuous support of my efforts, belief in my vision, a mind that is open, an ear that always hears and a shoulder when it is necessary. You have walked page by page with me through this book and this process, and I am eternally grateful.

To my mother, Mamie Sue Mitchell Pridgen, and father, Timothy Garfield Pridgen Jr., without whom, there would be no me. Although physically not here, I spend time with them daily and they are treasured moments. Thank you for the great gift of life that you have given me. My mother's love has sustained me during times of want and plenty. From her I know what the term unconditional love means. Pop, know that I am making peace with it, some days are better than others but I am getting to it. God rest your souls, be at peace; I love you both.

To Strebor Books, thank you for a home for my words and

opening the door to the possibilities. The welcome mat is out. Zane and Charmaine, Baby, let's roll!! Keith, thanks for the magic that you make. Christine, Yona and Adiya, thank you for the light that you shine on it.

To my brother, Tim, you have always been my hero; my sisters, Stephanie and Barbara; my aunts, Mae, Jacque and Edythe; my uncles, Jerry, Ulysses, Bill, Sonny, Donald "Duck," Leon and Freddy; nephews, Timmy and Antoine; nieces, Bria, Mariah and Brionna; in-laws, Sidney "June," George "Amp" and Mike; my second mother, Margaret, and my cousins, Richard, Thomas and Renee and friends, your presence in my life, no matter how long or brief, constantly shapes, shifts and molds me. I am a better man because of you. With any and all of you, there are new discoveries every day.

To my wife, Gail, my parents have given me life but the life we share gives me purpose. Thank you for accepting me as I am. With you I have transformed from a young man into a husband and a father. You are my rock and the foundation of our family. I will never be able to thank you enough for your support and for the two special gifts that we call children. Leondra and Leon Jr. are the best of whatever I will be. You, Gail, are an amazing woman who makes that all possible. Thank you for taking the time to listen to my Northern accent!

CHAPTER 1

A secret past was the fuel to Travis Moore's fire. It woke him up in the morning and daily, he put more distance between it and himself. It had driven him to the success that he now enjoyed as the internal auditor for Home Supply Emporium, a large hardware firm. His past also had led him to where he was now driving, the Garrison Addictive Disease Center.

Travis had volunteered a few hours a week at the center and its adolescent treatment program. The last two months at work hadn't allowed him to stop by Garrison. Home Supply was on the verge of going public, and Travis recently had uncovered an embezzlement scandal that could threaten its initial public offering. Today, he had to make an exception. Jarquis Love, "Baby Jar," was in trouble.

Baby Jar had completed Garrison's treatment and recovery program two months ago. Travis had heard that Baby Jar didn't last a month back home before he was deep into the street life again. Travis wanted to find out what had gone wrong.

He followed South Boulevard from downtown until he came to Fremount Road and made the right turn leading to Garrison Center. Its appearance had changed over the last three years since Travis had started volunteering his time there.

Garrison used to strictly be a treatment center for adults with alcohol and drug abuse. Gradually, it increased its emphasis on drugs, as the problem exploded among teens. Two years ago, Garrison applied for, and was granted a government license to operate a federal halfway house. So, in came the barbed-wire fences, wooden gates, and the division of the Garrison campus to separate federal inmates from adults in treatment. Adults were separated from the adolescents.

Garrison was lucky so far. There hadn't been any incidents among the federal inmates or the residents of the treatment center. Having teen males in close proximity to federal inmates begged for something to happen. If young men had observed what happened in a federal halfway house, they might have gotten the impression that doing time wasn't so bad.

Travis parked his brand-new black Volvo in a nearby empty lot. The administrative staff and the counselors called it a day between 4:30 and 5:00 p.m. It was a few minutes after seven o'clock. Travis wasn't able to get away from work as early as he wanted. The evening counselors were the only staff remaining at the facility. He had considered not going; he would be interrupting Group. Travis was compelled to find out about Baby Jar.

Group was when all adolescents gathered in a circle for a joint therapy session monitored by two or three counselors. A teen would read the story of a recovering addict and relate his personal issues to the story as best he could. Then the counselors encouraged everyone to share their thoughts if they wanted. If anyone had an issue they wanted to discuss, the floor was open to them. Other peers offered advice to help that individual develop coping skills for various problems.

Travis removed his tie, loosened his collar, and tossed the tie into the passenger's seat before stepping out the car and feeling the cold January night. He cinched up his black cashmere overcoat as he watched his breath escape into the night air.

Slim heard the bell ring. He nodded to his co-worker to inform him that he would answer. He then excused himself from the group meeting and entered the staff office.

Slim opened the door for Travis. He looked over his shoulder through the glass; he knew most, if not all, of the teens would have their eyes in the office instead of their circle. Slim glared at them and this did the trick; all eyes went back to the group. Not one of them dared to cross Slim. He was a dark-skinned, well-defined, two hundred forty-pound man that moved with the grace of a panther. He was hard on the teens because of their experiences and potential outcome. Clarke "Slim" Duncan would do anything he could to help them.

"Come on in the house, Travis." After the kids were admonished with his eyes, he turned his attention back to Travis.

"What up with you, man? Face all tore up, chest all swoll. Little cold weather didn't make you that hot, did it?" There was silence and they stared at each other. Travis was looking up at the six-foot-seven imposing figure in front of him. Slim was looking down at his five-foot-ten frame. It was a game of Chicken to see who would be the first to flinch. "What? C'mon, you ain't mad for real?"

Slowly, the corners of Travis' mouth began to arch upward and gave way to a devilish grin. "Gotcha!" He extended his hand.

"Ah, bulls…" Slim glanced over his shoulder again. "No, you didn't." He took Travis' hand and shook it. "I was scared, though." His voice was much lower.

"Damn straight, you scared." Travis dropped his voice as well, to be mindful of the teens.

"Scared I was going to have to mop up this floor."

The new linoleum tile was laid last week and the floor was spotless. Travis was confused.

"Mop the floor?"

"Yeah, from the blood you were about to spill 'cause of me bouncin' yo' butt off this floor." The two laughed.

"Don't let the height difference or this suit fool you." Travis unbuttoned the coat and took it off. He held it out for Slim.

"That's nice. What is that, cashmere?" Travis nodded. "That thing will be on the floor if you're waiting on me to hang it up." Slim moved his head in the direction of the coat rack. "There you go, playa."

"Had to try it." Hedging past Slim to hang up his coat, he caught a glimpse of the group in session. "Got another half-hour?"

"Nah, I think they're going to finish pretty soon. Running a short one tonight; they had a long day."

Travis spotted a few new faces since the last time he was at Garrison. "What you got? Twelve, thirteen?"

"Fifteen. Two of them are missing."

The group started to get up. "Group's about to end. You want to hit this Serenity Prayer?"

"Most def'."

The two walked out the office and joined the group. The seats were in the middle of the floor in a circle. The teens stood in place and draped their arms over one another's shoulders. The enclosed circle represented unity; when one couldn't stand on his own, there was a shoulder to lean on. Donny, one of the co-workers, and the two absent teens came in the main entrance in time to join in. The circle opened for them and welcomed their return. The group always welcomed anyone; the only requirement was a desire to stop drinking or using drugs.

In unison, the group began to recite, "God, grant me the serenity to accept the things I cannot change, the courage to change the things I can, and the wisdom to know the difference." The group disbanded and proceeded to take the chairs from the circle and stack them in the room that contained vending machines.

When Group was over, Donny and Rob, two of the counselors, divided them into smaller groups of six teens each to take to a Narcotics Anonymous meeting. Three of the newest teens had to remain at the center to complete their individual study. They weren't eligible for outside meetings yet. They were doing book work on drug and alcohol addiction.

Slim sat in the office, keeping a watchful eye. He filled Travis in on Jarquis Love. Slim could tell that Travis was unusually disturbed.

"You all right?" he asked. Travis nodded his head. "You know the drill, man; it happens."

"I thought that kid was ready to change his life. I mean, I spent a lot of time with him."

Slim was analyzing his answer. He was trying to get a handle on where Travis was coming from, and why this was hitting him so hard. He'd hung out with Travis. He'd even been over to his house. He knew what kind of work had brought him to Charlotte. But he was unaware about his past. Sometimes, he felt like he didn't know Travis at all. This was one of those times. If Travis didn't volunteer information, Slim didn't ask. He felt they were fortunate to have someone like Travis come by on a volunteer basis. They didn't want to make him feel unappreciated.

"What was it about him?"

"Don't know. Guess I saw a lot of myself in him."

"How's that? He's from the hood. He didn't come from Ballantyne Country Club."

"Neither did I," Travis responded flatly. The silence echoed in the room. "I grew up in a neighborhood like his. Neighborhood… a housing project. I was smart like he is; hell, he's a lot smarter than I was. I saw education as my way out. I thought he would, too."

"Some people need a bigger push than others."

"I thought I was pushing."

"Did you share your story with him, Trav?"

"Yeah…some."

"Some?" Slim's voice was full of skepticism. "Let me guess, you left the past vague. You showed him the big picture, but you didn't let him see the fine print."

"What?" The question was simply habit. Travis knew what he meant.

"You don't give it up, man. Your past. You're wide open about your life now, what you do, and who you are. But you keep that other life to yourself. I heard you talk about school at N.C. State, living in Raleigh, the job that brought you here three years ago. Telling him you lived in a project doesn't mean shit to him. In his mind, you don't see the same stuff he sees, unless you give it to him. If you don't, it's cool. I respect that. Some things might be better kept secret. You can make that choice. You're an example; shit, probably the exception. I'm saying all this because we want to keep you coming around here. We appreciate it and, sooner or later, some of these cats will, too. Just don't be disappointed when one of them doesn't."

"I feel you." Travis was pensive, pondering his next question. "So, how did he get himself out there so fast?"

"He hooked up with the right one. See that kid over there by the desk." Sitting by the wall closest to the rooms was a young man with his back to them. His hair was a matted Afro. "He's from Park Hills, where Jarquis is from. He said Jar was raw out there. I ain't for them war stories, but the other counselor, Donny, he hit me with that, too. After we saw him that last time at the meeting, I knew it was only a matter of time."

"Donny was sure?"

"Donny said he was down with a hitter. Cat named Kwame Brown, but they call him Bone."

Travis was staring at the floor listening to Slim, but his body became rigid at the mention of the name Kwame "Bone" Brown. Travis was all too familiar with Park Hills. But his outside demeanor didn't betray what he felt inside.

"We planted the seed. Maybe he'll come back. Man, don't let me talk your head off. You better get home to your woman."

"Yeah. Thanks for filling me in."

"Fo' sho'. I give it to you straight."

Travis had left Garrison with a lot more on his mind than he had anticipated. When he had left Charlotte fourteen years ago, he had left Park Slope behind. He wasn't the same person he had been then. Park Slope was six blocks away from Park Hills, but those hoods were like peanut butter and jelly; they always went together. Kwane "Bone" Brown was a name Travis could go the rest of his life without hearing again. When Travis had left Charlotte, he would have bet money that Bone would have been dead within five years. From the sound of it, he was rolling a lot deeper than ever.

CHAPTER 2

Hustling on the streets was his high and the promise of revenge was a constant motivator for Kwame Brown. That promise was close to being fulfilled. He had been successful in infiltrating his target's life without raising any suspicion.

Sixteen years had passed since he had looked him in the eye. They were friends until he had abandoned Kwame. He could understand Perry not being in touch with him when he was sent to the Jacksonville Juvenile Detention Center for a year. They had agreed on keeping a distance. To protect his partner, he would take the humble. After the year, they were supposed to be rollin' deep for real. After that one year, it wasn't like that, though. Perry was gone and nobody knew where. Perry had disappeared into thin air. He had left three keys and thirty-five thousand dollars in cash for Kwame. Bruce Bowen, a mutual friend, had kept it for him until he returned.

Bruce had advised that he was watching the store, but it was his store and he could get it anytime he desired. He wanted to get right back out there and start flipping that shit, but he was going to wait on his partner. Bruce kept running the show while Kwame waited to make his move. Four months later, he was tired of waiting for Perry to show up. He hadn't heard a thing from him. If that nigga didn't want to get down, then fuck Perry; it was time for Kwame to get paid. But the seeds of his contempt were firmly planted.

Over the next fifteen years, those seeds flowered and bloomed.

Kwame counted the days, knowing that the time would come when Perry would pay for his disloyalty. He didn't know when or where, but he could feel it coming. Six months ago, the opportunity finally arrived.

Kwame discovered Perry by accident. Kwame had gone to Garrison's halfway house to visit one of his homies after he was released from prison. As he entered Garrison and drove toward the back gate, he noticed a familiar walk nearing the front gate. The stride in the gait grabbed his attention. He'd never forget that walk. Nobody he'd ever known walked like Perry. Perry had upright nobility about himself, even when they were kids. Kwame barely got a glimpse of him. He was older and heavier, but he was sure it was Perry. By the time Kwame doubled back for another look, Perry was gone.

Parking the car and waiting was the only thing Kwame had on his mind. He never visited his homie that night. He parked his car among the other cars by the back gate. He leaned his seat back, turned on his music and waited. The thought of gunning him down right there in cold blood made his pulse race. The anticipation of watching Perry die at his hands excited Kwame.

As he sat, his mind raced through the memories. History had bound these two together and that motherfucker had quit on him, like he meant nothing. Kwame had done a year at the detention center and the thought of ratting Perry out never had crossed his mind. Yet, Perry had abandoned him when he had needed him the most.

They had played together in sandlots and the makeshift playgrounds in the projects. They had eaten fried bologna with the government block cheese at his mama's. Kwame was right there beside him when Perry had gotten his first piece; hell, they had shared it, like they'd done everything else. That was the day that Perry had nicknamed him, "Bone."

Kwame had had his back when his crackhead brothers had beaten on him and had tried to steal what little he had. He was there for Perry when his mother had started using drugs. He had watched over his boy when his mother would go missing for a day or two on the weekends. Later, it would turn into days at a time, then weeks. When Perry's mom had fallen off completely, it was Kwame who had known how to make some fast money that could keep Perry's mom off the streets. That's when they had started running dope.

Perry was always a good student and Kwame knew they could bust a knot, but he had no idea that Perry had the skills to take their game to another level. Within two years, they were running their own set. They had their own acquisition, manufacturing and distribution operation. The two of them were only sixteen. Perry was the square. He still went to school every day and ran their operation at night, a little CEO. Perry set everything up and Kwame usually executed it. That's the way Kwame liked it, though. He couldn't get enough of the streets; he loved it. The melody of the streets had him whipped. He loved the gunfire, drugs, the beat-downs, the money, the hoes and the jewelry. Everything the streets had to offer, he hungrily embraced.

Perry was constantly warning him to slow down and chill out. Perry used to tell Kwame that he was calling attention to himself. Perry tried to get him to understand that there were haters out there that would hand him over to the police. They had cats twice their age working for them who resented them. He knew if they weren't tied into the right people, their shit would be jacked. Perry cautioned that they had to be careful with the streets and how they played them. Perry knew it would be much worse to step on the wrong toes than to get jacked or busted.

Kwame didn't believe that shit stunk unless he smelled it himself. That had led to his downfall. It was one of those nights when

Kwame was itching with that street fever. He had wanted to get out there, put his hands on the product, crack some heads, and smoke some weed. He had gotten careless. Po-Po had caught him with four small crack rocks in a vial.

They did not waste any time. Before Kwame could blink his eyes, he was in a detention center in Jacksonville, N.C. The things he'd experienced in his two-plus years on the street hadn't prepared him for what lay ahead in the next year. The innocence of his youth that was left was ripped from him. Three seventeen-year-olds attacked him within days of his arrival. They had beaten him down and then taken turns raping him. Who he thought he was on the street didn't mean shit up in there. There was no one he could tell about his humiliation. He had suffered through it alone. He had survived that hell and had returned home to find out Perry had left him behind. Perry had moved on, without a trace. Until now.

Forty minutes had passed before Perry emerged from behind the wooden gate. This time, Kwame had gotten a good look at him and without a doubt this was his old running partner. Instinctively, Kwame reached for his nickel-plated Glock. As he sat up, he noticed Perry at the gate with a kid. He held the gun with the care that a mother takes with her child. His hesitation for the kid made him realize what he was about to do. He'd been swept up in his emotions and wasn't thinking.

Why was Perry there? What was he doing with a kid from the rehab center? He looked at the kid again and recognized him from Park Hills. He was a runner for one of Kwame's dealers. Why was Perry fucking with that kid?

That's when Kwame decided to take things slow. He didn't want Perry to know that he'd been discovered. So for the last six months, Kwame had tracked him. He discovered where he worked, where he lived, who his wife was and what she did. He knew they had a son. Kwame was envious of Perry's life and what he had become. He also had found out a lot about the kid he had spotted with Perry at Garrison. His name was Jarquis Love, "Baby Jar."

Kwame took Baby Jar under his wing. Jar was going to be his superstar. He was going to be the man to end Perry's life. Jar didn't know it yet, but this weekend he would do another man's bidding, or pay with his life.

CHAPTER 3

The grilled salmon with a twist of lemon was seasoned to perfection. The broccoli, carrot and cauliflower mix was sautéed in the wok with a drop of butter and a pinch of pepper. Not too much pepper. Although she loved it, she wanted to be considerate of Travis. Too much pepper and he would be sneezing his head off. The Mrs. Smith's pecan pie had baked in the oven. She had her mother's homemade recipe, but time didn't permit her to make one tonight. She had the whipped cream to go with it. Tonight, it would serve more than one purpose. The candles were lit and the wine was chilling. Michael, their three-year-old son, had already eaten, was bathed and ready for bed.

Kenya Moore wanted to make up for the tense conversation that she'd had with Travis earlier. Their fifth wedding anniversary was coming up on Sunday. There was no way that she was going to let the rut they were in continue. The dinner and the black body stocking with the crotchless opening that she wore under her plush Carolina blue cotton bathrobe would see to that. The time she had put in at the gym was still paying dividends. The brother was going to be in trouble.

That was the plan at six-thirty. She was still clinging to it at seven-thirty. But now, at a quarter of nine, the plan was aborted. The dinner was cold; the body stocking was even colder; and she had taken it upon herself to start in on the wine.

"And he didn't show up," Kenya said. The phone was cradled between her ear and shoulder. She was seething, but trying to keep her voice down. She didn't want to wake Michael who was asleep in her arms.

"He didn't?" Lisa responded.

"Hell no! Didn't call. Nothing." She laid Michael in the bed and covered him.

"Did you try to call him? Maybe something happened or…" She was offering an excuse for Travis.

"No, I didn't and I'm not going to. If he has better things to do than come home, then so be it." She left the room, closed the door behind her and started to raise her voice. "I'm tired of this shit. I go to all of this trouble and he doesn't even bring his ass home." She was headed back downstairs.

"You think he's creepin'? We can find out. Charlotte's not that big." So much for being a champion for Travis.

"No, I don't think it's anything like that."

"Girl, he's a man. Don't put anything past him. I wouldn't."

"Lisa."

"I don't wan…"

"Lisa!" Kenya didn't want to let Lisa get a good roll on the train tracks of negativity.

"Why is it that you want to turn my issues into sexual ones? I told you that our problems don't have sex at the core of them."

"That's what you think. Look, Girl, I…"

"Lisa!!" Kenya cut her off. She wanted to be heard, not lectured.

Any comment that Lisa was going to make would be held in check within the walls of her mouth. Lisa wasn't the ideal person to speak to, but she couldn't reach Jasmine. Lisa always had advice for married people, but she had no significant other to speak of. Since her divorce three years ago, she'd experienced a number of short-lived relationships with single men, almost single men, and a couple of straight-up married men. Jasmine, on the other hand, seemed to have everything together. The three of them would hook up at the gym tomorrow. Kenya would talk to her then, so Lisa would have to do for tonight.

"Sorry, Lisa," she said, after she had a second to cool off. "I didn't mean to snap at you. It's this other stuff on my mind."

"It's okay. I know I can get going sometimes. So, where do you think he's at?"

"Probably Garrison. He mentioned something about needing to get by there the other day."

"He's still messing around over there?"

"Yeah, but he hasn't been there in two months, maybe."

"Why does he do that?" She trailed off in thought.

Kenya could almost see Lisa's wheels spinning to figure out what Travis' motives were. "He has a need to try to reach some of those kids. At least, that what he tells me. I really don't know what else is behind it."

"Have you asked?"

"Yeah, but he just leaves it at that. I think it has to do with his past. But Travis won't go into much detail about it. He's like night and day sometimes, and the nights are getting longer. He's so open about our relationship and Michael, but he gives me nothing about his life before college. I thought that when we moved here, he would finally open up about his childhood, but it's been worse. It's like he's holding on tighter to that information and our communication has suffered because of it. Then, he's got more pressure at work and…" Kenya thought she heard a car approaching. "Hold on a second." She could hear the garage door opening. "Travis just pulled in. I'll call you back."

"Don't worry about it. I'll see you in the morning. Eleven o'clock sharp, right?"

"Right." She hung the phone on the cradle and went to have a seat at the dining room table. Surrounded by the cold food, she waited. Seven years of her life had been spent with Travis, the last five as his wife. She had borne his child and had discussed having more, but she wasn't willing to if their life was going to continue like this. Kenya felt like they had hit a wall. They were losing touch and she was tired of being patient. She would address all of her concerns tonight.

Travis entered through the garage and headed toward the kitchen. He stopped briefly at the hall closet to hang up his coat. He bypassed the dimly lit dining room and went upstairs. Kenya heard his footsteps leading to their bedroom, then the bathroom and back out. He went to Michael's room and stayed for a few seconds. Travis had developed the habit of holding his son for a few minutes every night, especially when he got home after Michael had gone to bed.

"Hey, Buddy," Travis whispered. "How ya' doin'? Your daddy was the man today at work. What'cha think 'bout that?" He waited for a response that he knew wasn't coming and gazed at his son nestled in his arms. Travis smiled at his boy. He noticed Michael returned his smile. Then, he heard the familiar sound of Michael popping off a little gas. "Thanks, man." Travis shook his head. "Where is your mamma, man?" He laid Michael back down. "Don't worry; I'll find her. Good looking out, Pup." Michael wasn't old enough to be referred to as his dog.

"Kenya?" Travis called from the top of the stairs. He waited for a response. Nothing. "Kenya."

Kenya didn't respond immediately. She was still trying to figure out how she was going to play this out.

"I'm down here," she finally said.

"Kenya? Why are you sitting in the dark?" Travis paused. For the first time, he smelled the hint of salmon that was in the air. *Shit*, he thought, *I hope she didn't cook*. He realized he was wrong.

As he took the steps downstairs, he could see her sitting in the dining room. She had used the good china for the place settings. He spotted the half-burnt, extinguished candle.

"You ahh…cooked, huh?" Travis asked nervously as he neared her.

"Yes," Kenya stated coldly.

"Hmm." His eyes roamed around the room aimlessly. "Sorry," he offered weakly.

"Yeah…So, what took you so long?"

"I ended up leaving work late. Then, I stopped by Garrison."

"And you couldn't call?" Kenya chided.

"I told you I was going to stop at Garrison one night this week." He was on the defense now.

"I go to all this trouble for nothing."

"I didn't know you were going to all this trouble for me."

"It was a surprise. One of the things about surprising someone is not telling them that you are going to surprise them!"

"Hey! Hold up…" Travis wasn't about to get in an argument with Kenya. He already had enough on his mind. "Don't you think you might be taking this to a level that we don't need to get to?"

"No, I don't. I'm tired of waiting on you for everything."

Travis looked at her and cocked his head. Her statement wasn't referring to only dinner. There was something that she needed to say.

"What's on your mind, K?"

"Nothing." She folded her arms.

"You sure?"

"Didn't I say nothing."

Travis studied her. Her body language screamed to say something more, but she did not. "Okay," he said calmly. He took a seat at the table.

If she wouldn't talk about what was bothering her, he wasn't going to try to figure it out. Although he knew what it was. It was what was at the heart of the majority of the arguments they'd had since they had moved to Charlotte three years ago. He didn't understand why she always harped on the life he'd left behind some fifteen years ago. His mother was dead and he had no family to speak of. He had taken Kenya to the cemetery to see where his mom was buried right after they'd moved. In his mind, that was a huge step. They had never really talked about it. As far as he was concerned, that was the extent of what he needed to share. He never took her back. Kenya always wanted to know more. He had given what he could and, frankly, he was tired of her asking. He had kept that part of his life to himself because it was in her best interest.

"Are you going to warm this up?" Travis was in the mood to agitate her.

No, he didn't. Kenya couldn't believe what she'd heard. "Excuse me?"

"I asked if you were going to warm this up."

"No." She stared a hole right through him.

"Fine. I'll do it myself." He went into the kitchen to heat the food. He was stalling for time. He wanted to divert the conversation from the direction it was headed. Once the food was sufficiently warmed, he went back to the dining room.

"The food looks delicious." He waited for Kenya to respond. She didn't. He could see she was not going to make this easy. He had to try another tactic. "Thank you for cooking for me."

"You're welcome." Kenya was still miles away.

Travis realized that he had to give her something to get the conversation going, but what? He couldn't talk about the potential embezzlement case at work. He damn sure wasn't going to talk about his past.

"How are things going with the charity event you're working on?"

"Fine." Kenya rolled her eyes. She knew he was trying to guide the conversation.

Travis wasn't getting anywhere. If the conversation was to move, he had to come with something stronger.

"Do you mind if I talk to you about something?"

"Nobody has ever stopped you." Kenya was hinting at something else.

"Kenya, can you give me a break? I'm trying to have a conversation with you, not an argument, okay? I should have been here sooner. There was something going on with one of the kids that used to be at Garrison." He stopped to take a bite of the salmon. "Mmm, mmm, this is delicious."

"Even though it's been sitting for the last three hours?" Kenya's comment was laced with skepticism, but she was giving in, a little.

"You know, once you put your foot in it, it stays there."

"Don't try to play me; you know I'm mad at you right now."

"You're not mad."

"Why not?"

"If you were mad, you'd be wearing flannel by now with your head wrapped. What you got on underneath that robe?"

"This doesn't mean a thing. I'm showing you what you could have had."

"Missed out on. Hell, you don't have to go to work tomorrow." Travis smiled. He spotted a hint of a smile on Kenya's face, but it didn't last long.

"No, but I do have some things planned for tomorrow."

"My bad. What do you have planned?" He was breaking the ice.

"Find me somebody who doesn't mind talking to me about anything." She was only half-playing. The tide hadn't turned for Travis yet.

"So now I don't like talking about anything?" Travis was agitated. He was trying to make an allowance for what he presumed to be the wine speaking, but there was only so much he would listen to.

"No, you'll talk 'til the cows come home as long as it's something you want to talk about." She looked at Travis while he took another bite of salmon. He acted as if she hadn't said anything. She thought, *the gate is open, what the hell? Let the flood begin.* "Let's talk about your mother."

"What is there to talk about? She's gone. It's done. I've said all I'm going to say about her."

"What do you feel about it?" She pushed for more.

"What is there to feel? I did what I could for her."

"You did what you could for her?" She was on to something.

"Damn it, K, just leave it alone! It's not the time." He stared at her. That conversation was over. There was silence.

"Like always." She sat there fuming. Why couldn't he share that part of his life with her? If they were supposed to be everything to each other, why was he holding back part of himself? This wasn't fair to her. If she was willing to give all of herself to him, then she deserved to have those feelings reciprocated. Why couldn't he understand that? Kenya thought they had a good marriage, but something was keeping it from being a great marriage. Maybe it was something about being in Charlotte. This never used to bother her. She was not near her family and friends in the Raleigh/Durham area. She missed that connection and sometimes felt alone here. Then, she was isolated from his past. She had introduced him to everybody she knew at home, but she never met any of his childhood friends. She knew his co-workers, and people he'd met since they'd moved to Charlotte, but nobody from his past. After all their years together, why was that?

"Did you hear what I said?" Travis interrupted her thoughts.

"No, I didn't."

"I was telling you about Baby Jar."

"Baby what?"

"Baby Jar. The kid at Garrison." Travis continued as if there wasn't a problem in the world between them. "Slim told me he fell off as soon as he got home."

"Who cares, Travis? I really don't want to hear about some kid on crack."

"What? I didn't say he was on crack. Are you listening to what I'm saying here? I'm trying to tell you about this smart kid who got caught up in dealing dope."

"He couldn't have been too smart for him to get caught up in that crap anyway."

"You think him getting caught in that life has something to do with his level of intelligence?"

"Who in their right mind would view choosing that lifestyle as an intelligent choice?"

"You don't know what kind of options that child was presented with."

"Nor do I care. I don't know why you do."

Wine or no wine, Kenya was out of control. Travis was going to put a stop to it. He had to make her understand what he was trying to do.

"I'm trying to give something to those kids. Eighty percent of the kids that come through Garrison are black. The role models they see are on the corners selling dope. By me being there, I show them that a black man can be anything he wants to be. Baby Jar can be anything he wants to be. He needs guidance. They need guidance."

"That boy is just like all the other ones that are selling that shit. It's who they are and it's who they will be. It's on them to change their lives, not you. You've got a son upstairs that you can influence. You're wasting your time at Garrison."

"So what you're telling me is that these kids, because of their current situation, aren't ever going to be worth shit."

"If you want to put it that way, fine. That's what I'm saying."

"You really don't know what some of these guys can be. They may not come from two-parent homes that resemble the Huxtables. Just because they don't have the same starting line as other people doesn't mean they can't run a better race." Travis pushed his plate away. At the moment, he didn't have a desire for her food or anything else. He got up from the table and went upstairs. Kenya could hear him grab his keys. Within minutes, he was down the stairs and headed for the garage. He snatched a coat out of the closet and reached for the door to the garage.

"Where do you think you're going?"

"For a drive, to get some air."

"Why?"

"You spit on something that I consider to be important and I don't want to be around you right now." Travis didn't want to say something that he would regret. It would be better for him to be alone for a while.

"What time will you be back?"

"I'm a grown damn man," he answered coldly. "I'll be back when I get back." He opened the door and slammed it behind him.

Kenya looked at the half-eaten meal, listening for the car to crank. She heard the car starting and Travis backing out.

Maybe it was too much wine; or she should have told him what she had planned. Perhaps she shouldn't have mentioned his mother. This wasn't how she had wanted to kick off the celebration for their fifth wedding anniversary.

CHAPTER 4

The black Volvo S80 made its way off the 485 loop and back onto I-77 heading north. Any other night Travis would be doing the speed limit, but tonight he wasn't paying attention to it. He had no idea he was approaching eighty in a fifty-five. When Mr. Do Right hit him with the blue lights, he took note.

"Ain't that a bitch?" Travis mumbled as he looked in his rear-view mirror.

He slowed the car immediately, hoping that the police car would continue past him. It didn't. The patrol car fell in behind him and slowed as he slowed, lights still blazing. Travis continued to slow down until he could pull his vehicle off the interstate and onto the shoulder. When he came to a complete stop, he killed the engine.

As Travis watched the rearview mirror, he could see that the officer had his head down, probably running his tag. Travis prepared for the officer by pulling out his driver's license and registration. Travis wanted to make sure that when the officer arrived, he didn't mistake any move he made for a sudden move. There had been a number of incidents recently where routine traffic stops had turned into unfortunate accidents. Travis intended to keep his eyes on the officer, making eye contact.

The interior light came on in the patrol car as the trooper prepared to exit the vehicle. As the officer stood, Travis could see him place his hat on top of his head. The side mirror gave Travis a better opportunity to watch him as he approached. He held his lit flashlight in his left hand and his right hand was on his pistol.

Travis put his hands on the steering wheel in the ten and two positions so they would be clearly visible. He damn sure didn't want to be an accident, and Barney Fife looked like he had an itchy trigger finger. Travis couldn't get a really good look at his face; he was blocked out by his headlights.

When the officer arrived, Travis waited to roll down the window. He stared straight ahead until the officer knocked on the window with his flashlight. Travis hit the automatic button.

"Is there a problem, Officer?" Travis was still trying to get a good look at him.

"License and registration."

Travis moved slowly to hand the information to the officer. He didn't want to alarm the officer, and it was cold outside. He handed the information to the officer; their eyes met briefly. Strange, there was a familiarity about the officer, but Travis dismissed it.

As Travis rolled up his window, the officer turned and walked to his patrol car. His steps were quick in the cold weather, but the further away he got, the slower his pace became, until he stopped. The officer had his flashlight on the information. He studied the license. The face was familiar to him. Older, yes, but he definitely remembered the face. He looked back at Travis' car, then at the license again. P. Travis Moore. That was the face. The officer walked quickly back to the car.

"Excuse me, Sir. Is your name Perry? Perry Moore?"

Perry Moore. Travis hadn't been referred to as Perry...since he'd left Charlotte. Hell, he couldn't remember the last time someone had called him Perry; that was another life.

"Sorry, Officer, my name isn't Perry."

"Perry Moore. I know that face! From Park Slope."

Oh shit, Travis thought, *who is this and how the fuck does he know me like that*?

"You don't know me, man? Rick Nixon."

"I don't....Rick Nixon?" The mention of the name caught him.

"Lite Brite!" Rick stepped back to let Travis get a good look at him.

"Lite Brite!" Travis yelled. "Nigga, what you doing? A cop? State trooper, you got to be kidding me. They're taking anybody, ain't they?"

"Yo, P, get out the car, man." Rick couldn't contain his excitement.

Travis stepped out and the two gave each other a pound, then embraced.

"Man, look at you. You lost some weight and stretched out, didn't you? You look good, boy!" Travis said.

Rick was real light-skinned with green eyes. He stood six-foot-one and looked to weigh about two hundred pounds. The last time Travis had seen him, he was only five-foot-seven and weighed over two hundred and thirty pounds.

"Where the hell you been, man? I haven't seen you since the night after you graduated. Don't tell me you been here all this time?" Rick asked.

"No. I just moved back here about three years ago."

"No shit."

"What about you? You the policeman."

"Yeah, I took your advice and got my shit together," Rick said.

"My advice? What are you talking about?"

"You don't remember?"

"What?"

"You beat my ass down." Rick eyed Travis. "You don't remember. I was a freshman when you were a senior. You caught me trying to sell some dope. It was my first time and you beat the shit out of me. You told me if I quit selling, you'd put some money in my pocket. Ten bucks for an A, seven for a B, five for a C, and nothing if I got anything else. That was when I was fourteen."

"Shit, I remember coming off that paper, but I don't remember beating you up." Travis gave a slight grin; they both knew he was bullshittin'. Travis recalled what Slim had said about planting a seed. "You used to be on me like a bill collector with those report cards. That first one was five B's and two C's."

"Forty-five dollars." Rick smiled and then it faded; he became hesitant. He could remember where that money had come from. He looked at the car Travis was driving. "What do you do nowadays?" He hoped he wasn't into the stuff he used to be.

"I'm the manager of internal audit for Home Supply Emporium."

"No shit." He was relieved. Even if it was a lie, he wanted it to be true. "That Home Supply is growing."

"It's getting ready to go public. You better get you some of that when it hits."

"I'll keep my eyes open." There was an awkward silence. "So what happened to you? It was like you disappeared after you graduated."

"I didn't waste any time leaving for school. I left the day after graduation for N.C. State. Didn't want anybody to know where I was. Just was ready to leave it all behind."

"I feel you." He looked down at the license and registration. "Here, take this back." He handed them to him. "Do you remember what you told me when you gave me that money?"

"I asked you how you felt when you got that report card," Travis said.

"That's right. I was proud of myself."

"That sense of pride, nobody can take away from you," Travis added.

"You told me that the money would be spent, but I'd still have that grade. I may not have always gotten what I was due, but I'd always have what I'd earned."

"There you go." Travis got back inside his car and reached over to his glove compartment and pulled out his business card. He jotted down his cell number. "Give me a holler, Rick." He handed Rick his card.

"No doubt. I want to find out more about that stock. Take mine, too." Rick pulled out his card. "Have you been back to the old hood?"

"I've been around that way a couple of times, but I haven't been up in it."

"Me either. Ain't nobody over there for me to see."

"I know what you mean," Travis agreed.

"Slow it down, Perr…I guess it's Travis, right? All us troopers didn't grow up in Park Slope."

"Good looking out, Rick. Thanks." He gave Rick a smile.

Rick stared at Travis. "Thank *you*. Good looking out."

There was mutual respect between these two old hoodrats. Rick went back to the patrol car, turned off the lights, put the cruiser in gear and pulled up beside Travis. He honked his horn, pointed at him and hit the gas.

Travis thought about his good fortune. He was lucky to have been pulled over by Rick; otherwise that would have been a one hundred and fifteen-dollar ticket. He considered going home but he wasn't ready. He put his car in gear and eased onto the interstate. It was up to the car to take him wherever it would lead him.

CHAPTER 5

A half-hour had passed since Rick had stopped Travis. The road had led him to Park Gardens on Statesville Road. It was the cemetery where his mother was buried. The cemetery had a twelve-foot-high gate that surrounded the perimeter. The graveyard at night wasn't the most inviting place to be, but it had been too long since Travis had visited.

He had only been to his mother's gravesite three times in the fifteen years since her funeral. The first was on graduation night, before he'd left for college the following day. The second time was when he'd brought Kenya, right after they'd moved to Charlotte. He wanted to tell her the story then—where he'd come from and who he was before he'd left Charlotte. He couldn't bring himself to do it. He had come to the gravesite again the following day. He didn't know why. He had stood in front of her grave until he had lost track of time. Maybe he had wanted to make peace with her and the life she had led. Maybe it was his own forgiveness he had needed, but it never came to him.

Travis drove into Park Gardens and followed the road he had driven in his mind many times. The road went to the right, dipped and curved back to the left. As he came up the hill, he spotted his mother's headstone. He had ordered and paid for it himself. He had first noticed the headstone when he'd brought Kenya with him; the sight of it had moved nothing in him then or now. He came to a stop right in front of her grave. Travis got out the car and stood at the same place he had stood three years ago.

The gravesite sat in such a way that it overlooked Park Slope. Travis had picked the plot. When she was alive, she couldn't escape her circumstances. Now she rested above those circumstances. She was above the Kwame Browns and Jarquis Loves and all the madness of Park Slope and Park Hills. She was let go—and then Travis realized: it was time for him to let go of what he'd held on to for so long.

Travis got back into his car. He finally had what he needed from this place. He put the car in gear and headed for the front gate. As he neared the gate, his mind gave way to thoughts about Baby Jar and Bone. If he was to make peace with his past, he was going to have to revisit it.

Travis turned right onto Oaklawn Road. It was two miles of road not to venture off if you were not familiar with the surroundings. Travis wasn't familiar with the area anymore. He steered off Oaklawn into Park Hills and his instincts took over. He remembered these streets and his eyes shifted from left to right. Travis knew that eyes were on him. A shiny, new, black Volvo couldn't hit this neighborhood without calling attention. It wouldn't be long before somebody would be looking to jack him or turn him out. It was a shot in the dark, but he hoped to run across Baby Jar in this concrete jungle.

Activity on the street was already brisk. The street pharmacists were busy plying their trade. Travis rolled through the streets slowly. Everything was different but, at the same time, nothing had changed. The hustle was still the same. Lookouts were on four corners, within two blocks of where the deal goes down. Then he noticed something different as he circled the block for the second time. Technology had made its way into the game. Some of these brothers appeared to be communicating with one another with smartphones. A block away from where the pickup was made was the money man. You placed your order and gave him the money. He'd give a signal and send you to the pick-up spot. If they had headsets on, you'd mistake this for a McDonald's drive-thru.

This was the hot spot. This is the kind of shit that Bone would be running—nine-man operation. Those were the people that Travis could count, so he knew there had to be at least three other people involved that he couldn't see. Travis was surprised at how quickly his street sense had dissected this operation. This was the kind of setup he had put together when he had played the game. This was Bone's operation. He could smell it and feel it. Somewhere in this mix was Baby Jar.

Travis had thoughts of seeing what was happening in Park Slope, but had decided against it. Instead, he looped around Park Hills two more times. He hoped to draw the right attention to himself; maybe Bone or Baby Jar might find him.

He stopped his car near the hot spot. Travis watched the activity and pondered it. All this hustling wasn't for any real money. Street-level hustlers had a little flash money. They could get some sneakers, clothes, jewelry, or gold fronts. Maybe a hooptie and throw some rims on it. They could eat, but they weren't getting anywhere. They couldn't buy a house or a new car. At the end of this road was nothing but problems. They could only run the game for so long before they had to take a humble. The game was set up for the fall, and the street was the only thing that would welcome them back. Jails, institutions or death were at the end of these roads, unless they knew how to get out of the game. And nobody was showing them that. There wasn't a mentoring program to get the young brothers off the street and out of this life.

Travis wasn't comfortable here anymore. It was time to shit or get off the pot. He needed to see if his suspicions were right, but after watching this circle of insanity, he thought it might be best for him to go home to his wife and straighten that out before he tried to save the world. Baby Jar and Bone would be there when it was time to step to them. This was their world; let them have it.

FROM THE THIRD FLOOR OF AN ABANDONED APARTMENT building that was adjacent to the corner, there were two sets of eyes watching the black Volvo. One pair of eyes had a trace of fear when they watched the car. He recognized the car that belonged to Travis Moore. Travis had showed it to him before he had left rehab. He had told him he could have one identical to it if he continued to work to improve his life through education. He was inspired. Now, two months later, seeing Travis, he was shocked and ashamed of how far he'd fallen so quickly. Whatever he was feeling, Baby Jar dared not show that kind of weakness to the man standing next to him.

The other pair of eyes was cold and calculating. The revenge he had been seeking for the past fifteen years was coming to fruition. His plan was falling into place and that motherfucker was taking the bait. He was banking on Travis to come looking for the kid. Kwame cut his eyes toward the sixteen-year-old on his left. The boy had no idea how valuable he was to him.

"Like I said, boy, you always got to keep your eyes open. That ma'fucker right there, in that Volvo, that nigga didn't pick up, right? Didn't drop. He up to some shit. That ma'fucker up to some shit! He'll be back. Always keep your eyes open for Po-Po. They could be driving anything."

"Uh-huh," Baby Jar stammered. He figured that Bone was going to ask him if he recognized the car.

"Ma'fuckers like that, you got to be ready for 'em. It's them or you out here. Anybody threatens your shit; they got to go with the quickness. Don't matter who it is. You feel me?"

Baby Jar gave a nervous nod. His mind told him to form words, but his mouth wouldn't obey.

"Don't crack on me. To run this here, you got to be ready to lay anybody down for it. Could be your best friend, your brother, sister, mama, daddy or your favorite bitch. Hear me? You don't put nothing before this shit right here." Bone pulled out a vial of crack and held it up for Jar to see. "This is what makes you money, cuz. This right here can make your life worth living! Do you feel me!?"

"Yes, sir," Jar answered with conviction. He was over the shock and shame. He was going to play Bone's game and come out on top.

Bone loved what he heard. He had Baby Jar's ear; he was getting in his head. Occupying some space in there. Soon, he would manipulate his puppet to do whatever he wanted him to do.

CHAPTER 6

Home was where Travis belonged. Visiting his mother's gravesite had done him good. He was finally making some peace toward her. He didn't know why it had taken so long. For so many years he had resented her, her weakness and what she had forced him to become. He had come so close to losing himself to that life. When she had died, Travis had to get away from what he was becoming. He'd lost a mother and two brothers to that lifestyle. There was another brother that was in prison and Travis had no idea if or when he would get out.

His childhood best friend, his dog, Kwame Brown, was still locked into that life. Travis couldn't recall a time when he didn't know Kwame. They'd started running dope together but, by the time they were seventeen, their relationship had been severed. It wasn't their decision. Kwame was in the custody of the juvenile correctional system and Travis couldn't have any part of him. Tonight, when he saw what his old life involved, he was glad that he had left that all behind him.

Travis realized it was time for him to share this part of his life with his wife. There was a lot of ground to cover and a lot of it wasn't pretty, but it was time to trust her with it. It was up to Travis to tear down this wall that was building up between them. He could already feel some of the burdens of his past rolling away.

Travis pulled up to a dark house, but he was aware that Kenya was inside wide awake. She could never go to sleep when he was out of town on business until he would call to tell her good night.

Truth was, Travis couldn't go to sleep until he heard her voice either.

Once in the house, Travis didn't waste any time getting to their bedroom. He stood in the doorway and allowed his eyes to adjust to the dark. He focused on his wife and could see that she was lying under the comforter. Mentally, he retraced the symmetry of her body; her caramel skin and the thighs that his hands took pleasure in massaging after a strenuous workout. He wanted to caress her body and make love to her, but there were other things he needed to address at the moment.

"Kenya." He spoke in a whisper. He didn't want to risk waking Michael.

Kenya's body stirred. She pushed the comforter back and strained to see Travis. She could see his silhouette leaning against the doorway. She didn't respond but looked over at the clock.

"Are you okay?" Travis asked.

Kenya rolled her eyes. "Does it matter to you?"

"Yes, it does," Travis said after taking a deep breath. "I'm sorry for anything that I may have done to upset you." His voice was absent of any of the sarcasm that it had held earlier.

"Uh-huh." Kenya was still skeptical of him.

"I am."

Kenya sat up. She sensed something different about Travis. "Travis, I shouldn't have said som…"

"Don't worry about it," Travis cut her off. "You wouldn't have said those things if it weren't for me. The way I can be." Travis started to move toward Kenya slowly. As he walked, he began to drop his head. "I'm sorry."

"Travis, are you okay?"

"Yeah." He lifted his head and gave a half-smile in her direction. "Thanks for asking."

Kenya was still upset over how things had gone earlier, but she was willing to let that slide for the moment. She could read Travis. There was something on his mind and her instincts took over. She opened her arms to him. Travis sat on the bed, faced her, closed his eyes and gave himself to her warm and tender arms. Her loving and gentle touch reassured him.

"Five years," Travis said in a hushed tone. "I don't know why you've put up with me."

Kenya continued to hold him and not speak.

"The last three years since we've been here, I haven't been there for you. Not the way I should have been. It's like I've been keeping some distance between us, not letting you in on certain things."

"Travis, what happened to you tonight?"

"I finally realized that I needed to make peace with my past, to accept it. I've been trying to go around it. Trying to find other ways to avoid it instead of taking it head-on."

"What are you talking about? Where did you go?"

Travis drew a long breath. "I went to visit my mother." Travis could sense Kenya's body tighten ever so slightly. "It was time for me to. I felt like that was where I needed to start making peace."

"Did you?"

"I'm starting to; I need your help, though."

"I'll do whatever you need me to do."

"Just listen to me. Don't pass judgment; try to understand."

"I will."

Travis knew how his wife thought; she had no idea of the things she was about to hear. He sat up so he could look at her. He wanted to stay in the comfort of her arms, but what he was about to share with her needed to be said face to face.

"K, I left a life behind because I didn't want to live it anymore."

Travis waited for the inevitable questions that would be forthcoming. She was going to start the inquisition as she had done so many times before. There were no questions; Kenya waited for him to continue. Travis stood, turned and walked back toward the door.

"You want anything?" Travis waited for a reply from Kenya. He turned halfway toward her. He was trying to stall for some time. He wasn't sure if he was ready to tell her about his previous life in Charlotte. He also knew that if he left the room, he wasn't going to ever tell her. He looked into Kenya's face. She still didn't say anything. Her words were absent. Her silence spoke volumes. They locked eyes on each other. Without saying a word, Kenya persuaded him to free himself of his past.

"My mother was a crackhead." His voice quivered as he spoke those words. "That's why she got killed when she was thirty-seven years old. She was messing around with a drug dealer and got caught in the middle of his bullshit." Travis walked over to Kenya. "I was sixteen. That's when I knew I couldn't keep doing what I was doing."

"What was that?"

Travis stopped walking and took a deep breath. "I started selling dope when I was fourteen." His voice was low. He was recalling a dark time in his life.

"You did what?"

"I sold dope." He spoke louder. "I was fourteen when my mom got into using crack. I remember her smoking weed all the time. She even used heroin; but once she smoked crack, she was gone. She did whatever it took to get it. Didn't matter when it was, she would do anything to get high. My mom prostituted herself to get high." The contempt was building in his voice. "She would suck a dick so she could suck a crackpipe. That ain't the kind of shit a fourteen-year-old kid should see his mom doing. She wasn't paying the bills and there wasn't ever any food in the house. She would go missing for days at a time. I had three older brothers and they didn't care about her or me. They were all involved with drugs in one way or the other. One of my brothers tried to deal, but he became his own best customer. They never looked out for her or me. I was a smart kid but looking at the situation, I didn't know what to do. I had to get my mom off the streets. I tried to stay away from it, but I got sucked into dealing dope. I rationalized it by going to school and keeping my grades up. I paid the bills and put food on the table. It worked for a while; my mother started staying home. It didn't take long to realize that she was staying home because I was in the game. I figured if it kept her home, why not hit her off with what she needed? No matter what I did for her, it wasn't enough. She started stealing the dope from me, more than I could cover. That's what led her back out to the streets. The further down she went, the higher I started rolling.

"I would be out on those streets at night, figuring out how to work them, but I never missed a day of school. By the time I was sixteen, a partner of mine and I ran our own operation. Buying the coke, cooking it and having our own runners distribute it. I ran the show from behind the scenes, but my partner wanted to be on the streets and it cost him. At the end of my junior year, he got busted. I never saw him again after he got sent away. I don't know what happened to him after that." Travis wasn't being completely honest, but he didn't see any need to go into depth about Kwame. "He's probably dead. That junior year was an eye-opener. My mom was killed in February; my oldest brother committed suicide two weeks later; and my boy was sent away by the end of April."

"My God."

"That's why I had to get away from that life. Everybody around me was either dead or en route to it. I saved money from the time I started running for somebody else and I deposited money everywhere. Small banks, big banks; it didn't matter. I must've put money in every bank within a forty-mile radius of Charlotte. I used that money to pay my way through school."

"Dirty money?" Kenya was numb, stunned and overwhelmed by all the information.

Travis became pensive. He wasn't comfortable with Kenya's response. Not that it was different from what he had expected, but there was much more to tell and he wasn't sure if she was ready for it.

"I guess you can call it that," Travis said. "I mean, there's no other way to put it."

"No, there isn't."

"I don't expect you to understand, but that was the only way out I could see at the time. I keep those things in the past. I keep it to myself because I realize how people will look at me if they know where I came from, what I was." He waited for her to say something, anything. She didn't. "Even you. Right now, you don't see me the same."

For fifteen years he had kept the secrets of his past to himself and he wasn't free of all of them yet. As good as it felt to release some of it, he had no idea what it might cost him.

"No, I don't. That part of you...it's like I never knew you."

"You never knew me? K, c'mon, you've always known me. You know my heart. You didn't know *that* me, but that's not who I am. Not anymore."

"How do I know that? How do I know you're still not leading another life? You can't bring all this to me and think that everything is okay."

"What are you talking about? This is the shit you wanted to

know! It's taken me a long time to get to this point and now that I'm giving it to you, it's too much for you!! I...."

The sound of Michael crying stopped Travis from continuing. He looked toward Michael's room and then back to Kenya.

"I'll get him." Kenya took the opportunity to get away from the conversation. The distraction would give her time to process the information Travis had given her. She quickly moved from the bed and went to Michael's room.

Travis was left to contemplate the decision he'd struggled so long to make. Maybe it wasn't fair to keep this information from Kenya, but when they'd met eight years ago in Raleigh, that life was irrelevant. After moving back to Charlotte, being so close to where he'd grown up, he had begun to think more about his past. It started to weigh on him. Volunteering at Garrison was supposed to be a bridge that helped him make amends with his past, to make it right. It had worked for a while. He was able to maintain his distance. He presented himself as a positive role model, listened to their stories and offered advice—that was, until he met Baby Jar. Hearing his story caused him to struggle even more. Baby Jar's life was the mirror image of his own.

Kenya re-entered the room with Michael in her arms. The crying had stopped, but he was still awake. Kenya couldn't bring herself to look at Travis. She went to the bed and placed Michael in the middle of it. Without a word, she lay down on the right side of Michael and pulled the covers up. Their conversation for the evening was over.

CHAPTER 7

Baby Jar sat in an abandoned apartment, counting money by candlelight. It was money brought in by some of the street runners. His count was interrupted when Bone's cell phone began to vibrate. He had strict orders to answer any call that came through on the line and inform him immediately. He smiled when the phone rang. He'd been given responsibilities.

They had fallen into Jar's lap because of the woman that had rolled in fifteen minutes ago. Bone was off in another room handling that piece of business. The noises coming from that back room kept drawing Jar's attention and messing up his count. He was glad when the phone interrupted him; that way he had a legitimate reason for losing count.

"Hello?"

"Where's Bone?" the woman on the other end had demanded.

"He's, ahh..." Jar had hesitated.

"Never mind. Look here, Lolly's got something for him and it ain't got no heat on it." Then she had hung up the phone.

Baby Jar was confused. He had no idea what that meant. He grabbed the stack of money that he'd managed to count, bound it with a rubber band, and set it aside. He wrote down what he counted so far: six thousand, seven hundred and forty-five dollars, and the night wasn't over. He wrote the figure down and stuck it between the rubber band and the money.

Jar checked to make sure the front door was locked and then went to the room where Bone was and stood outside the door. The sound of him and the woman going at it caused Jar to hesitate. Though the room was dimly lit when the woman had entered, Jar could see how attractive she was. He couldn't believe a woman that fine, dressed the way she was, would be coming out on this cold-ass night to a rundown project house. There was no electricity; boards covered the windows; and this dime was willing to subject herself to this, to get with Bone. Jar looked over the cold, abandoned apartment that was lit by nothing but candles and realized that the dope game had some real power. He continued to listen to the noises inside. He smiled as he heard the makeshift bed banging against the wall. The rhythm of the bed hitting the wall began to quicken and the noises became louder. Jar didn't want to barge in; he could hear Bone and the woman saying something back and forth to one another, but the banging of the bed didn't allow him to hear what was being said.

Jar knocked on the door to tell Bone about the message and the door opened slightly. Jar peeked. He could see that Bone was behind her on his knees with his hands gripping her hips.

She was on her hands and knees and looked like she was having the time of her life. She had no idea the door had opened and she was being watched.

"What?!" Bone shouted while he continued to thrust himself forward. He looked toward the door, in the direction of the knock. Bone never stopped his movements. He could see that Jar's attention was on the woman that was in front of him. Instead he thrust himself harder and deeper.

"What do you need?" he asked. He smiled as Baby Jar turned his attention to him.

"Phone call," Jar said, shocked that he had been caught watching.

"Well, what they say?"

"Ah...ah..." Jar wasn't sure what shocked him more—that he'd been caught watching or that Bone continued like he didn't give a damn. "Lolly's got something for you and there ain't no heat on it," he repeated from his phone call.

"Alright; I'll be out in a minute."

That was Baby Jar's cue to leave, but he couldn't help himself; he couldn't tear away. He watched Bone thrust himself toward her one more time. He stayed and growled in ecstasy before finally releasing himself from her.

Jar shut the door and went back to his money table. He scrambled to count as much money as he could before Bone emerged from the other room. Jar knew that Bone had taken a liking to him, but he also knew that Bone wouldn't hesitate to flip on him. He tried feverishly to manipulate the cash with his stiff fingers.

"You finished counting?" Bone shouted as he came out of the room. He was still adjusting himself and pulling up his clothes.

"Not yet," Jar responded nervously.

"Give me what you got counted and put the rest back in that bag. We getting ready to move to someplace warmer."

"You just gonna leave me in here?" the woman asked from the room.

"You don't hurry your ass up, hell yeah, I'ma leave your ass in here. And blow out the ma'fuckin' candles when you leave."

"No, nigga, you ain't leavin' me in here!"

"Hold the fuck up. Who the hell you think you talkin' to? Gotdammit, I was just playin' with your trick ass." Bone was headed for the room and met the woman on her way out. He snatched her by the throat. His voice was deathly serious. "You ever raise your voice to me again, that'll be the last time anybody hears your fuckin' voice."

The woman did not take the threat lightly. She rushed back into the room to gather her belongings without uttering a word.

Seconds later, she was on her way out of the room. She tried to squeeze by Bone without pissing him off any further.

"Oh, you ain't gonna say goodbye to a nigga?" Bone said, smiling at her. His whole attitude had flipped right back.

The woman didn't know what to say or how to take him. She stared blankly at him.

"Jar, give that fine-ass ho a hundred dollars," Bone said and he waited for Jar to comply. "She got some good shit, boy; you need to get you some of that."

Baby Jar handed her a hundred dollars in twenties. He was too embarrassed to look at her. There was some embarrassment on her part, but not enough to keep her from snatching the money out of his hand.

"Go on and catch my man outside; he got that blindfold for you. The car's downstairs waiting for you. They'll take you wherever you need to go."

She didn't waste any time getting the door open. A hand holding out a blindfold met her and ushered her out. The door was shut behind her; then there was the sound of her shoes walking unsteadily toward the stairs.

"I hope she don't fall down them steps. That was a good damn ride there, Dog," Bone joked.

Jar shifted his eyes back and forth. He wasn't sure if he should say anything. One wrong word and Bone would be on his case.

"How come you so quiet?" Bone shot at Jar.

Jar looked at the door and then toward Bone. "I...can't believe you talked to her like that," Jar said nervously.

"What? C'mon, Jar. Fuck that ho. That phone call, it was about money. It's time to roll. Look, I had to talk to that bitch like that. She'da been up in here tryin' to hang out all night long, no matter how cold it is up in this joint. Them hoes be clingin', man. That's why you gotta make them as uncomfortable as possible. Ain't no damn way I'da left her ass up in here. They be tryin' to run all through your shit." He studied Baby Jar. "Lighten up, Jar; them hoes like that. It's part of the game. She came up in here with this place like it is, she down for the game. You either run game, or you get gamed. Bet you fifty dollars she'd be back twenty minutes from now if I wanted to ride that ass again."

Jar smiled; this game sure had its perks. He gathered up the rest of the money after handing the counted money to Bone. He watched Bone as he went back into the room. The light that was cast by the candles grew dim, until finally the room was dark.

"Yo, get them candles out," Bone said as he re-entered the room.

Baby Jar snapped to it. He blew out two candles and was moving for a third when he got the courage to ask his next question.

"So, what was the deal with the blindfold?" He didn't look at Bone.

Bone turned to look in the direction of Jar. He instantly stopped what he was doing. Even though Jar couldn't see Bone, he knew Bone's eyes were on him. He could feel the heat from his eyes burning up the side of his face. *This was it*, he thought. It was his turn to catch hell.

"What have I been telling you?" Bone said calmly. "It's about protecting everything you do. I can't have no ho knowing where my money spot is. That's why she blindfolded. She don't know how she got here or where the fuck she was. All she knows is that it was cold and dark. Even if by some chance she knew where she was, my money spot will change in a couple of days. Next time I hit it, I might bring that ass to a spot where I got people cooking the shit. Remember, you can't trust them hoes. It's all about puttin' this game first. That's all this is about."

Jar, still not looking at him, nodded his head.

"Make this run with me, yo. School ain't over for the night yet."

With all of the money gathered and the candles blown out, Bone whistled as he walked by a boarded window. Then the two of them headed out of the apartment and into the dark hallway. Bone stopped and listened for any sound. He stuck his arm out to quiet Jar. Satisfied that there was no one lurking in the shadows, he gave two taps on Jar's chest, walked slowly and quietly toward the steps and then downstairs. Bone paused again at the bottom of the steps to make sure the coast was clear. They walked out the apartment building and Flake, one of Bone's flunkies, pulled up to meet them. He was driving Bone's 1984 black Datsun 280ZX. As he stepped out of the car, he held the door open like a bellhop. It had a tan leather interior and gold pinstriping. It was over twenty-five years old but looked showroom new; the car was off the hook.

"We're riding in that?" Jar asked in disbelief. He'd seen Bone drive the car a number of times, but he never had seen anyone ride with him. He'd let Flake fetch his car for him, but that was it. He definitely wasn't riding shotgun.

"Yeah, Little Man. You get to chill in the classic tonight."

Jar opened the passenger side door. He was anxious to get inside.

"Jar, what the hell are you doin'?" Bone snapped. The stern look turned into a smile. "You drivin' tonight, Little Man... You can drive, can't you?"

"Hell yeah!" Jar was like a kid in a candy store.

"Calm down and go on over to the driver's side."

Jar hopped from the passenger side, dashed around to the driver's side and got right in. Flake took notice of that. It was apparent that he couldn't believe that Bone was letting this kid run around like this.

"You got a problem, Flake?" Bone caught the way Flake watched Jar.

Flake looked down and shook his head no. He knew better than to say otherwise. Being Bone's yes-man was the best job he'd ever had, and with his lofty career expectations, this was probably as good as it was gonna get.

"Good." Bone watched Flake for any sign of slipping. Once he was satisfied there weren't any problems, he scanned the area and eased into the car's passenger seat.

Jar was already bouncing in the driver's seat. He found his favorite radio station and Drake's hit, "Best I Ever Had," was pumping.

"That Bose system you got in here is bumping," Jar said. "Too bad you don't have a CD player. I got the *Thank Me Later* CD; all them joints is hot." This new sense of trust had put Jar completely at ease.

"What makes you think I don't have a CD player? Because you can't see it? Everything ain't the way it looks." He looked at Baby Jar and gave him a slight grin. "You can drive this, can't you?"

"Ah yeah, sure," Jar said while he checked out the driver's cockpit. "I just got one question." He looked down. "Why does this thing have two brakes?"

"Two brakes?" Bone looked over at the floor on the driver's side. "That's a clutch. Can you drive a stick?"

"Yeah, I was just messing with you." Jar laughed.

"Hmph. Calm down, Jar. That was a little funny, but this is still business. Turn that radio down. Don't need to call no attention to us, alright?" Bone waited while Jar complied. "Now, throw that thing in gear and let's roll."

Baby Jar pressed the clutch, threw the car in first, hit the gas twice to rev the engine, then he let the clutch pop. The car lurched forward and then stalled.

"So, you drove sticks before, huh?"

"It's a...been a while." Jar restarted the car. This time he eased off the clutch and they were on their way. Flake watched the car pull off. He stood there with his hands in his pockets and once they were sufficiently out of sight, he shook his head.

"So, where are we going?" Jar asked.

"Over off Nations Ford. Bramblewood Apartments."

"So, we going to see about Lolly?"

Bone nodded.

"What was she talking about, when she said there wasn't no heat on it?"

"She got some mail for me, probably FedEx. Stuff I been waitin' on. She was lettin' me know it was cool to come get it."

"What is it?"

"You'll see soon enough. Just drive…like you got some sense."

With the exception of the music and occasional directions given by Bone, the two rode in silence until they reached their destination. Jar pulled into a parking space at the apartment complex and killed the engine. It was the first time he'd ever been on this side of town. He loved the way these apartments looked. They weren't the most expensive in Charlotte, but they were a hell of a lot better than what he was accustomed to living in.

"You want to come up?" Bone asked as he checked out his surroundings.

"Is it okay?" Jar was a little hesitant.

"Yeah, everythin' cool."

Bone and Jar got out the car and Jar followed Bone to the apartment. They walked through the entrance door and up one flight of stairs to 2B. Bone knocked on the door and waited. Jar stayed behind Bone, but he was trying to peek around him. The sound of someone walking toward the door could be heard, although they were approaching cautiously. Then the noise stopped. The person on the inside was apparently looking through the peephole.

"You alone?" the feminine voice asked.

"Open up, I ain't got all night," Bone ordered and the person inside complied.

When the door opened, standing in the doorway of the well-lit apartment was a beautiful, five-foot-nine sister wearing a black bathrobe. Jar got a good look at her curvaceous body. She noticed Baby Jar behind Bone and it didn't seem to bother her one bit. Neither of them said a word.

"Where the package at?" Bone was all business. He was heading into the apartment.

Baby Jar followed, but didn't take his eyes off Lolly's body as he walked by her.

"It's in the kitchen," Lolly said.

"Lolly, this Baby Jar," he muttered as he went for the kitchen. "You talked to him earlier."

"There's five in there."

"That's straight."

As Jar followed Bone to the kitchen, he picked up the scent of a pungent odor.

"What's that smell?" Jar asked.

"Cinnamon. It kills the scent of cocaine when we running shit FedEx. We got to kill the scent so them dogs don't fuck with it when it comes through. We also put a couple of hits of mace on it. Them dogs don't like sniffing that shit. If one of them dogs sniffs through the mace, then all they smell is cinnamon. Coffee grinds are good, too." Bone examined the five kilos that he had in the packages in front of him. "Looks good. You test it?" he asked Lolly.

She nodded. "It's on point," she said slowly and seductively, letting the words roll off her lips.

"Look, I'ma go 'head and take care of this here," Bone said as he looked up and down Lolly's voluptuous body. "Why don't you take care of Baby Jar over there? Walk him down the path to manhood."

Without a second to ponder what had been said, Lolly's attention was directed to Jar. She inched closer to him and began pulling at the sash on her robe. When she was within three feet of the sixteen-year-old, she held open her robe, revealing her ample bosom to him. This all happened under Bone's watchful eye.

"What you waiting for, boy?" Bone was giving Jar his permission.

"Why don't you come with me?" Lolly asked.

Jar stood and was shocked that this beautiful woman was offering herself to him.

Bone chuckled. "Go on; I'll be right here waiting on you."

Lolly walked past Jar, dropping her robe as she went by. Jar turned to follow her without a word. He started pulling off his clothes as he followed her. Her stride, her long legs and the way her hips swayed her beautiful ass from side to side mesmerized Jar. The tension in his pants had already risen. Lolly led him to her bedroom; she turned on the light as she entered the room. She stepped aside to let him enter.

"Finish taking your clothes off," she demanded sexily.

Jar eagerly tore off his clothes while he continued to stare at the woman from head to toe. He was oblivious to what the room looked like or anything else, other than Lolly and his erection. After he was nude, he waited for her to tell him what to do next. He'd only gotten some twice from girls who were as scared as he was, and they did it in complete darkness. Lolly was letting him see everything here.

Lolly walked her fine body slowly to him. She extended her right hand, got a good grasp of his member, and began to stroke it. "I'm impressed."

Hot damn!! he thought. Nobody had ever touched him down there. He couldn't muster a single word. He reached out both of his hands and grabbed her breasts. Nothing ever felt so good to him. Lolly used his member to back him toward the bed.

"Lay down," she said.

Jar gladly obliged. He sat down, scooted back and lay flat on his back. She never let go of him. Jar didn't know how much more of the stroking he could take. When he'd centered himself on the bed, she eased onto the bed to join him, still holding onto his rigid body part. She let her body graze against his member as she crawled up him. Jar shuddered with anticipation. Lolly sat up and straddled him. She then placed his member inside her walls. Jar was breathing heavily now and watched everything as it unfolded. Lolly lowered her twenty-three-year-old body onto his sixteen-year-old one.

"Oh shit!" he finally said, filled with delight. "Ah fuck!" he said as her gyrations picked up pace. Within minutes, Baby Jar hollered as he exploded into Lolly's womanhood. He never stopped watching. She continued her motion to drain every ounce of fluid out of him. He reached up, put his arms around her and buried his head in her breasts. He wanted to hold her close as she finished her ride.

After it was over, Lolly got up and left him lying on his back with a smile on his face. He couldn't believe what had happened. He was replaying the ride in his mind, over and over. With perks like this, the dope game was "sho nuff" the life for him.

CHAPTER 8

As the sunlight crept into the bedroom, a sharp pain in his left kidney woke Travis up. It had been hard enough for him to finally fall asleep last night. Judging by the way Kenya had tossed and turned, Travis would have bet money that she'd had the same difficulty.

Everything he'd told Kenya last night was obviously weighing on both of their minds. Although neither of them spoke another word on the subject, it would take some time for her to sort things out. He would let her make the next move. His pressing concern at the moment was dislodging little Pele's foot from his kidney. How this little foot, that was a size four in baby shoes, could exact so much pain and punishment during the course of one night, staggered his imagination. Having Michael sleep in their bed was a habit that wasn't going to continue. Michael wasn't getting any smaller and the blows were beginning to land with more power.

Travis moved away from Michael to create some space between them. As he turned over to take a look at Michael, he narrowly avoided an elbow.

"Okay, buddy. That's it. Time for you to go," he joked as he took his son into his arms.

"What are you doing?" Kenya asked.

"I was going to put Michael back in his room." Travis was keeping his voice down.

"It's almost time for him to get up." Her voice was still distant.

"Then I'll get him dressed. I was going to drop him off anyway."

"I'll get him dressed."

"I thought you wanted to sleep in. You..."

"I will get him dressed," Kenya stated firmly. She reached over and pulled Michael into her arms. "You can take care of yourself." She left the room hastily.

Travis resisted the urge to respond. The conversation wasn't about Michael. It was about what was left unsaid last night. There were things thrown at her that had hit her like a ton of bricks. Kenya was always so full of questions. Now she was the one who didn't want to take the conversation any deeper and Travis fully understood. After knowing Kenya for eight years, being married for five and sharing a child, he was finally able to let her in on his past. She definitely needed some time.

Travis also had needed a break. With all that he'd experienced since arriving at Garrison yesterday, the last thing on his mind was work. But today promised to be a big day; now was the time to get geared back up for it.

Travis got out of bed and went into their bathroom. He opened the shower door and turned it on. As he prepared to brush his teeth in the sink, he looked at his face in the mirror and debated shaving. The stubble that he usually wouldn't bother with was going to have to go. The dog and pony show was on for the heavyweights. He brushed his teeth, gave himself a quick shave with the electric razor and jumped into the shower.

Kenya walked into the bathroom as Travis finished his shower and began to dry off. They eyed each other. Travis didn't want to say the wrong thing and Kenya wasn't in the mood to talk.

"Is Michael ready?" Travis finally broke the silence.

"Yes," Kenya answered flatly. She appeared to have something to say, but couldn't get it out.

Travis looked at her as he wrapped the towel around his waist.

His eyes tried to convey to her that he would answer any questions; there were none. She edged past him to her sink to brush her teeth. Travis went into their large walk-in closet. He pulled out his blue, conservative, single-breasted suit, white shirt and burgundy tie. He capped off his ensemble with a pair of black, spit-shined wingtips.

With everything in hand, he stepped out the closet and headed back to the room. Kenya was still at her sink. She'd finished brushing. Travis could see her watching him in the mirror and she could see him. He slowed his pace as he waited for her to speak.

Once he was back in the room, he began to get dressed. He wanted Kenya to come into the room, to say anything to him. Then he realized he'd forgotten his belt so he made the trek back through the bathroom to the closet. When he had his hands on his belt, he started back to the room. This time he stopped at his sink, reached down to get his deodorant and cologne. All he was really doing was stalling to see if any conversation would begin. Kenya was still in front of the mirror, staring. Again, he was denied.

Travis went back into the room and finished dressing. He had a challenging day in the office ahead, and he did not want his focus to waver once he was there. If he were to have any peace of mind after leaving their home, he would need to take the steps to clear it.

Kenya had not moved from her spot in front of the mirror. Her mind was spinning at a million miles per hour. She didn't notice Travis had re-entered the bathroom until he reached out his hand and touched her. Startled, she turned and looked at her husband but still couldn't find any words.

"I'm sorry," he started. "Kenya, I'm sorry. I should have told you about this long before now. The truth is, I was scared to. I had been running from my past since the day I left Charlotte. What

I did and who I was in high school, it was completely different from who I was in college. By the time I met you, Perry Moore was a distant memory and all that was left was Travis. If any of the people that I worked for knew about my life as a dope dealer, they wouldn't have given me a chance. Kenya, you wouldn't have given me a chance, not if I came to you with all that baggage up front." Travis paused; they both knew it was the truth. "So I kept it from you because that lifestyle has no bearing on what my life has become. Honestly, I never thought that it would. Then we moved here. I don't know, being so close to home, my past started coming back to me. All the stuff with my mom, I don't know. That's why I started helping out at Garrison. It was my way of trying to clean up some of the dirt I left behind. I also realized that I needed to come clean with you. I'm tired of carrying it alone and I need your help. There is nothing that means more to me than you and that boy in there. K, you have to know me."

"I know you, Travis. I know what you've shown me. All I've ever seen is that you are a good man. What I'm having a hard time believing is that you could have lived that way, that you *did* live that way."

"I didn't know any other way to live. I was only trying to survive."

Travis looked at Kenya and she nodded. Everything wasn't fine, but it was better. There would be plenty of time for conversation. Kenya needed a little more time and she'd come around.

"Kenya, I love you. You make my life better."

Kenya fought the urge to hug him. She could feel her thoughts being played against her emotions. "This isn't over."

"I know." He reached out and grabbed her hand. "Let me get ready to go." He hoped she might want him to stay a little longer.

"Michael's bag is packed. All you have to do is drop him off."

"Seems like an idiot-proof task."

"Let's hope so." The attempt at humor didn't fly with Kenya.

Travis was not going to let anything or anyone stop him from getting home this evening. He was running short on time and work was calling. Tonight they would talk more and they would get themselves back on track.

THE PRECIOUS MEMORIES DAYCARE OPENED at 6:00 a.m. every morning, Monday through Friday. When Travis pulled in the parking lot at 7:20, they were wide open. With his windows up, he could hear the voices and stomping feet. Travis wanted to make sure that Michael was well bundled before they got out the car.

"Your dad has been involved in some pretty bad things in his life." Travis was reaching over his seat and pulling Michael out his car seat. "Things I hope to God you never get involved with." He sat Michael in the seat beside him. "That's why I bust my butt every day. So you'll grow up learning what an honest man does for a living. I've got an opportunity to give you something I never had. A father." Travis saw a smile go across Michael's face. "I can't wait to see what kind of man you grow into, but I'm going to watch you every day from now until then. Bet money on that, kid." Travis got out the car, hurried to the passenger side to get Michael, and then scurried him inside the daycare.

TRAVIS NEVER NOTICED THE BLACK 280ZX that had tailed him to the daycare. It had stopped four hundred yards from Precious Memories. Bone watched as Travis got out the car, grabbed Michael and entered the building.

"I'ma give your ass some precious memories." He was alone in the car with his obsession. Bone felt nothing but contempt for the loving father. His redemption was getting closer with every second that passed.

CHAPTER 9

Today had promised to be an interesting day. Yesterday, Travis had informed the chief financial officer and the vice president of marketing and development that one of Home Supply's trusted employees had been embezzling money.

So far, Travis had been able to document a little over $1.9 million that Patricia Bradshaw had collected for herself. Patricia was an attractive woman. At the age of thirty-seven, her physical attributes were the envy of most twenty-five-year-old women. Blonde hair and perky breasts; the hair wasn't natural and neither were the breasts. Patricia, the marketing director, oversaw all of Home Supply's promotional campaigns. Every seasonal campaign or event had in some way crossed her desk, and she was keeping a piece of the pie.

Home Supply didn't need this type of publicity as the corporation approached its initial public offering. The market was unpredictable due to the current recession, corporate mismanagement, bailouts and inflated bottom lines; this had the potential to destroy its position in the market.

Ordinarily, it would be easiest to expose the person who was embezzling funds. The corporation would show potential investors how they had rooted out a thief within the company and assure anyone with doubts that their money would be guarded with the same dogged determination. That would be a simple solution—if it were the only problem.

Brad Johnson, the vice president of marketing and development, had come to Travis, after being informed of the potential problem.

He had urged him to handle the situation discreetly. Travis didn't know why, but he had followed Brad's wishes. It wasn't until he had realized that Patricia was involved, that it made sense to him.

Tom Miller, chief financial officer and one of Home Supply's co-founders, was an upstanding citizen in the Charlotte community. He was a deacon in his church, benefactor to his alma mater and a corporate sponsor to many charities. Tom was the perfect family man and doting grandfather to three grandchildren as he neared the age of sixty. His life was nearly ideal except for one thing—he had been laying the wood to Patricia for the last six years. If that information got out, it would put a little more than a blemish on the corporate image.

The stunned look on his face when Travis had laid out this information yesterday looked like a man who really had stepped in it this time. Tom was slightly overweight and he had sat rubbing his short, stubby fingers on his temples. He had expressed concern about the corporation and what this could mean. However, what he didn't say was that if his affair were to be exposed, he would never be able to repair his reputation and his family life would be in shambles. He wanted to discuss this situation with the chief executive officer, Walter Hill, and begin exploring the best way to pursue some type of damage control.

Travis was deep in thought when his intercom buzzed.

"Travis Moore."

"Travis, Mr. Hill would like to see you in his office," the receptionist said.

It was show time. Travis gathered the nineteen-page report he'd prepared and shared with Tom and Brad yesterday, then proceeded to make the trek two floors up to Walter's office.

The pinging sound of the elevator reaching the fifth floor was the only detectable sound from the elevator. This was the top floor of Home Supply. As Travis stepped out the elevator into the plush surroundings, he felt like he was reporting to the principal's office.

"Good morning, Travis," the attractive young receptionist spoke in a sweet and chipper manner. "Mr. Hill is in there with Mr. Miller and Mr. Johnson. They're waiting for you."

This struck Travis as odd. He was the one with the goods on the embezzlement, yet he was the last to the meeting. He kept his cool and never flinched. The big boys were in charge. He was going to lay out everything he had and let them sweat the decisions.

"Thank you."

Travis opened the door to Walter Hill's office. It was immaculate as always. Walter sat behind his mahogany desk in a black leather, wingback chair. Facing him were three smaller leather chairs that swiveled. Seated in the chair to the left was Tom Miller and Brad Johnson was in the chair to the right.

"Travis, come on in, son," Walter said, smiling.

On cue, Tom and Brad turned their chairs toward him as he came further into the room.

The three of them seemed to be very much at ease for people whose livelihoods were at stake. Tracing fraud and embezzlement wasn't part of his audit duties, so he was going to follow their lead.

"How are you doing this morning, Travis?" Walter asked as he stood and rounded his desk. He extended his right hand to Travis. His grip was firm and his left hand gripped Travis on the forearm. His eyes never lost contact when he spoke.

"Doing fine, sir. Yourself?"

"Good, considering some of the things that have been brought to my attention." There was a break in his eye contact, but only to look at Tom and Brad. "Are you gentlemen going to speak?"

"Morning, Travis," Brad said with an even tone.

"Morning," Tom said, without looking at Travis. There was a hint of embarrassment in his voice.

"Gentlemen."

"Have a seat, Travis." Walter was motioning to the chair in the middle.

Travis took his place and was barely in the seat before Walter got started again.

"Might as well cut to the chase. It is my understanding that we have a situation with a Patricia Bradshaw."

There was a bit of uneasiness that entered the room.

"That is the young lady's name, is it not, Tom?" Walter said, as he sat on the corner of his desk.

"Yes, sir," Tom responded. The shame of his indiscretions caused him to shrink in front of everyone.

"One-point-nine million dollars." Walter's eyes were fixated on Tom but he was addressing those present in the room. "Tom brought me your report yesterday. One-point-nine million over the last three years." His eyes were shifting to everyone present. "At least that is what Travis was able to find. By the way, good work," he directed to Travis. "If you found one-point-nine million, I'm sure there's more out there."

Travis started to tell Walter that he'd only begun to scratch the surface. There was little doubt in his mind that there was more money out there; probably a lot more. Travis had plenty of experience when it came to hiding money, but there was no need to let them know.

"This is an embarrassment to our company. We are about to take this company public and there are concerns out there about corporations mismanaging funds. People are not as trusting of corporations right now. Needless to say, this situation must be addressed immediately. No one outside of this room, with the exception of Ms. Bradshaw, knows that she has been caught."

"How does she know she's been caught?" Travis asked before he realized. To his knowledge, Patricia had no idea what was going on. He looked at both Brad and Tom. Brad was poker-faced, while Tom continued to shrink.

"As I said, this situation needs to be addressed immediately," Walter continued, sending the signal that he was not to be interrupted. "Tom and I talked at great length last night. We looked at this from every possible angle."

There was a wrinkle that began to form on the forehead of Brad's poker face. Travis was trying to get a read on him. It was apparent that this was news to both Brad and Travis.

"What immediately came to mind was having this woman arrested and indicted for embezzlement. One-point-nine million dollars is a lot of money. The question is though, can we afford to prosecute her? If money was the only issue here, it's a no-brainer." Walter's eyes went back to Tom. "But there are some other things to consider." His eyes went back to all three. "The primary concern is the position of the company. Tom, do you care to elaborate?"

The tone in Walter's voice let everyone in the room know that this wasn't a request.

"Ahh...she... Our greatest concern is making sure the company is shown in its strongest light as we go public. There are hundreds of millions that are at stake here. Two million dollars, we can eat. If it becomes public knowledge that amount of money was stolen in-house, the damage caused could be into the hundreds of millions. That is something we are not willing to risk. The decision has been made to terminate Ms. Bradshaw. She is clearing out her office as we speak. Walter and I spoke with our corporate attorney last night and they are drawing up documents for her to sign. Basically, she can never discuss this incident, and we will recover all assets that are traced to the one-point-nine million that you have documented, Travis."

"And the money that hasn't been traced yet? There was money

found in offshore accounts," Travis said, maintaining his composure.

"We don't want to know that," Walter stated solemnly.

There was a noticeable uneasiness with Brad now. Travis was stunned, but all of his years in the dope game had taught him to never be fazed by what transpired. Keep your composure and keep rolling. Tom looked to be relieved that this probe wouldn't go any further. The fire on his ass was about to be put out and he barely got burned.

"She knows she's in hot water and she has agreed to get out of it," Walter continued. "I think it's the best thing. We don't expose how much we've lost. We don't look weak to potential investors and, more importantly," Walter looked squarely at Tom, "we avoid further embarrassment from other scandals that could arise from this situation." Maybe ol' Tom wasn't completely out of the hot water yet.

"Where is the woman now?" Brad asked. He was usually very calm and reserved, but the little circus that had been concocted by Tom and Walter had agitated him.

Walter looked to Tom. It would be left to him to finish and answer whatever questions came to the table.

"She's clearing out her office," Tom said.

"Is security with her?" Brad hounded.

Tom looked to Walter as if to say, *do I have to answer*? Walter folded his arms and sat back on the corner of his desk. There was no assistance coming from him.

Tom cleared his throat. "Ah, no… She's alone."

"A woman who has stolen over one-point-nine million dollars from this company is being allowed to clear out her shit without anybody keeping an eye on her?" Brad shot at Tom. "That woman is walking out of here scot-free. You know damn well if there was two million found in two months, there's at least another two to four million out there. Is that ass worth that much to you?!"

"You son of a bitch."

Tom struggled to get up from his chair as fast as he could, but his weight slowed him. Brad was out his chair much faster. He stepped over Travis and shoved Tom back into his chair. Travis looked at these two middle-aged men who were having a physical confrontation about money and a little bit of poontang.

"All right. All right! That's enough!" Walter barked.

The confrontation was over as quickly as it had begun. Tom's face had turned beet red during the little skirmish. Brad, who was wire thin, had his fist cocked. He looked like he had been waiting to do that for years.

"Begging your pardon, sirs, but I think this may be a good time to table this meeting," Travis interjected calmly. Deep down, he wanted to laugh at these two men behaving like nine-year-olds. He also wanted to laugh because he was pissed; the work he'd put in, it being discounted and she was walking away with a slap on the wrist. He had seen enough and he was ready to leave.

"Very good then. Travis, remember, not a word to anyone," Walter cautioned.

Travis nodded as he stood to acknowledge his understanding. He squeezed himself away from Brad and a heavily breathing Tom.

"There are some documents that we all will need to sign. Confidentiality statements. The attorney is having them sent by courier. We should have them in the next two hours. I'll make sure they get down to you."

"Confidentiality statements, huh?" Brad was hunched over, fist still clenched and his eyes had never left Tom.

"Yes, like I said, we don't want this information spreading."

Brad unclenched his fist and began to stand erect. He shook his head in disbelief. "I'll be going back to my office now." He looked at Tom and then over to Walter. "You know, the office that is next to Ms. Bradshaw's office on the third floor."

"Brad, you will be getting yours as well," Walter added as Brad headed for the door.

"It's not the first time." Brad intended to make this comment under his breath, but if everyone had heard it, so be it.

Travis waited until Brad opened the door before he made his move to leave. He didn't want to appear too anxious, but he wanted to get more of Brad's thoughts on the matter without going to Brad's office. Crossing the path of Patricia could be a little uncomfortable. Since she was being terminated, she had to know why. Even if she hadn't seen his report, she had seen more of his face lately around Brad's office. She wasn't a dumb woman; the way she was hiding money told him that. It wouldn't be long before she would put two and two together, if she hadn't already done so.

"I have to get back to work myself. Is there anything else I can do for you two before I go?" Travis said, hoping that there wasn't.

"That's it for now. Thank you for the good work. This company and its entire vested employees will benefit as a result of what we've decided on here today. Once the company goes public, you will be a wealthy young man, Travis."

Travis nodded and smiled subtly—not a big, opened-mouth gaping grin, but a casual smile. He'd already done his calculations as to what his value would become. His job paid him a base salary of one hundred and forty-five thousand dollars annually. His annual bonus had averaged eighteen thousand dollars the last two years. He had over one hundred and seventy thousand dollars that he had rolled back into the company. By conservative estimates, he would be approaching millionaire status. Moderate projections would take him near three. The numbers that the other executives were hoping for would put him slightly over five million, though. He didn't want to read too much into it, but he certainly hoped

Walter didn't think that mentioning the money would encourage him to keep quiet. Although the money was nice, Travis had vowed years ago that money would never rule him. He let it pass and made his way to the door.

"That would be nice," Travis said over his shoulder as he reached for the door.

Travis caught up to Brad while he was waiting for the elevator doors to open. Getting out of the office hadn't cooled Brad's heels yet.

"Is everything all right?"

"Those sons of bitches," Brad said through lips that barely moved. "This doesn't surprise me one bit."

"What do you mean?"

"They're covering. Surprise, surprise. Everybody here is focused on the bottom line. Understand, I like that bottom line myself, but I'm tired of Tom's so-called indiscretions." Brad turned to study Travis. "You do know what's going on here, don't you?" Brad made sure to keep his voice down.

"It became clear to me pretty early when I started looking at this that Tom was sleeping with Patricia."

"Exactly. Tom has built up this image of himself as this loyal and upstanding pillar of the community. He's chased damn near every skirt that's come in here, if they looked halfway decent. Married or unmarried. It's not the first time he's tripped over his dick, and this company ignores it and continues to make him a wealthy man."

The elevator doors opened. Travis listened to what was being said and wondered if Ol' Tom had tried to make a move in Brad's yard. He wasn't sure what kind of angle Brad was working, but there was definitely something else going on between the two.

CHAPTER 10

Kenya was soaking wet with sweat as she continued to pick up her pace and push herself on the treadmill.

Kenya was supposed to meet her girls at the gym at eleven, but she had arrived early. Lisa and Jasmine were never on time. She wanted to make sure she got started early because she knew Lisa would be dying to pick up the conversation they were having last night. She didn't want to go there today. She enjoyed having their company at the gym. A little conversation while they worked out was nice, but when they were around, it was more conversation and less working out. Today, the gym was going to be her stress reliever.

What Travis had told her last night didn't allow her a good night's sleep. She'd thought she'd get some sleep once Travis and Michael were gone, but that didn't help either. She was up after they'd hit the door. She cleaned and dusted, but it wasn't long before she was on her way to the gym.

At a few minutes before ten, Kenya was on an exercise bike trying to pedal the thoughts out her mind. A half-hour passed; she moved to the Stairmaster and the thoughts were still with her. Her husband, who never talked about his past, had told her everything. Never had it crossed her mind that his past would be anything like it was.

Her head was swimming in confusion and she didn't notice the arrival of Jasmine and Lisa.

"Damn, girl! You sure couldn't have gotten none last night with the way you moving on that thing. What? You climbing Mount Everest?" Lisa said loud enough for everybody in the room to hear. Kenya was caught off guard.

Jasmine rolled her eyes at Lisa. "You are so ghetto."

"Lisa's just Lisa," Kenya said between pants.

"So what's up? You couldn't wait for us?" Lisa said, hardly paying attention to Jasmine.

"There's two more Stairmasters right here waiting on you. Nobody's stopping you two from getting on," Kenya shot back.

"Might as well get started," Jasmine stated.

"Shit, I was hoping we'd get to talk a little bit before we got started."

That was precisely what Kenya wanted to avoid. "You two came dressed to work out, didn't you? So, let's work out." Kenya had no intention of stopping. She immediately turned up the resistance on her Stairmaster to let them know it was time to be serious. Talk would come later.

Seeing the conversation wasn't going to go anywhere, Lisa reluctantly put her gym bag down. She was about to get on the Stairmaster next to Kenya, but Jasmine was already there.

"Ahem!" Lisa cleared her throat, indicating that she wanted to be on that particular piece of equipment.

Jasmine looked at her, then at the Stairmaster that was next to her on the right. It was still free. She turned her attention back to Lisa. She blinked and then rolled her eyes. It didn't matter to Jasmine which machine she used, but now that she was set on this one, she wasn't about to move. Plus, no matter how ghetto Lisa thought she was, she would break her off a little something if she showed out. Lisa recognized that look and moved to the next one.

"So, how long we gonna be on this thing?"

"Jas, you just got on it," Kenya said.

"And I just got off work a little while ago."

"Aren't you cranky this morning."

"Girl, I've been at it since seven last night. I got a right to be cranky."

"I had to beg her to come this morning," Lisa added as she was getting started.

"Why did you get up so early last night? You don't usually get up until nine-thirty," Kenya said.

"Go on, tell her. Your slutty self." Lisa turned her nose up at her.

"Slutty. Girl, I'm married, and anything I do with my man don't make me a slut, but it sho'nuff makes him happy. Ever since I've been getting to the gym regular, he can't seem to get enough of this." The thought made her start stepping faster.

"You better slow down before you have a cardiac up in here." Lisa grinned. "Now come on; give us the details."

"Lisa, how long you known me?"

"About four years."

"And in that time, when have I ever given you any intimate details about the goings-on in my bedroom? Or my living room, or my bathroom, or my laundry room?"

Lisa thought for a moment. "Never, now that you mention it."

"Right. So, what makes you think I'm going to start now?" Jasmine turned to Kenya, but made sure Lisa heard her. "People who aren't catching any on a regular always want to get the four-one-one on somebody who is."

"She's always trying to get the scoop on me, too," Kenya chimed in.

"Oh, I got the scoop on you. Ain't nothing happening at your house," Lisa said, laughing with Jasmine. Kenya, drenched in sweat, chuckled, but Lisa was right. Last night there was "nothing" happening at the house.

"Girl, be quiet and get to work," Jasmine said. "Kenya's way ahead of us."

"I can't push it too hard today. I think that brother Keith might be back up in here today," Lisa said.

"Keith? Who? That thug-ass brother you were kicking it with the last time you was in here?" Jasmine recalled.

"Thug nothing. That brother looks like Wesley Snipes with a better body."

"Sheeoot! A knock-off Wesley Snipes," Jasmine shot back.

"Who are you talking about?" Kenya asked.

"You know that dark-skinned brother. Face looks like it was hit by a brick, but his body looks like it was cut out of them," Jasmine described.

"Yeah…wait, wait, hold up. Lisa was kicking it with him last week?"

"We were just talking. No big deal," Lisa said defensively. "We talked a couple of times, whenever I'd see him here."

Jasmine gave her a scrutinizing look. Lisa didn't talk to simply anyone. She was almost thirty and had no husband. She had her hook in the water and she'd told them on a number of occasions that she was fishing for a husband.

"You know that trick is trying to give him some," Jasmine said to Kenya.

"Forget ya'll married sluts; I ain't trying to sweat all my cute out before he gets here."

"I wondered why you busted out the new workout gear. You should have seen her at my house. She tried out two other outfits before she settled on that one."

"I was making sure I had the right gear with my shoes."

Fifteen minutes later, they were finished. They moved into the weight room and secured a bench for themselves. Kenya was amped, ready for more. Lisa was true to her word; she'd barely broken a sweat. Jasmine tried to keep pace with Kenya. The effort was admirable, but the cramps that she was nursing let her know she might want to scale down her pace a little bit. Jasmine separated from the other two and sat on the floor to stretch and loosen her calves. Lisa took the opportunity to move in on Kenya.

"So, what's up?"

"What are you talking about?" Kenya was dabbing sweat from her forehead and trying to avoid the inevitable.

"You know what I'm talking about. What happened when Travis got home?"

"Nothing."

"I could tell nothing by the way you were working out. So, what did he have to say for himself?"

"He was at Garrison," Kenya responded. She wanted to leave the conversation at that. She didn't want to go into the argument that had ensued or that Travis had left the house angry. She definitely didn't want to tell her what she had found out about her husband when he'd returned.

"And?" Lisa pushed for more details.

"There are some things that we need to figure out."

"Uh-huh."

"Uh-huh, what?" Kenya could see Lisa trying to figure something out.

"I can see right through him." Lisa squinted her eyes. "That man of yours, he's up to no good, isn't he?"

Oh hell, there it is, Kenya thought. Lisa didn't have a man, so everybody else's man was under suspicion. If Lisa could get some, even a booty call, maybe that would chill her out.

"Lisa, we are not going to have a conversation where you berate my man."

Jasmine listened to every word that was being passed between Lisa and Kenya while she continued to work her cramps. She noticed Keith as he entered the weight room. Lisa was so busy trying to get into Kenya's business that she didn't notice him. Jasmine observed his track sprinter athletic body, a well-defined build on a slim frame. She also noticed that his eyes were on the move, checking the area he'd just entered. When his eyes caught sight of Lisa, they stopped. The menacing look on his face softened somewhat. He didn't waste any time approaching Lisa.

"Excuse me, you don't mind if I get a set in?" Keith interrupted.

"We were in the middle…" Lisa started to snap until the voice registered with her. She turned toward Keith and flashed all thirty-two. "Hello, Keith."

"Look at you. You got that thang on point today," he said, admiring her outfit.

"Thank you." She blushed.

Jasmine observed the interaction and cut her eyes to Kenya. Not more than ten seconds ago Lisa was bashing men as if they were all wrong for being men. Now, one man was showing her a little attention and she had turned into a schoolgirl. She and Kenya made eye contact and Kenya understood immediately. They were thinking the same thing; look at this heifer.

"Oh, Keith, these are my friends…" Lisa started.

"Let me guess," he interrupted. "Kenya," he said in her direction at the bench. "And you're Jasmine." His eyes darted quickly from one to the other. "It's a pleasure."

"I guess somebody's been doing more talking than she's let on," Jasmine said.

"Keith, can you help me with some sets on the incline bench over there?" Lisa was separating her calf from the herd.

"We'll get to talk a little more later," Keith said to Jasmine and

Kenya. His eyes were darting again, but he held his attention on Kenya for a half-second longer.

Kenya was oblivious to this, but Jasmine didn't miss it at all. For Lisa to always have her eye out watching other people's men, she certainly had blinders on when it was a man in front of her.

"So what do you think about Keith?" Jasmine asked.

"Not much. Nice body, but he doesn't look like Wesley," Kenya responded.

"Shit, I told you that. But, Lisa needs to watch him."

"Why do you say that?"

"Something about his eyes. You notice how they jump around a lot?"

"No, not really."

"I did. Eyes are the windows to the soul. If his eyes are shifty and jumpy, something about him is, too."

"What's that? An old wives' tale?"

"Maybe, but you mark my words, my intuition is telling me that the brother is something else."

CHAPTER 11

Aside from the morning distraction, it was back to his office for Travis, reviewing audit reports as usual. He had expected more from the dismissal of Patricia Bradshaw—a show, with her being escorted out by security, while she shouted derogatory comments about Tom and his sexual prowess or lack thereof. That would have been a big bang, something the people in the company would have talked about for years to come. Maybe that was Brad's motive? Cause enough internal embarrassment to get Tom out of here.

Instead of the big show, what Travis received was the hush-hush, keep it quiet and sweep it under the rug scenario. According to Tom and Walter, this would put the company in the best position possible. It would never reach the board of directors and it definitely wasn't going to reach the public. Travis felt indifferent toward the situation; it was business. There was no mistaking where Brad stood. He didn't agree with how it was handled. He was out of the loop when Tom and Walter had concocted the plan, which was designed to keep Tom out of trouble. They had told Patricia what was happening without letting him speak to her first. To top it off, they had let her clean out whatever she wanted from her office and go on her merry way without anyone keeping an eye on her.

"Travis, this just came for you," Emily said. She leaned halfway into his office and held out an envelope. "It came by courier," she said as if she was already trying to figure out the contents.

Emily was a senior auditor. She was one of those people who had to know everything, whether it was her business or not. Travis had to steer numerous of their conversations away from his background. She spent more time in people's business than she did with her work. Travis had given her a verbal reprimand. It was worse that she shared her life story to anybody that would give her two minutes. No matter what was going on with somebody else, she could always relate to the situation.

"What do you think it is?" Emily walked quickly toward his desk.

"I don't know. I haven't opened it yet." Travis took the letter from her and placed it on his desk.

"It's from our corporate attorney's office," she pressed.

"And how did it end up in your hands?" Travis was letting her know that she was on thin ice.

"I...ah...wanted to help you out."

"Right." Travis nodded and smiled. He could see her nervous feet starting to shuffle. Another question was working its way up.

"So what's going on with Patricia?" Emily finally got around to the real reason why she had stopped by.

"Patricia who?" His attention was already back on his work.

"Bradshaw. In marketing. She got fired today."

"Really?" Travis feigned surprise.

"You haven't heard. Got her out of here this morning. I hear it was a big old mess. She was throwing stuff everywhere. The police came; they had to shut off the floor so they could get her out of there."

"Who told you that?"

"Didn't you hear all the commotion?" she asked as if that validated her point.

"Did you?"

"Well, actually, I wasn't here yet."

"Uh-huh." Travis knew she wasn't at work by the time Patricia was gone.

"I guess sleeping with management doesn't guarantee job security." It was Emily's last attempt to bait Travis into gossip.

"Thank you for dropping the letter off," Travis said, ending the conversation.

"Oh...you're welcome."

Travis watched her as she left his office. He waited a few seconds, then started tearing a piece of paper. Before the paper was completely torn, Emily was back in the doorway. Travis stared at her as she stuck her head in. She almost tripped as she tried to get away from the door.

"Emily, do you mind closing that door? With you on the other side of it; thank you."

Emily shut the door and Travis waited for a few more seconds before he opened the envelope she had handed to him. As he scanned the confidentiality statement, he smiled to himself. He'd signed these before, but they usually were concerning employment in one way or another. This was the first one he was signing involving a cover-up. The rules in the corporate game differed from the street game. Here, they take away your money and maybe a little pride if you crossed somebody. You pick up and take your skills elsewhere. Cross somebody on the street and that's it. Game over. There weren't any confidentiality statements out there. The smile was for his good fortune and for where he was in his life. As tough as it was for him to discuss his past, he was relieved that he'd finally shared some of it with his wife.

Travis' brief moment of reflection was interrupted by a knock on his door. If that was Emily again, job or no job, her nosy butt was about to get cussed out. The door was already opening before the knocks stopped.

"Emily! What do you need?" Travis growled as he stood.

Her eyes doubled in size as she continued to enter. "I…wa…I," Emily stuttered.

"Let's go, Emily; spit it out."

"I was showing someone where your office was. I ran into a gentleman who was talking with the receptionist. I volunteered to show him to your office." Emily opened the door wider to reveal the gentleman behind her.

The impeccably dressed African-American male was wearing a charcoal gray, two-piece suit. Draped on his shoulders was a full-length, lambskin coat. He sported black gators and he topped off the ensemble with a leather cap that was turned to the back.

"That will be all, Emily," Travis said in a low voice. His attention stayed on the gentleman beside her.

Emily resisted the urge to speak. A sense of fear overcame her. She cleared the way so this stranger could move further into the office. This time she knew to close the door behind her. The two men looked at each other. Slowly, Travis moved from behind his desk.

"So, this is what you do now?" the man said, as if he was not impressed. "Yell and bully poor little middle-aged white women."

"Sometimes. But trust me, she might be little and she might be middle-aged, but in about two weeks she ain't ever going to be poor again," he continued as he smiled. "And she ain't the only one leavin' po' street behind."

"Black Man, when was the last time you been on po' street? This ma'fucker got people hoppin' for him. I mention the name Travis Moore and people start runnin' to help. That's a name with some pop on it." He laughed.

"Bruce Bowen! Man, you are still a trip."

"Always have been, always will be. Don't let that music thing fool you." He gave his good friend a pound and a hug. "You looking good, dog. Conservative, but good." He backed up to take another look.

"This is how I play now. But look at the pot calling the kettle black. I wouldn't mind trading my suit in for yours."

"Your wife ain't gonna let you run my kind of life."

"Sho' you right. Man, what are you doing down here slumming?"

"Slummin' my ass." Bruce looked around the office. "You straight out here. Look here, man, I got them tickets for you."

"Anthony Hamilton at the Coliseum. Did you get front row?" Travis almost had his fingers crossed.

"No, I couldn't get front row." He pulled out what he had. "Can you settle for backstage passes?"

"Hell yeah!"

"Said it was your anniversary, right? I had to hook you up."

"I appreciate it; I hope my wife will, too."

"Come again." Bruce made his living in the music industry by being able to read people. He could hear a hit from two miles away. He could also pick up any sign of trouble before it presented itself. "You just came past me with some troubles. What up?"

Travis had one connection to his past that he would occasionally visit. Bruce was it. They might get together more if Bruce wasn't traveling all the time. Bruce was a year younger than Travis and he, like Travis, had left most of his past behind him. Bruce was the only person Travis had had contact with while he was at school.

When Travis had left for college, Bruce was the last person to see him. When Travis had turned up missing, some presumed that Bruce was somehow connected to his disappearance. Bruce was left with his hands on the operation that had been started by Kwame Brown and Travis aka Perry Moore. Two days after Travis had left, Kwame was back in town and ready to move product. Bruce had shown him how everything was running—the stash location, the workers, and the suppliers.

Travis had cautioned Bruce not to stay involved with Kwame. Make the transition and get it out of his hands. Then let Kwame do his thing. If Bruce stayed around Kwame, he would be stuck in the game. Travis was also aware of Bruce's music interest. So he put Bruce on with a promoter that was dealing above and below board. He fronted Bruce twenty thousand dollars to get down with the promoter for a show that was being put on that July. It helped get Bruce on his way in the music game. Travis felt it was the least he could do for the keeper of his biggest secret.

"So what gives, dog? What's stressing you?"

"Work."

"All right, let me run this down to you right quick." Bruce spoke at a rapid pace. "I know you; I know how you handle business. You ain't sweating that, 'cause you quick with your head and your feet. I didn't bring your worker no backstage passes; I brought you and your woman some. Now you the one who's hopin' she appreciates it, not your office. Now, I ask again, what's stressing you?"

Travis nodded his head in appreciation for Bruce's sense of perception. "Got any lunch plans?"

"I do now. Where can I get some sushi?"

"You eating sushi?"

"Been eating it. You?"

"Hell yeah. But none of these Japanese restaurants serve it during lunch. We got to do some riding to get to the nearest spot."

"Good, it will give you some time to ride in my new Benz."

"Benz? Must be nice."

"It is, my brother, it is."

CHAPTER 12

Continuous knocking at the front door had awakened him from his peaceful slumber. Lolly's hips, thighs and beautiful skin danced through his dreams. As Baby Jar came to, he was hoping that last night wasn't only a part of his dreams.

Jar scrambled to put something on and then reached between the worn-out mattress and box spring to retrieve the Glock Kwame had given to him. *Who could be looking for him*, he wondered. His mother was keeping her late nights again, but it couldn't be her. She had developed the habit of leaving her key with Mrs. Pearl, a neighbor she used to get high with. Mrs. Pearl had given her life to Christ, gotten clean and took every opportunity to preach to his mom. Jar sure didn't want to see her; he had been out all night himself and if she got wind of it, her preaching that was reserved for his mother would start rolling over to him.

When he reached the door, the knocking that paused briefly, started again. Definitely not Mrs. Pearl. She would be saying something by now.

"Who is it?" Jar barked. He dropped his voice to get more bass in it. The knocking stopped. He cocked the Glock to get a round in the chamber. He let the person on the other side of the door know that he meant business. There was no reply.

"I said, who is it? You don't say shit, I blast shit!"

"It's Evan, man," the scared voice replied nervously.

Great, Jar thought. *Why doesn't that goody-two shoes have his butt in school?* Then Jar noticed the time; it was almost three in the afternoon. Time had gotten away from him and there was no sign of his mother. She hadn't bothered to come home and surely had no idea that he had arrived home about seven in the morning. That familiar feeling of abandonment was smacking him in the face again. It had started creeping in two weeks after he had gotten out of rehab. Two weeks was all his mother could stand being off the streets.

"What do you want?" Jar demanded as he opened the door. He made sure the gun was visible.

Jar needed to interrupt any thoughts of self-pity. He wouldn't admit it, but he wanted somebody to keep him company, even if it was that knothead, Evan. This would be an opportunity to show him that he was now a hardened thug.

"I came by to check on you," Evan said, standing outside the ground-floor unit.

"The fuck? You gonna stand out there all day. It's cold out," Jar said, holding the door open. To put Evan at ease, Jar tucked the gun into his pants. "You coming in?"

"Is everything okay?" Evan asked as he cautiously hedged past Jar.

"Yeah." Jar checked outside the door like Kwame had taught him. He turned toward Evan. "Everything's straight."

"What are you looking for?"

"Making sure nothing funny is going on. You know how it is."

Fronting a thug image in front of his peers was easy. Around Kwame, Jar was careful not to say too much. He would absorb as much as he could from Kwame and emulate that persona in front of the people he knew.

Evan went into the living room and stood by the worn blue sofa with the mismatched cushions. There was a half-empty bowl of milk and Cap'n Crunch cereal sitting on an old coffee table.

"What are you waiting for? Sit your butt down."

Evan quickly grew tired of Jar's thug act. He continued to stand. "What's up with you?"

"What you talkin' about?" Jar knew full well what the question was.

"How come you weren't in school today?" Evan took it upon himself to be Jar's personal watchdog.

"Come on, man, you ain't gonna trip on me about that again, are you?"

"You know you supposed to be in school or they're going to send you back to that rehab place."

"Who you supposed to be? My mama?"

Evan looked around at the mess in the house. There were no visible signs of Jar's mother. "Somebody's got to look after you."

"Fuck you! Get out of my house."

Evan had succeeded in touching a nerve. He took a seat in satisfaction and defiance. "I'm not leaving until you tell me why you didn't go to school."

Rushing Evan was the first thing that came to Jar's mind. Evan was his partner; everybody knew that. If he knocked his teeth out, that would send a message to anybody who knew him. Baby Jar was not to be played with. The truth of the matter was that Jar was not willing to take that step yet. He didn't want to be left alone. He looked around the apartment and saw the same thing that Evan saw. Hopelessness. Evan was still waiting.

"I'm trying to get paid," Jar boasted. "I'm getting paid and then I'm gonna be up out of here."

"You gonna be up out of here alright. You'll be right up in a jail, messing with that bullshit."

"They ain't gonna catch me, dog. I'm getting schooled right this time."

"What's that mean? 'Schooled right'! There ain't no such thing when you messing with drugs."

"There ain't no such thing if it's personal. This is a business. You run it like a business and you can be successful." Jar regurgitated Bone's words verbatim. He was trying to convince himself as much as Evan.

"Did you hear that crap you tried to dump on me? Who's feeding you that shit?"

Jar had been warned not to mention Bone's name to anybody. He was in no rush to find out what would happen if he didn't heed the warning.

"It may be crap to you, but let me ask you something. What did you do last night?" Jar steered the conversation in a different direction.

Evan was dumbfounded. "Nothing, really. Why? What did you do?" Evan threw the conversation back at Jar. He didn't know where Jar was coming from, but he was going to see.

"Made some money. Two hundred bones."

"Damn! For real."

As principled as Evan was, he was taken by surprise. He knew the money was dirty, but two hundred dollars was a lot of loot in the hood.

"For shizzle!"

"Let me see it," Evan responded skeptically.

Jar started to run to his room to retrieve the money, then he hesitated. Bone had told him not to be too flashy with his shit. Even though Evan was his boy and wouldn't cause him problems, he was going to respect the game.

"How long you know me, E?"

"All my life."

"And my word is bond, right? So if I tell you I clocked two hundred dollars, then…"

"You clocked two hundred dollars."

There was a time when these two were inseparable. Over the last two years, they had changed a lot. Evan was thriving academically and Jar had found himself in trouble. Evan had missed all the clues when Jar had begun to slip the first time, but he had vowed that he would keep Jar on the straight and narrow.

"There is money to be made out there. I'm telling you. We could be paid, kid. I'm gonna hang with this old head for a while. Then I'm gonna be boomin' with my own thing. You want to get down?"

"I pass," Evan said without hesitation. He lived by the motto that all money wasn't good money.

"You gonna pass without hearing about the perks?"

"What perks? You act like you have a job. Perks? Brother, you hustle dope."

"Yo, ease up, man. I'm sayin' there's an upside to this, if you know how to work it."

"What are you talking about?" Evan was a little curious.

"Kid, I was up all night last night." Jar sniffed the index and forefinger on his right hand as if they were fine Cuban cigars.

"What? Bullshit. Where? Who?" Evan responded with excitement and disbelief. "Was it Dee Dee?"

"Hell nah. I done already broke that. I was with a woman."

"For real."

"E, that old head I'm rollin' with, he's puttin' me on, kid. He's got fine hoes comin' into apartments with no heat or electricity, and they still giving him play. I was sitting in another room counting money and this redbone, fine as she want to be, was back there serving him."

"Did he let you hit that?" Evan was almost drooling at the mention of sex.

"Hold up, you missing the point. This fine-ass woman was up in there, in check, because of the game."

"So, big deal. That doesn't mean anything for you." Evan was rushing to get to the point.

"After he was done, I took a ride with him. It was across town. He had to pick up some weight. So he tells me to come up to this spot with him. There's this fine, brown-skinned sister in that piece and that mug was thick. She must have been about twenty-four."

"Word."

"Dog, she had on one of them long, warm robes."

"How could you tell she was thick."

"That robe couldn't cover up all that fine. Anyway, my man was making a check on his weight so I started to check old girl out. Lolly, that's her name. I asked her what was up with her and the old head. She was like, never mind him; she wanted to know what was up with me." Jar was scared as hell last night, but Evan wasn't there and he didn't know the difference. Jar figured he might as well embellish. "So, I kept it cool. I nodded at my man and he nodded back. I looked at Lolly and told her to drop the robe. She was butt naked under there."

"No shit! Where she live? Can we go over there?"

Jar cut his jabbering off. "Man, you can't take your virgin ass over there. She'll hurt you. So, I told her to show me her room. Ol' Lolly couldn't wait to get me to her room. She tried to turn the light off in the room, but I told her to leave it on. I wanted her to see this thing comin' at her. I was layin' it down on her for about an hour." Jar was really spreading it on; he was lucky if he'd made it to two minutes.

"So, this bad sister let you get up in it like that?" Evan was both aroused and skeptical.

"Yeah, man, but it wasn't about me. It was all about the dope game. Lolly saw me kicking it with my man. She was down for whatever. Man, I have a harder time trying to get with these chickenheads we see at school or on the block. But out there, game recognizes game." He let Evan ponder those words for a few seconds. "E, we can run this. You want to get down?"

"That's not for me. You're too smart; it's not for you either. I mean, it sounds good. You got some money and some good pus, but that's the upside. You just got back from rehab. You know how it goes down out there. You ready for that?"

"It ain't goin' down like that no more. I got my man..."

"That doesn't change anything! That dope game leads to three things: jails, institutions and death. You've already been to an institution. If you're lucky, you might get to another one. The other options are jail and death. I'm down for you, but I'm not trying to get there with you. I'm going to stick this school thing out. If you want to get down with me, we can roll." Evan had heard enough and headed to the door. "I'll keep checking on you. Sorry, man, but I can't flow with you." Evan reached for the door.

"Maybe not today, but you'll see what I'm talking about," Jar said, slinging his last-ditch effort.

Evan paused and considered the words that had fallen on his ears. That was it; Jar finally had his ace in with him.

"And maybe you'll see what I'm talking about before it's too late."

Evan knew that if Jar stuck with his present choice, Jar would pull him down before Evan could pull him up. He walked out the apartment.

Jar thought he might be able to change Evan's mind if he worked on him some more. Jar didn't want to admit it, but Evan's words had hit him harder than anything Jar had thrown at Evan.

CHAPTER 13

The Kyoto Japanese Steakhouse was located six miles away from Home Supply's office. Travis and Bruce had spent the last three hours hanging out together. Like two high school kids, they were playing hooky. They went joy riding in Bruce's Benz and caught up on some old times. When they settled in for lunch, the conversation began to take a more serious turn. Travis filled Bruce in on Kwame and Jarquis Love and the events that had transpired at Home Supply that morning.

"See, that's bullshit. A brother like you, or me, we hit that ass for one-point-nine mil, what do you think we're doing? Won't be clearing out no desk, that's for damn sure."

"It's the game. No matter what walk of life you in, there's always a game being played," Travis said.

"The truth has been spoken, hustler to hustler." Bruce paused, rethinking his words. "Legitimate hustler to legitimate hustler. So?"

"So, what?"

"We've been dancing around the real issue all day. Don't get me wrong, I like hanging out with my dog, but what gives with you and the woman?"

"It's not her. It's more about me than anything," Travis said with hesitation.

"So, we're talking about those days, right?"

"Yeah, they were weighing on me and causing problems between Kenya and me. Stuff started coming back to me when we moved to Charlotte. I've been married to Kenya for five years. She's given me her life and a son. It was time to give it up to her or give her up. I wasn't willing to give up this life I built for myself. So, I decided it was time to let her in on who she was married to." Travis looked at Bruce.

"You told her everything?" Bruce watched Travis. He could see Travis replaying his past, then Travis looked away. "How much?"

"I told her about my mom and why I started slinging. There were no names mentioned. I just told her about me and hustling."

"You didn't tell her about Kwame? I mean, that nigga is still out there running shit. I've seen him once or twice since I left that life years ago. That nigga ain't right. He was still asking about you. That brother still got beef with you."

"I'm not tripping on Kwame. His beef is his beef. I told my wife I used to hustle with somebody, but I wanted to tell her about me, That's it."

"Did you tell her about...?" Bruce was reluctant to ask the question.

"No. I didn't get that far. She had enough going on in her head. She was looking at me like she didn't know who I was anymore. She came up so different from me. She can't fathom what that kind of life is like. She doesn't understand the dope thing. She'd never understand me doing what I did, no matter what the reason was. That's going to have to come at some other time, if ever."

"I feel you. It's good to have finally laid that shit down though, right?"

"For me, yeah. For her, I don't know. It caught her off guard. We'll have to wait and see."

"She'll come around. The more you try to keep something hidden, the more power you give to it. Some things need to stay under wraps for a while, but it all eventually comes out. What you let her in on, it ain't that bad. Give her some time." Bruce knew the story of Perry Moore got much darker, but there was no need to dwell on that now. "Man, I got to get movin'. I'm in the studio tonight. I got this kid that we're doing some work with. He's about to blow up." Bruce took out a roll of bills, peeled off a hundred-dollar bill and laid it on the table. "You want a limo for the show?"

"No doubt."

"I'll get you straight with your lady."

"Thanks, man. I've been getting hooked up by some of the old fellas lately."

"What are you talking about?"

"I was speeding last night and I got pulled over by a state trooper. You wouldn't believe who's the police now. Rick Nixon."

"Rick...Rick...Nixon." Bruce furled his eyebrows, trying to recall the name. "Light Bright? That brother's the police?" he asked incredulously.

"That's what I said."

"He give you a ticket?"

"No, he let me pass."

"Hell, all them passes you gave him back in the day, he need to let you slide on about fifty tickets. I'll be damned, that crooked-ass brother is Mister Do Right."

"A whole lot of crooked brothers from back in the day are doing right these days."

"True that." Bruce picked up his last piece of sushi with his chopsticks and dipped it in some soy sauce. He looked around before he spoke his next words. "You ever figure out what you're going to do with that stuff I'm holdin'?"

"I'm working on some ideas, but I'm not ready to move on that yet." Travis' voice was cold and calculating. It took Bruce by surprise.

"Yo, dog, for a second, I didn't know if I was sitting here with Perry or Travis. That nigga Perry could be cold-blooded."

"No, Perry is long gone. I just remember how to look out for me."

"Let me know what to do when you're ready. I got your back."

Travis nodded. Whenever they talked about the incident, their conversations were extremely vague. They never mentioned the gun that Bruce was holding for him. Travis knew he needed to leave it with Bruce some fifteen years ago. Knowing that Kwame was still kicking it around town, Travis had the feeling that the gun would later be of some use to him.

CHAPTER 14

Kenya's plans for the afternoon had been drastically altered. Instead of completing her to-do list, she'd decided to hang out with Lisa and Lisa's new friend, Keith. Keith had hooked up with one of his friends, Fred, at the gym. Fred was muscular and could throw weights around with anybody in the gym, but he didn't strike Kenya as being particularly bright.

When they'd decided to eat lunch at Carolina Place Mall, Kenya had left her car at the gym and had ridden with Lisa. Keith and Fred had followed in a black Datsun 280ZX.

The lunch conversation over their Chinese food was boring Kenya to no end. Kenya's initial impression of Fred proved to be true. He said nothing of interest. Keith, on the other hand, was talking a mile a minute to make up for Fred's lack of conversation. But for all of his gum flapping, he wasn't saying a thing. It reminded Kenya of sitting in a high school cafeteria, listening to a sophomore boy throw some weak rap at a senior young lady. But Lisa was hanging on to every syllable he uttered. Keith picked up the tab for lunch and the four of them began to do some window-shopping.

Keith, the big spender, didn't let his generosity stop there. When they reached the storefront for the Lady Foot Locker, Keith put a stop to his little entourage.

"You know what I want to do?" Keith said to Lisa. "I want you to go in there and pick you out some more of those outfits that you look so good in. Kenya, you're more than welcome to get something."

"That won't be necessary."

"It's on me."

"Really!" Lisa was glowing.

That was the only bit of hesitation Lisa offered before she was in the store and lifting outfits off the racks. Moments later, Lisa was gracing everyone with her presence as Keith's personal supermodel. The more outfits Lisa tried on, the giddier she became. Conversely, the more irritated Kenya became with having to play chaperone.

Lisa was barely able to contain herself when Keith picked out three of his favorite outfits and purchased them for her. Kenya watched as her friend turned to putty; it was only a matter of time before she was ready to hand over the booty. If she'd said, "no, thank you," or had shown some kind of backbone to redeem herself, Kenya thought it would have shown Keith that she had some control in all of this. As long as Lisa was being showered with presents, she wasn't going to let the opportunity pass her by. Lisa picked up her bags, ready to head back in the mall area for more window-shopping. Kenya watched her friend and thought, *If she runs out of here, holding her bags in each hand, looks up toward the ceiling and starts turning circles à la Mary Tyler Moore, I'll leave her where she's standing.*

"I need to use the restroom," Lisa blurted as they walked. "Would you two excuse me?" she asked of Keith and Fred.

"Sure." Keith smiled. Fred nodded and gave a half-smile.

"Kenya, dear, will you come with?"

"Uh-huh." Kenya was surprised she'd even asked. She looked at the two guys in their company and knew she sure as hell wasn't going to make small talk with them. The two women ducked into the nearest restroom and Keith and Fred found the nearest rail to lean against.

"Girl, you are tripping," Kenya said.

"What are you talking about?" Lisa was dumbfounded.

"Kenya, dear, will you come with?" Kenya barely got the words out before she started laughing. "Some free gifts can do that to you, turn you proper?"

"You liked that, didn't you? They were impressed; I could tell."

"Impressed? I don't think so." Frankly, Kenya didn't know if either one of them had any inclination that she was using proper English, especially Fred. Regardless of what was said, he'd only nod and smile.

"Shit, they were impressed. So, what do you think of Keith?"

"The same, I mean, he's okay." Kenya still had other things on her mind. Evaluating Lisa's love life didn't rate that high on her priority scale at the moment.

"Okay, nothing. That man just bought me over two hundred dollars' worth of workout gear. Girl, he's feeling me. He could be the one." She checked her face in the mirror. "You know, if you weren't married, you could hook up with his friend."

No she didn't just say that, Kenya thought. *Lisa's lack of a man must make anything walking with that third leg in the middle seem eligible.*

"No thanks," she replied politely. "Not even close to my type."

"Oh, girl, give him some play. It's not like your husband is getting with it." As soon as the words had left her mouth, Lisa knew she had screwed up.

"Lisa..." Kenya's voice was monotone and she was pissed. "I don't give a damn what kind of man you're in to and what the hell you do with him. But obviously, since you don't have a regular one, I don't think you are the one to make an assumption about mine. Now, it would be wise for you to shut the fuck up about my man before I break my foot off in your behind. If you are so impressed with that muscle-bound, thick-necked, muted ogre, why don't you show the two of them the time of their lives."

"I'm sorry. I didn't mean..."

"Save it. After I'm finished in here, you can take me back to the gym so I can get my car."

"Okay." Lisa's mouth had succeeded in opening wide enough to stick her foot in it.

The two of them continued to straighten themselves up in silence. Lisa searched in vain for the right words that would make everything okay. Kenya waited for one more wrong thing to be said. With all the things on her mind, a straight right to Lisa's jaw would be what the doctor ordered to relieve her stress.

Keith and Fred were having an intense conversation themselves at that moment. Fred had more to say after Kenya and Lisa had left than he'd said during the entire time that they were present.

"So how long I got to keep this up?" Fred's patience was growing thin.

"What the fuck else you got to do?" Keith snapped. The charming person who was entertaining company at the gym was nowhere to be found.

"Bone, I don't..." Fred started.

"Nigga, shut up before I cut your throat." The voice was low, but the intensity was deafening. "You call me Keith."

"C'mon, man. This is whack. You callin' me Fred. Just call me Flake; them tricks don't know me. Man, what's going on? Why we hangin' with these hoes?"

"What I told you was goin' on. You need to hang tight with that uppity-ass bitch and get as much info as you can from her," Keith, a.k.a. Kwame "Bone" Brown, responded.

"Bone…Keith, you trippin', man. I don't know what the fuck's goin' on, but you trippin'. Look, I done kept my lip on some bullshit lately. You sportin' that kid every night while you out hustlin'. Last night, that little punk was pushin' the 280 and now we up in a mall frontin' like buppies with these two uppity broads. This ain't you. What's goin' on?"

"Flake, who runs this show?"

"You."

"Damn right. Me, and I pay your ass, right?" Bone waited and Flake nodded. "When I tell you to do something, you do it. You don't ask no questions. All you need to know is that I'm workin' on something." Bone eyed that thick, muscle-bound Flake for a second and realized that Flake was concerned. "Now, when you ready to buck again"—the voice was cold and heartless, almost hollow— "you let me know so I can call your fat-ass mama and tell her to get her best black dress. There'll be a whole lot of slow singin' after they find your ass gutted."

Flake hung his head. He was ashamed because he showed concern and Bone would view that as weakness. He also knew that no matter what he did for Bone, no matter what roads they traveled together, Bone wouldn't hesitate to burn him like anybody else on the street.

"Nigga, you best to get your head up. Them bitches is coming and you get me my info. I want to find out as much about her as I can."

Flake nodded his head in compliance. He prepared himself for the next round of lies and deceit. He still had no idea why it was important to get any information on Kenya. The thought of failing Bone and the repercussions from it would motivate him to find out something for him.

"Well, welcome back, ladies," Bone said with all the warmth

and charm he could muster. In the blink of an eye, he was back in Keith mode.

"It'll be a short welcome. I've got to go," Kenya said as she and Lisa approached them. "I've got some other things to take care of."

"Are you leaving us, Lisa?" Bone inquired. "I haven't finished shopping for you yet."

The thought of more free gifts was enticing and Lisa wanted to continue to stay in Keith's company, but she needed to do some making up with Kenya. While she was contemplating Keith's offer, Kenya interjected. "I'll catch a cab, Lisa. You go on and enjoy yourself. It was a pleasure meeting you two," Kenya lied.

"And you as well," Bone added. He cut his eyes to Flake.

"Can I walk you?" Flake asked.

Kenya was shocked to hear him speak. "That won't be necessary." She was already on her way. "Lisa, call me," she said pleasantly. At the moment, she felt that if Lisa called next year, it would be too soon.

"So, are there any more outfits you want to see me in, Keith?" Lisa asked with a hint of seduction in her voice.

Lisa's attention was only on Keith. It ticked Kenya off even more as she continued to walk to the nearest exit. Lisa was on her own. Flake didn't know what to do next. He started to take off after her until he noticed Bone dart his eyes in his direction. Without uttering a word or moving a muscle in his body, Bone told him to stay put. Like a trained Doberman Pinscher, Flake quickly obeyed his master's wishes.

Once Flake was held at bay, he was content to engage Lisa in conversation. She was a talker. Although he would have preferred to have Kenya with them, he would use Lisa to extract whatever information he could get on Kenya and use Flake as his cover. After all, the information wouldn't be for him; it would be for Flake.

"You keep talkin' like that and you're going to get more than just another outfit out of me," Bone said as he winked at Lisa. He knew this broad was ready to fall for anything. "Fred, looks like you missed out." His eyes followed Kenya as she moved further away from them. "Don't worry, you can hang with us." Bone knew this would help to put Flake at ease.

"She's a trip anyway. She and her husband, they can be a little uppity." Lisa couldn't wait to kick some dirt on Kenya.

"You know them pretty well?" Bone asked innocently, but he was starting his deep-sea fishing. He shot a quick nod to Flake.

"I know them overextended bourgeois Negroes," Lisa lied to sound as if she had the scoop on all their business.

"Can you tell me more about her?" Flake asked. That question met with Bone's approval. Flake now understood his job. He would spend the rest of the time with them milking Lisa for information.

CHAPTER 15

As the five o'clock hour approached, Travis was ready to call it a day. After the long lunch he'd taken with Bruce, he wasn't much good for the remainder of the day anyway. He was counting the seconds as they passed. To his surprise and disappointment, he hadn't heard from Kenya. Under normal circumstances, he would have called her by now. But at the moment, the circumstances weren't normal. He thought it was best to give her some more time.

Travis had seen what he thought was going to be an eventful day turn into a rather uneventful one. Patricia had lost her job as a result of her embezzlement, but little else. Actually, she had been rewarded. Brad had gotten word to him that part of the settlement in her termination allowed her to remain vested in Home Supply. Although she had to give up $1.9 million, she stood to gain roughly $4.5 million when the company went public. That put her $2.6 million ahead. She must have had some really good stuff on Tom to work that out.

The phone rang and Travis picked it up almost before it finished the first ring.

"Hello?"

"Damn, Travis. Can you pick the phone up any faster?" Slim said.

"How are you doing, Slim?"

"I'm fine. How's the brother?"

"Good. What's going on?" Travis was concerned that something was wrong at Garrison or with Baby Jar.

"Everything's cool. I just wanted to check on you. You know I threw some weight on you yesterday."

"It's all right. It helped me to look at some things. You were right; I needed to open up."

Slim paused to see if any of that openness was going to come his way. There was none forthcoming.

"So when are you swinging back through?"

"Sometime next week. I would try to slide by tonight, but I'm heading to the house. I'm off tomorrow and I'm going to spend some quality time with my wife, if she'll let me."

"Let you?" Slim was about to get started.

"You know what I mean." Travis tried to squirm out of his statement.

"Hell no, I don't know nothing about that. Let me ask you something; you are the man, right?"

"Are you going somewhere with this?"

"Okay, let me school you real quick. You got the wrong terminology. See, you gonna let her spend some time with you."

"I'll keep that in mind, but right now I'm trying to get with my woman to celebrate our fifth anniversary."

"It's your anniversary?"

"Saturday, but I'm taking tomorrow off and I'm going to see if I can get it started tonight. No need to stay around here. They have some snow in the forecast."

"Yeah, I heard. I don't want to get snowed in here. I've been through that before. I won't keep you. Congratulations to you and the Mrs."

"I appreciate it. I'll holler at you next week."

Travis hung up the phone. Opening up to Kenya was one thing and that was hard. Sharing information about his personal life with Slim wasn't something he was prepared to do. Plus, there was no need for Slim to know the situation between him and his wife. Travis grabbed his coat and briefcase and was on his way out the office.

Travis got into his car, plugged in his cell phone and debated the pros and cons of calling Kenya. The debate was short-lived. He quickly called his house, but the machine picked up. Travis hung up and dialed Kenya's cell phone.

"Hello?" Kenya answered.

"K, it's me." Travis was silent. He didn't know what he wanted to say. He could tell by the sound on the other end that Kenya was in her car. "Do you need me to pick up Michael?"

"No, I already have him."

"Are you near the house?"

"No." She paused. "I'm on my way to Raleigh. I'm near Greensboro."

"Greensboro?" Travis was surprised. She was almost an hour away and headed in the direction of the bad weather. This concerned him because he knew how she was about driving in bad weather.

"I'm taking him to Mom and Dad's. I'll be back later tonight." There was a pause. Kenya had decided to take their son to her parents for the weekend to give her some time alone with her husband. Driving to Raleigh and back would give her more time to think things through. She'd heard the weather forecast for the Raleigh area but didn't let that deter her. "You don't mind, do you?"

Hell yeah, Travis minded; those roads were going to be hazardous. "No, I don't mind. It's a great idea. You be careful on those roads."

"I will."

"I'll see you when you get home. You want me to get you something for a late dinner?"

"Yeah, surprise me with something."

"Done. I'll talk to you in a little while." The words came out pleasantly enough as he hung up, but his mind was already somewhere else entirely. The time alone would be good for them. Kenya leaving for Raleigh without telling him had caught him off guard though. That was not like her at all. Travis wasn't comfortable with her actions, but he excused it. With everything that he had confided in her, he'd let her have some time to do whatever it was that she needed to do.

Without Kenya at home, there was no need to rush there. Travis considered dropping by Garrison. That thought was halted abruptly, almost as quickly as it began. Tomorrow, he would be on vacation; he was going to have some fun tonight. If it wasn't with Kenya, it would be with somebody else. He could act as irresponsibly as she could. Travis looked for another phone number in his cell phone to dial.

"Holler at me," the voice on the other end stated as the phone was answered.

"What's going on, Bruce?"

"Travis? What up, playa?"

"I'm cooling."

"Cooling?" Bruce mocked. "You've been out of the hood too long. You're chillin', or at least coolin'. Drop the g, partner. What can I do for you?"

"You in the studio yet?"

"I take it things didn't work out with your lady and the tickets?"

"Don't know. I haven't had the chance to play those yet."

"Uh-huh." Bruce paused. "We're getting ready to get busy in a few. If you have some free time, swing over to 1938 Morehead. This kid is off the heezie." Bruce rethought his wording. "That means the boy is bad."

"I know what you meant," Travis said flatly.

"Come by. We can run the gift of gab; plus, you can see how we make a number one hit. It's True Beats."

"I got it." Travis hung up. He was anxious to get to Morehead Street. It was time to discover if life in the music business was like the life in the music videos. Travis would get the opportunity to see for himself.

CHAPTER 16

"This ain't making sense to you, is it?" Bone broke the silence they had been riding in.

Flake simply shrugged his shoulders and kept his eyes on the road. All the years of running with Bone had taught him many things—most importantly, when to keep his mouth shut. A lesson he'd briefly forgotten earlier in the day. He opted to drive silently. Given enough time, Bone would continue the conversation on his own.

"There is a method to the madness. I'm on another level and you ma'fuckers ain't ready to see me. But you'll see me when I post the nigga up."

Flake didn't know what the hell Bone was talking about. He was tripping and it was beginning to make him uneasy. Bone's behavior had been strange the last couple of months, but the last couple of days were something else. If getting stranger by the passing minute was taking it to another level, he was there.

"You back that ma'fucker down, shoot him an elbow, then throw that shit down on him!" Bone was visibly rocking in the passenger seat.

Flake thought the window would crack when Bone shot an elbow to it. Bone growled as he mocked a thunderous dunk. Flake remained calm, but his fingers and forearms told a different story. The forearms flexed as his fingers tightened their grip on the steering wheel.

"What up with you, nigga? You tense?" Bones darting eyes picked up the rigidity in his arms.

"I'm trying to figure out what's going on?" Flake kept his eyes on the road.

"You ain't ready to see me." Bone waited for a comment but Flake wasn't going for it. "Oh, you can't talk to a ma'fucker now?"

"What you want me to say?" Flake picked his words carefully.

"What you want to ask?"

Flake hesitated. He was worried about Bone. He felt like the brother was slipping and he didn't know why. Flake knew Bone wasn't playing the game smart. Bone was his meal ticket. He kept him around the game and money in his pocket. If Bone fell off, then Flake would be short. Flake knew his limitations; he wasn't smart enough to run game on his own. He needed to be the muscle for the big man. He needed Bone to stay on point. It was time for him to say something to get a handle on what was happening.

"Why did you blow a g on that broad?" Flake finally asked.

"I'm working on something." Bone smiled.

"Some ass? You didn't have to drop a g on her to hit that. You frontin' like you somebody else, talkin' all proper."

Bone chuckled and shook his head. "It ain't about droppin' a g on that broad. The information I got out of her was worth five g's to me." He waited for the light bulb to go off for Flake. "You don't get it, do you?"

Flake waited to be enlightened.

"Getting info on the other broad is what I was after. I needed to get the lowdown on her for something else I got planned." Bone's mind went somewhere else. "I know where she lives, where she works and where she works out. I know what perfumes she wears and where her snotty-nosed little bastard goes to school. I needed to know all this to get inside his head. I can mess with it before I blow it up. I'm gonna get mine back for all I lost to that shit."

All he lost? Flake thought. He wanted to press for more answers but he knew Bone well enough. He wouldn't be forthcoming with many more revelations until he was ready. "So you got this in check?" Flake asked wearily, trying to bring him back.

"It's on lock, playa."

"Cool." Flake paused. "What about the kid?"

"Now you're seeing things. That's the trump card."

Flake wasn't sure what that meant. Lisa, Kenya and Baby Jar figured into some plan of Bone's.

"I took the kid over to Lolly's last night, to make that pick-up."

"You did?" Flake was stunned by this news. He wasn't sure what surprised him more—that the kid had made the run with him or that he'd gone to Lolly's. It was a cocaine pick-up and Flake knew firsthand how Lolly got down.

"Oh yeah. She served him up, too, dog. Knocked his brains out."

"Lolly let him hit that?" The car swerved as Flake asked the question.

"Don't even trip like that. Lolly's down for the game, you know that. She ain't nobody to be real with."

"Sho you right. She a bad thing, for real though." Flake played it off. He didn't want Bone to know how pissed off he was that a sixteen-year-old kid had the opportunity to lay up in the same guts that he was trying to lay claim to.

"She was badder than a mug last night, too. All her shit was poppin'. She did the kid with the lights on. That little brother is loving the game right about now. He could be a true baller out here. He's right at the edge of doing anything for it. I'm going to take him to the pit that there ain't no coming back from. He's gonna step up for me. He's gonna do what I need him to do, too."

Flake kept thinking this was getting stranger by the moment. Bone's words had left him behind again. He put his eyes in the middle of the road and decided to keep his head down. Flake wasn't sure where any of this was going. With Bone's behavior the way it was, he was sure the road ahead would be a rough one to travel.

CHAPTER 17

The snow that had begun to fall an hour-and-a-half into her trip had gotten heavier as she approached Raleigh. Kenya wasn't a big fan of driving in inclement weather since she had had an accident on an icy bridge in Charlotte three years ago. She didn't get hurt in the accident but the Toyota Avalon she was driving did. The Lexus LX570 that she was now driving was a result of the accident. As sturdy as the SUV was, there were two occasions where she'd considered turning back to Charlotte, but she kept pressing forward. She thought the farther she got from Charlotte, the less Travis would be on her mind; she was wrong.

Kenya turned into the secluded Glenhurst subdivision that was the home of her teenage years, and took the familiar route to her parents' house. Kenya told herself she would make a quick drop-off with Michael and get back on the road before it got too late. She was also getting leery of the road conditions and wondering if coming here was a good idea. Kenya honked the horn to get her parents' attention. It dawned on her that she'd never bothered to ensure they would be home. Her parents were semi-retired and would take off on a trip at the spur of the moment. She left the car running while she prepared to get Michael and his bags out the car.

"Girl! What is wrong with you?" Kenya's mother shouted as she opened the double doors at the front of her house. Lillian Jackson's face was all smiles at the pleasant surprise. She dashed out the door to greet her baby girl and her grandson.

Kenya smiled in relief when she caught sight of her mother. She gave up on trying to free Michael from the seatbelt. Her mother would have him in her arms before she could get him out the carseat.

"There's my baby boy!" Lillian exclaimed as she reached the car. It took her no time to reach inside to grab hold of him. "Look at you! You have gotten so big." She was filled with pride as she freed him from the seat restraints.

"Mother...your daughter. Hello," Kenya said to call attention to herself.

"Oh, hey baby. This is such a surprise. Why didn't you tell anybody you were coming? I would have straightened up."

Kenya shot her mother a look that said *I don't believe you*. Not one day in her entire life growing up with her parents could Kenya recall her mother ever having anything out of place in their house.

"Now, you cut this car off and come inside." The mother in Lillian was coming out. "You have no business driving in weather like this."

"Mama, I have to. I've got to get back to Charlotte."

"Not tonight, you're not."

"Mama, Travis and I are celebrating our anniversary."

"Well, then he should have come with you." Lillian put an end to the conversation.

Kenya knew it was over, too. Deep down, she knew this would happen and probably wanted it to. That's why she'd kept driving toward Raleigh. Kenya wanted to deal with Travis but she wasn't quite ready. The inclement weather in Raleigh and her mother would see to it that she didn't have to. Kenya feigned reluctance as she turned off the Lexus. That settled, Lillian took Michael out the car and made her way back to the entrance of the house. Kenya grabbed Michael's bag and her gym bag out the trunk.

"You'll just have to call Travis and tell him you can't get back on the road tonight." Lillian passed through the entranceway.

"Yes, ma'am," Kenya responded as she entered the house.

She set the bags down in the foyer and made a dash for the den. Lillian eyed the bags and shook her head. Her house would be in disarray. Once Kenya crossed over the threshold of her childhood home, she was the baby girl once again. She was hoping to see her father; she was always a daddy's girl. He wasn't in the den so she hopped into his favorite chair.

"Where's Dad?"

"Downstairs in the basement. He's building something else we can't use." Lillian rolled her eyes. "Something for me to clean up."

"Daddy's still dabbling with the woodwork?" Kenya listened for the sound of wood being cut. She couldn't hear anything.

"Dabbling? I think he's trying to build an ark down there."

"Oh, I gotta see that."

"I'll call him up for you." Lillian managed to balance Michael in one arm and grab the bags with her free hand: years of practice had prepared her for a day like today. She walked by the closed basement door and used her elbow to nudge a button to the right of the door. Lillian paused for a second as if she was listening for something, then she turned back to her daughter. "He'll be up here in a minute. Won't he be surprised?"

"What did you do?"

"Your daddy doesn't know what to do with his money. He soundproofed the basement so his working down there won't bother me up here," Lillian explained as she continued walking to Kenya's old bedroom.

Before Eddie Jackson had retired, he had been a partner with the prestigious Colby and Sturgis law firm. Now that he had time on his hands, he loved to play with different gadgets. Power tools to electronics—you name it, he had it. The house was full of high-definition TVs and digital cameras, and video cameras on the outside of the house. Eddie could check any part of his house, inside or out, by simply turning any TV in the house to channel 98. The button by the basement door and the soundproof room were the latest additions. He knew Lillian was calling for him when she pushed the button beside the basement door. It set off a series of red lights that blinked intermittently to let him know that Lillian needed him.

"What is it, Lil?" Eddie had rushed up from the basement and cracked the door to make sure that nothing was wrong. He was fifty-eight and in great shape. "Lil?"

"In here," Kenya said, trying to imitate her mother.

"Well, what is it?" he said moving toward the voice and knocking the sawdust off his clothes. "Baby Girl!" he said when he caught a glimpse of his chair. He opened his arms and Kenya jumped out the chair to hug him.

"What's with all the sawdust?" she asked as she stopped in her tracks and backed away from the embrace.

Knowing that she was trying to get away, Eddie grabbed her and hugged her tightly before letting her go. "What are you all doing here? It's your anniversary. You kids can't be spending it up here with your parents?"

"No, I brought Michael for a few days so Travis and I could spend some time together."

"Hmm." Eddie paused and squinted his eyes at his daughter. "Are you two trying to double up on us?"

"Daddy?!"

"Edward!" Lillian said, laughing. She held Michael by his hands and helped him walk toward the den.

"What did I say?" he asked innocently. "Give me my grandson."

"Not until you get cleaned up."

"This is a manly smell, Lil. He needs to get some of that on him. Make him hard."

"Hard, huh? This from a man who gets a facial more often than me."

"Facial?" Kenya chided him as well.

"You tease me now, but you don't hesitate to get up under me when I've just had one," Eddie shot back. Lillian didn't say a word. She knew he was right.

"I guess I'd better get back on the road. I can't stay." It was Kenya's last attempt to convince herself that she really considered driving back to Charlotte.

Eddie read her choice of words. Kenya was in the habit of making definitive statements. She had done that since she was a toddler. He always knew when she had something else on her mind when she didn't make definitive statements.

"I don't know what road you think you're going to get on. I already told you that you're staying here." Lillian was done with this foolishness. She gave Kenya the same type of look when they'd had disagreements when Kenya was in high school. "You are not too grown to go out back and get your own switch," Lillian teased to break the tension. "Baby, call Travis like I said. He wouldn't want you out there driving in the snow. Why did he let you drive here anyway?

"It was a spur of the moment idea. I didn't tell him I was bringing Michael here until I was an hour away." She could have put her foot in her mouth; her mother would have a thousand questions. "I'll give him a call."

"I'm going back downstairs to finish up. Baby Girl, I'm glad you made it home safely. Tell Travis I'm sorry he couldn't make it when you talk to him. Come down and check out my new digs in a little bit." Eddie rambled to get himself out the room. He knew it wouldn't be long before his daughter came to hang out with him. No matter how much bickering went on between his wife and his daughter, Lillian was Kenya's confidante. He would let them have their time together. Something was going on between Kenya and Travis. Once he was out the way, Kenya and Lillian would be free to talk.

Lillian watched Eddie as he went to the basement and watched the door close behind him. Lillian picked up the remote to the television and flipped to the Cartoon Network. *Scooby-Doo* would keep Michael's attention.

"This has got to be real good," Lillian started.

"*Scooby-Doo*?"

"Don't play with me. You show up here unannounced."

"Unannounced? I have to announce myself now?" Kenya said with a smile, trying to find humor in the moment.

"Unannounced." Lillian's look was back, this time for real. "You drove through a snowstorm."

"The ground's barely cov…" Kenya paused when she noticed her mother's look.

"The ground was barely covered when you ran into the side of that bridge, too." She paused, but still watched her. "Kenya, you are a grown woman with your own responsibilities, and to take off and come here without telling anybody, tells me that something is wrong. Now are we going to play cat and mouse, or are you going to tell me what's going on?"

This was her chance to talk to someone she could trust. She was relieved and almost happy to get the thoughts out in her mind. She would have confided in Jasmine but Lisa was around. For the next twenty minutes, she told her mother about what had happened the previous evening—the missed dinner, the argument, which had led to the revelation of the hidden secrets of Travis Moore's life.

Lillian handled the details of the dinner and the argument well enough. Those things are to be expected in a marriage. But she sat in stunned disbelief as Kenya talked about her husband's past life. From the moment Travis had stepped into her daughter's life, she knew he was the one for her child. When they'd married, Lillian viewed him as no less than her own son. Kenya was her only child and he was the son she would have wished for. She knew that he had no family to speak of. His mother had died before he'd gone to college. She had always been drawn to him. But now this! She empathized with her daughter's confusion. She was confused herself.

Nothing about Travis ever gave her any indication that he would have anything like this in his past. Lillian's motherly instincts told her that she had to protect her child and her grandchild. She had no idea what kind of dangers Travis and his past life could present. For all she knew, he could still be involved in that type of life.

"Kenya, is it wise for you to go back?" Lillian resisted the urge to tell her daughter that she wasn't returning. "Is that why you and the baby came home?"

"Excuse me? No, it's not why I came home. I'm not here to stay. Maybe I needed a break to clear my head a little, but being home with my husband is where I belong."

"How do you know that he's not involved with that mess now? You could be in danger. You said he left you for a couple of hours last night." Lillian stared at her daughter and let her ponder the thought.

"Don't do that, Mama. It took my husband more than seven years to reveal that to me. He was tired of carrying that secret. If he tells me it's done and over, then it's done and it is over." Kenya wasn't backing down from her point. "I trust that this conversation stays between us."

Kenya wanted to show her mother that she believed in her husband. She had to; otherwise, everything they'd built together was a lie. One thing that she couldn't deny was that Travis Moore's past did bother her, and Lillian's seeds of doubt certainly didn't help any.

CHAPTER 18

Donna Love sat in her room and contemplated which lie to tell her son tonight before she escaped into the streets. Donna's nickname was Sugar. Sugar Love, for her caramel-colored skin that tasted so sweet. She could remember a time when men lined up around the block for a piece of that hot, sugar-coated, caramel skin.

When she looked in the mirror to stroke her long, thick, rich black hair, she couldn't help but marvel at how fine her body was. It was no wonder she could still drive the men crazy.

"Girl, you still the bomb diggity!" she told herself.

What did she know? She was staring at herself with bloodshot eyes that didn't hesitate to lie to her. The mirror reflected a body that was worn down by prostitution, heroin and crack; she had nearly overdosed on two occasions. She was bone thin. Her body smelled of the cold winter streets, and her hair was a dingy black with gray streaks. The once-beautiful caramel complexion was now ashen; it gave her a ghost-like appearance.

Sugar couldn't see any of this. She wasn't living in reality. Her world was consumed with finding that next high or that next guy. If she were lucky, she would get a two-for-one.

Once Donna was satisfied with her appearance, she went into the kitchen. Food wasn't on her mind; finding the right excuse to get out the house was. When she opened the refrigerator door, she had it. The refrigerator was near empty as usual.

"Baby Jar! You drink all this damn milk in here! Ain't nothin' but a damn swallow in the jug!" Donna yelled as she raised the half-gallon carton. The small quantity of milk made some noise as it sloshed from side to side.

There goes that crazy-ass woman again, he thought. This was part of her routine. Jar kept his mouth shut and continued to watch the music video on BET. He was forced to watch television on the thirteen-inch secondhand TV; Donna had pawned their thirty-one-inch Sony when he'd completed rehab two months ago.

"Nigga, you hear me talking to you!"

Jar slowly blinked his eyes and thought, *why does she keep doing this*? She was a grown woman, entitled to do anything she wanted. There was no need for these bullshit excuses.

Donna had stayed at home three nights after Jar was released from rehabilitation, and it was killing her. By the time that third night rolled around, she was jumpy at any sound and she could not keep still. He knew that look she had about her. When he was a runner, he could spot a mark from three blocks away. He couldn't miss a mark that was sitting in his face, even if it was his own mother.

"Nigga, I will smack the shit out of you!" Donna yelled, as she flung the milk container in his direction. "I got to go to the store and get some more."

"Ain't no store near here open at this time of the night. All you got is Peso's and they started closing at eight o'clock since they had that shooting up there at the corner. It's almost nine." Jar thought she could make up a better excuse to get out the house than that.

"You ungrateful little smart ass." Donna rushed him. It was time to teach this boy a lesson.

Baby Jar sat patiently. Her slapping and grabbing would be over soon. He felt the first slap on the side of his face, then the second and a third. She reached for his neck and he felt both of her hands tightening around him. Enough was enough; he wasn't going to sit idly and take another beating from this woman.

"Why don't you just go?" Jar snatched her hands from his neck. "Go to the store; go out into them streets, wherever. Just leave me alone. All this shit ain't necessary."

Donna was shocked to hear her son speak to her this way. She was also surprised that Jar had removed her hands with such ease.

"Don't you disrespect me and my house. Don't you cuss at me."

"Ain't nobody disrespecting you, but you."

This rant and rave act of Donna's was getting old. Jar held her hands in check. She wasn't fooling either of them. They both knew what she wanted. She wanted to leave the house. There was a moment of shame that Donna felt. She realized that her son saw her for what she was. Donna Love was a crackhead. The woman who was in front of him disgusted Jar. Knowing that the confrontation was over, Jar released her hands.

The silence that followed smothered Donna as she searched for something to say. Nothing she could think of would fit. The bottom line was that she still wanted to get the hell out that house.

"I guess I'll go get that milk. Is there anything else you need?"

Jar knew that was a load of crap she'd thrown at him; as well as she did.

"No, thank you." Jar's disgust resonated in his voice, but he was also torn. He longed for his mother to behave responsibly. He wanted to feel like a sixteen-year-old kid who was loved by his mother.

Donna didn't have any idea what was on Jar's mind, nor did she particularly care. She could not find any motherly instincts in her that would make her reach out to her son. She had her mind set on one thing, getting out the house. The tantrum she threw didn't work. Her son was older now and stronger, mentally as well as physically. She could feel his strength when he grabbed her hands. There was a time when he cowered if she raised her voice; not now. She would deal with him later. Right now, she was focused on getting on the other side of that front door.

"Ma, why don't you wait until tomorrow to get the milk? We could watch some TV together. There's some popcorn in there." Jar's need for his mother's love was beating out his contempt for her. He didn't want to appear soft, but he needed his mother and she needed him. He wanted any validation, some sign that showed that his mother loved him.

"I got to get this milk. If I don't, ain't nobody going to go." Her voice was choppy and anxious. She and Jar both knew how this was going to end. She was going to be out that door.

Knowing that he would have no impact on her decision, Jar decided to say nothing more. He had made his plea to her. He wasn't going to lower himself and beg her to stay.

"I'm going to get that milk. Don't be up too late. You got to go to school in the morning." Donna was backpedaling toward the door. She stopped briefly to pick up the coat she had slung on the floor a few hours earlier.

"Uh-huh, I'll be ready to go," Jar replied. If she'd spent any time at home, she might've known he hadn't been to school on a regular basis in the last couple of weeks. And if crack logic didn't have a grip on her, she'd realize the snow on the ground would put a halt to anyone trying to make it school tomorrow.

The sixteen-year-old man-child settled back in to watch more television. BET wasn't able to hold his attention anymore. His mind was on his mother. No matter what he did, he couldn't keep her at home. Moments ago, when he had grabbed his mother's hands, he had prevented her from continuing to whale away at him. What he really wanted to do was crack her in the jaw. His lifetime of rejection and frustration was coming to a head.

He was alone with his mind and he thought the person he needed the most wasn't there for him. The drug game had found him; he didn't go looking for it. His mother had introduced him to it the first time around. She'd told him he couldn't get caught and even if he did, nothing too serious would happen to him. She was right about that, at least. When he'd gotten caught selling dope, he was sent to rehabilitation. He'd gotten three hots and a cot and away from his mother for nine months. He thought the time away would do his mother some good, too; maybe she would get herself together. When he'd returned home though, it didn't take a genius to realize how deep his mother had sunk.

He wouldn't continue to go any deeper with her. His good fortune had landed him under the guidance of Bone. He would never let his mother in on that tidbit of information. Like Bone said, "You don't let nobody come between you and your shit, not even your own mother." He could see her and admit what she truly was—an addict. Jar wouldn't let her come between him and his thing. She wasn't going to bring him down. The road he had in front of him presented steeper consequences if he was caught, but he didn't see any other options.

He didn't fit in with the kids in school. He was smarter than most, but he'd already seen the snickering and finger-pointing in the short time he'd spent back in school. When he'd gotten out of rehab, he was told to get a sponsor, do ninety meetings in ninety days, and keep yourself clean. He wasn't dirty; he didn't do dope and he damn sure wasn't doing no ninety meetings with any junkies. As for getting a sponsor, those old cats couldn't relate to him, or vice versa. Bone was his sponsor now. He stayed clean because of Bone. Bone let him know he couldn't function in the game if he was getting high; even weed was a no-no in Bone's book. The dope game was introducing him to a whole new way of life and what he was experiencing couldn't be matched anywhere. He didn't know if he wanted to be doing this for the rest of his life, though.

There was another way out. There was somebody he could call on who would listen to him. He should have called before now, but guilt and shame had prevented him from making the call. Jar didn't know what to say to him or where to begin, but he had to make the first call. Jar went to his room and started searching frantically through the things he had packed away from rehab. The card he was looking for would be right where he'd left it; tucked inside an empty can of Murray's hair oil. It was his favorite hiding place while he was at Garrison. If he had something he wanted to keep, that's where he'd put it. Some of the kids in the rehab program would sneak weed or pills or whatever they were into, back to Garrison after a weekend pass. They would use their toothbrush holders, soap holders and even dirty clothes.

Jar opened the can that he considered his lifeline. He'd filled it with Post-it notes that would serve as reminders for him. "Keep it Simple," "One Day at a Time," and "Let Go and Let God" were some of the sayings he'd picked up while he attended some Narcotics Anonymous meetings. At the bottom of the can was the business card for Travis Moore. Jar looked at the back of the card. Travis had put his home number on it. Travis had told Jar on the day he'd left Garrison that he was welcome to call him and now Jar needed to.

Jar went to the nearest phone in the kitchen. He looked at it in its cradle. He took a deep breath, picked up the phone and dialed the number. He listened as the phone rang, then he heard a knock at his front door. Couldn't have been his mother; she had a key. He listened for an answer on the phone, but heard the answering machine pick up. It was Travis' voice. *Good*, he thought, *it's the right number*. Before he could leave a message, there was a second knock at the door.

"Baby Jar!" came the voice on the other side.

Jar hung up the phone and put the business card in the drawer next to the refrigerator. He knew that voice also. It belonged to Bone. He reluctantly opened the door.

"Get your shit, boy. We rollin' out. We got work to do." Bone's quick eyes picked up the hesitation. "What's the matter?"

"Nothing." Jar's emotions were being worn on his sleeve.

"Bullshit! Let me in. Snow's falling out here."

Jar opened the door wider to allow Bone to enter. Bone quickly scanned the surroundings. It was the first time he had been in Jar's house. Knowing the streets, he knew about Donna. His ideas about how she provided for Jar were confirmed by giving the apartment a quick once-over.

"Your mama here?" Bone posed the question, already knowing the answer. Bone had watched as Donna had left a few minutes earlier.

"No, she's not," Jar answered.

"Yo, kid, you alright?"

The head nodded but Jar's body language and lack of eye contact told a different story.

"Kid, if you got anything on your mind that you need to get out your head, you can holla' at me." Bone exhibited a softer, caring side of himself that he rarely ever showed to other people. He knew the kid was in need. Jar needed somebody to lean on and Bone was happy to oblige him. He was sinking his claws deeper and deeper into him. It was part of his manipulation.

If Travis had picked up the phone, Jar would be talking to him now instead of considering confiding in Bone. He was having a problem with his mother and it was difficult for him to handle alone.

"It's my mother. She's out there." Jar struggled with the words.

"I'm sorry. I've seen it before. It's hard to handle, but it's not your fault. You can't be expected to live other people's lives, especially grown people that's supposed to take care of you. So you have to make a decision to come out of this the best way you can. I'm going to show you how."

The lost boy with limited options needed something to cling to. This was a lifeline that was being thrown to him; it was all he could see.

"I'll get my stuff."

"Tell you what, before we get to work, I'm gonna show you a little something that I'm working on. This is a tough game and you got to be careful out here. I have; that's why I'm still holdin' my own out here. I'm going to show you where this game can take you, if you play it right."

CHAPTER 19

Rick had hoped for a peaceful Thursday evening. He had reached the point in his career where he liked the twelve-hour night shift he pulled for one week every two months. Nights like tonight, though, he'd come to dread. The snow was coming down and accumulating fast. Snow was pretty, but it would cause some hazardous driving conditions. That meant accidents and they were more work for the highway patrolman. Working the accident scene, helping people in need, was fine with Rick. The paperwork that accompanied it was what aggravated Rick.

Most of the accidents involved cars that had hit a guardrail, or had skidded off the interstate into a ditch. Usually it would be some Billy Bad Ass in a sports utility vehicle that was involved in a wreck. This, Rick had to admit to himself, was a little funny. Charlotteans had enough trouble driving on a rainy day; you'd think they would have enough sense to slow down for snow and ice. Let somebody behind the wheel of an SUV and they think that they are ready to take on any road conditions. The three accidents that Rick already had worked were a testament to the fact that no matter what SUV you drove, if you didn't drive carefully, you'd be calling your insurance company the next day. Fortunately for the victims, the only thing hurting on them was their pride.

When he heard the dispatcher on his radio report an accident on I-77 and Brookshire Boulevard, he knew there had to be a major problem. An accident had been reported there less than a half-hour earlier, and an officer was already dispatched to the scene. If another accident was reported in the same area, something must have gone wrong at the scene.

"Charlie eleven-four to dispatch. My ETA is five minutes to the site," Rick responded into his handset.

"Roger that," the dispatcher responded.

"You got any info for me?"

"There was another accident involving Trooper Wyatt. We don't have much information. Apparently, he was working the accident scene when he was struck by another vehicle."

"I'll be there in three minutes!" Rick hung up his handset, turned on his blue lights and wasted no time getting to the scene.

Flashing red, orange, blue and white lights lit up the accident scene. The paramedics were already at work. Rick pulled onto the shoulder and scanned the scene to make an assessment of the situation. Three cars appeared to be involved in accident number one. Two paramedic crews were behind that accident. Trooper Wyatt's cruiser had struck one of the emergency rescue vehicles. An eighteen-wheeler had clipped the back end of the cruiser and it had smashed into the rescue vehicle. Then Rick spotted Wyatt. Another set of paramedics was tending to him. Rick called for additional backup before he got out the car and started flagging the area with flares. Once traffic was diverted, Rick went to check on Wyatt.

Rick was nervous as he approached Wyatt. While he was setting the flares, he could hear Wyatt in pain and he caught the sight of what appeared to be Wyatt's blood on the snow and ice near the stretcher he was on.

"How's he doing?" Rick asked as he approached the EMT's.

"He's doing good," the older-looking of the EMT's said as he looked up. The other heavyset EMT continued to work; his look did little to reassure Rick. The older EMT noticed Rick watching the other one.

"New kid," he said as he nodded toward the heavyset EMT.

"What's wrong with him?"

"Dislocated right hip. Right leg is broken in three places, two fractures in the femur and a compound fracture in the tibia. He's barely feeling a thing now, though."

"But, I can hear," Wyatt barked.

"How are you doing, Captain?"

"Like he said, I'm feeling no pain. Shit! Seven days and a wake-up from retiring and this happens. I never got this jammed up in 'Nam."

Wyatt was on his second retirement at age fifty-seven. He was a twenty-one-year veteran of the North Carolina Highway Patrol. He also had done twenty years in the U.S. Army, sneaking in at the age of sixteen.

"Well, you did it right this time. What the hell happened, sir?"

"I was working the three-car accident, while the EMT's were checking the victims. Some bitch in the eighteen-wheeler didn't slow down. Damn fool was driving like he didn't see none of this snow and ice out here. Bastard lost control and rear-ended my cruiser. When I realized what was happening, I pushed the EMT and one of the victims out the way. I got clipped before I could get out the way."

"He was pinned between the cruiser and the ambulance for a few minutes," added the heavyset EMT.

"How long before you get out of here?" Rick asked to either one of them.

"We were just finishing up," the more experienced one answered.

"Good, you fellas take good care of him. He's one of the good guys. He's got a retirement party coming up." Rick looked back at Wyatt. "Don't worry about a thing out here, Cap. I'll take care of everything. I should have some backup here soon."

"I wouldn't count on it, officer; not anytime soon. Emergency calls are coming in left and right. Wreckers are slow; everybody is spread pretty thin," the experienced one added.

The EMTs carefully loaded Wyatt into the vehicle. Rick watched as they eased away on the snow and ice. He could see Wyatt lift his head in the back of the vehicle. Wyatt gave Rick a thumbs-up. Rick shook his head as he thought about the captain who was a little more than a week away from retirement. He busted his butt all this time to end up like this. The vibrations of his personal cell phone broke Rick's train of thoughts. He pulled it out and recognized the all-too-familiar number. Now wasn't the time to answer it; there was an accident to clear.

Fifteen minutes at the accident scene passed before Rick's backup finally arrived. During that time, he'd begun to interview the driver of the eighteen-wheeler. Rick picked up the scent of alcohol and performed a street sobriety test on him. The driver failed miserably. Rick took the man to his cruiser and gave him a Breathalyzer test. Again, he failed, blowing a .24, which was triple the North Carolina legal limit of .08.

"Did you like working for that trucking company?" Rick asked, resisting the temptation to shove the Breathalyzer down his throat.

"Excuse me," the driver slurred.

"After your company gets this accident report, I seriously doubt you'll have a job. Have a seat in the back of the vehicle, please. I'll have your ticket ready in a few minutes." The driver obliged Rick and he finished the ticket. Rick let him sit tight while he got out the car to talk to the new officers that were on the accident scene. They were both Charlotte police officers.

"What you got there, Nixon?" Officer Jacobs asked, anxious to find out what Rick had going. He was also anxious to get into Highway Patrol School.

Rick gave him a quick rundown of what had happened in the accident involving Officer Wyatt. He made sure to tell them that Wyatt had given him a thumbs-up as the ambulance pulled away.

"True Blue, huh?" Jacobs chimed in. He was all smiles and looking for something. "Isn't he retiring?"

"In a week," Rick said quickly. Jacobs irritated the hell out of him. All of Jacobs' statements were questions.

"So, what do you hear about my package? Am I going to get in?"

"Man, I done told you, I don't have information on your package." Rick was out in the middle of an accident scene and this guy was begging for information on Highway Patrol School. He was about to go off, but before he did, his cell phone began vibrating again.

"You could put in a good word for a brother, right?"

"Yeah, sure." Rick checked his phone. It was the same number that was recorded earlier. "Do me a solid and I'll see what I can do." He put the phone back on his hip.

"Anything you need."

"I'm finished with the guy in the back of my cruiser. Can you run him in for me? I want to clear this scene and get the traffic moving again."

"You got it."

Twenty minutes later, the traffic was moving. There weren't as many cars on the road. Once Rick was in his car and driving, he decided to return the call he'd received. He picked up his personal cell phone and dialed the number.

"Yo," the voice answered.

"It's Rick."

"Where the hell you been?"

"I'm a state trooper. I'm working. I can't always drop what I'm doing to hit you back, Bone."

"I feel you. Rick, are you ready to get this money?" Bone knew Rick was already counting his cut.

"What do you need?"

"Got a dark-green Lexus LS 400, chrome rims, headed north. It will be exactly six miles per hour over the speed limit. I got your backup covered, too. Got twenty keys in it. I say you tax them for six."

"How many in the car?"

"Just two. My guy and Ray Griffen."

"The ball player?"

"That's the one."

"No shit."

"When have I made it hard on you, playa."

Rick smirked as he recalled his history with Bone. The dirty money Rick had made with Bone was always easy. The way Rick saw it, it never hurt anybody. His allegiance to Bone was blind to a fault. "True," Rick agreed.

"After we finish with this minnow, we going after some bigger fish. All of this is part of a plan. You make contact?"

"Last night. I pulled him over for a ticket, and then I let him go. It's all love boat. His car is marked. I can track him anywhere. But I don't need to know too much on that tip though."

"Nuff' said." Bone appeased Rick for now. When the time came, he would have his greedy ass do whatever he wanted. "Go on and get that cheddar."

"Fo' sho." Rick hung up the phone and made a beeline for I-85.

Ten minutes of thin traffic and waiting had passed when he spotted what he believed was the green Lexus as it approached. Rick tracked it with the radar gun as it passed. The vehicle was traveling precisely six miles per hour over the speed limit. Rick spun the rear wheels as he skidded on the snow in an effort to return to the interstate. He trailed them for a half-mile before he hit them with his blue lights. He would've loved to have heard the conversation in the other car as the lights went on.

The driver of the Lexus was reluctant to pull the car over, but they eventually came to a stop. Rick could see that the person in the passenger seat was motioning toward the road. This caused the driver to become animated as well. As Rick opened the door of his car, he noticed the driver and passenger stiffen. Apparently, their conversation had reached a conclusion. Rick unsnapped his Glock and put his palm on the handle. He wasn't taking any chances.

The window rolled down as Rick neared it. The scent of lemon drifted from the car, but it could not mask the pungent odor of marijuana smoke. Rick almost laughed as he thought, *Easy money.*

"Is there a problem, officer?" the driver asked nervously.

"License and registration, please."

"Yes, sir." The driver fumbled to get his license while the passenger's jittery hands scrambled around in the glove compartment for the registration.

"Is this your vehicle, sir?" Rick looked at the documents that didn't match. "It's registered to a Mister Griffen."

"No, sir. This is Mister Griffen beside me."

Rick leaned into the car window. "It's a pleasure, Mister Griffen." Rick smiled as he saw fear run across the face of the man in the passenger seat. This was going to be like taking candy from a baby. "Do either of you have any idea why I stopped you?" They shook their heads in unison. "The roads are too slippery for you to be traveling at a high rate of speed, don't you think?"

"Yes, sir," the driver said.

"Seems to me that since you're smoking weed, it would have slowed you down a little bit."

Griffen dropped his head. He could already see the headlines. It would be another spoiled, rich, high-profile athlete in trouble. Smoking weed would be the least of his troubles if the officer found out what else was in the vehicle.

"Do you have any drugs or weapons in the vehicle?"

"Officer, what is it going to take to make this go away?" Griffen asked.

Rick had him where he wanted him, but he wasn't ready to let him go. "What do you want to make go away? You fellas get away with smoking weed all the time. Call a press conference, apologize to the team and the fans for getting caught, submit to the weekly drug testing, and you're good, right?" Rick waited for Griffen to say something, but he was at a loss for words. "Now, if you gentlemen don't mind, I need you to remove yourselves from the vehicle, one at time, please."

Griffen was scared as hell. This wouldn't be about some league-imposed treatment program; this was going to be it for him. He had twelve kilos of cocaine in the vehicle. He faulted himself for being so greedy and allowing himself to get caught in this position. The coke wasn't even all his. His attempt at bravado, showing his boys back in Cali that he was still real was blowing up in his face. Everything Griffen had accomplished was about to come to an end. Running away wouldn't do him any good. The officer knew who he was. Griffen had a loaded gun under the seat; killing the trooper wasn't a viable option. The state would give him death for that.

Rick asked for the keys to the car and the driver complied. Rick then handcuffed him to the steering wheel. He escorted Griffen back to his cruiser; he kept his hand on his gun. He could see Griffen's nerves unraveling as they walked toward the cruiser.

Rick opened the door to the backseat for him. "So, what am I going to find?" Rick asked. Griffen kept his mouth shut.

That was fine with Rick. He closed the door behind Griffen and started back to the Lexus. The knocking on the window stopped him. Rick paused to let him sweat a little bit before turning back to him. When he turned back, Griffen was motioning for him to come back. Griffen's eyes appeared to be welling up. The man, who wreaked havoc on the fields of play, was not an able participant when it came to playing the dope game. Rick almost felt sorry for the guy; he had no idea he was being played.

"What's on your mind?" Rick asked as he opened the front passenger door and sat inside. It was time to deal; he turned off the blue lights.

Griffen struggled as he started to say something, but instead he began sobbing uncontrollably. Rick fought to contain his laughter. How could this guy ever think he had the balls to run dope? Rick knew he had enough money to get some other peon to make the run for him. *There must have been more to it*, Rick thought.

"This is the big boy world, Griffen. Stop crying like a bitch," Rick snapped. There was no more "good cop" in him. "Tell me what's in there that you don't want me to see."

"I didn't..." Griffen struggled as he started.

"Save the drama, boy. What's up? You only have so much time before my backup shows up."

"Cocaine," Griffen blurted. That's it. He was done. The good life of the pampered athlete was over for him.

"Cocaine, huh?" Rick echoed with no surprise. "How much you got?"

Griffen was stunned. This officer sounded as if he wanted to deal. This wasn't the direction he thought the conversation would go. "Twelve."

"Twelve ounces?" Rick baited him for fun.

"Twelve kilos." Griffen was ashamed of his admission.

"Twelve kilos? What the fuck is wrong with you?" Rick waited for an answer that wouldn't be coming. "I ought to shoot your dumb ass right now." Rick watched Griffen drop his head in shame. "Where the shit at?" Rick was done with the small talk.

"Under the dash and in the trunk. There's a double back to the trunk. I swear, that's all there is."

"You know, I love the team, so I'm going to look out for you. Now, if I find something that you haven't told me about, you're going to jail."

Rick picked up the knife he kept under the driver's seat and got out the car. He jabbed the right rear tire of the Lexus with it. He uncuffed the driver when he reached him. "Get every ounce of cocaine from up under that dashboard. Pop that trunk so I can get the jack out. When you finish up here, get the rest of the shit out the trunk."

"You supposed to just get half from him?" the driver questioned.

"Did I stutter, motherfucker? The shit changed. You can either do that or be a dead nigga out here tonight. Don't make me none." Rick waited for the driver to buck. "Get to work. I'll let Griffen out so he can help you."

When Rick had possession of the twelve kilos, he got back in his car. There was no sign of Bone's backup and he did not have any intention of waiting for them. He'd settle up with Bone later.

"Fellas, 'preciate your help." Rick looked at Griffen's solemn face. "Griffen, buck up, you got your life back. It only cost you, what? A hundred and fifty thousand? Not bad. If my name or tonight ever comes from either one of your mouths, both of you are going to have some problems."

The crooked cop pulled off, already planning to give Bone his six kilos and he would keep six for himself. He considered it a luxury tax for all the work he was putting in for Bone. He left the two men standing in the falling snow with a flat tire. Griffen was filled with both anger and gratitude. He and his source were out a hundred and fifty g's, but he still had his life. He could lose his seventy-five g's and be okay with it, this time. But Griffen was giving serious consideration to changing his life.

CHAPTER 20

Travis sat on a stool near the motherboard as Bruce continued to work diligently. The room was overcrowded with engineers, producers and a couple of people from Soul's entourage.

Soul was the name of the artist singing his heart out behind the glass partition in the soundproof room. The kid was only twenty and his slight frame gave no indication that it contained the type of voice that would make Marvin Gaye stop and listen. He was appropriately named; every time he opened his mouth to sing a note, he'd let the audience in on a piece of his soul.

Travis couldn't put a name with the sound of the kid's voice. It was an old-school sound. Somewhat like Percy Sledge, but more up-tempo. Bruce told Travis that a voice like this kid's only comes along once every twenty years. The voice was so unique that no one could pin it down with one comparison and the boy could blow. Bruce agreed with Travis. The kid did have a shade of Percy, but Bruce described the voice as a blend of Johnny Gill, D'Angelo and Sam Cooke.

Travis was surprised and impressed with the way Bruce ran his studio session as a tight ship. It wasn't the same type of musical session that Travis had seen on BET and MTV; he thought it was much better. He was looking for half-dressed women, alcohol and drugs. Travis was both relieved and disappointed by what he found. Disappointed because he was looking for a little harmless mischief and relief because he didn't have to ward off any temptations. Not from the drugs or alcohol; those dragons had been slayed a long time ago. But scantily clad women, hanging out and digging the music vibe; he was up for a peek or two.

"All right, folks, let's take a twenty," Bruce announced. He hit the intercom button for the soundproof room. "Soul, that's beautiful, man. We're taking twenty. We changed some lyrics on the next verse. I want you to check them out." Bruce turned the switch off. Soul took off his earphones and backed away from the mic. "This kid picks up on shit faster than anybody I've ever seen," he said to Travis.

"Shoot! And that voice? Where does it come from?"

"I know, it's sick, right?" Bruce was all smiles.

"Nobody mentioned any changes to me," came an agitated voice.

The young man that interrupted them was Harold, Soul's twenty-four-year-old first cousin who was now Soul's manager—not by Soul's choice, but by the mother's. Bruce rolled his eyes and slowly turned his attention to him.

"Is there a problem, Harold?" Bruce's voice suggested to Harold that it would be best to let it go.

"It's my song and ain't nobody saying nothing to me about it." Harold was marking his territory. He didn't know who Travis was. All he knew was that every chance Bruce had, he was telling Travis something about Soul.

"Ain't nothing to worry about." Bruce was talking about more than the song. "We just tightened up a few words. If you want him to sing that version, you can rent the studio time and have him sing it. Right now, my dime says we're going to change it. Any problems with that?"

"So, it's okay?" Soul asked as he emerged from the studio.

"No doubt. Soul, take your cousin out to the lobby. Food and drinks, whatever you need. It's out there. If they don't have it, let me know and I'll get it."

Brief introductions were made, and then Soul took his cousin/manager out the room, leaving Bruce and Travis alone.

"Good kid?"

"For now. Once the madness starts and he blows up, we'll see where his head's at." Bruce paused to look at Travis. "All right, we don't have long before the crowd starts flowing back in."

"So where's the wild party? I thought people would be drinking and smoking; maybe a couple of butt-naked honies."

"It's not that type of flow. Soul's not there yet, so I don't want anything to mess with his focus while he's in the studio. That's my time. Now, what he does when he's on his time, that's his business."

"I see. How did you find that kid?"

Bruce sat in silence for a moment to contemplate the answer. "You gonna keep bullshittin' or are you gonna tell me why you're sitting here instead of at home with your woman?"

"I'd be at home with her if she was there. I left work early so I could try to get home with her. I caught her on her cell phone and she was halfway to Raleigh."

"She'll be back though, right?"

"Yeah, sure." Travis frowned and nodded. That's what Kenya had told him, but with the tension between them, who knew what could be going on in her head? "She was going to head back here tonight."

"She just blowin' off some steam. She'll be straight, though."

"I'd like to think so." Travis had no confidence in what he was trying to assure himself of. Last night, he was relieved to have finally come clean with his wife. Today, he was still sure he'd done the right thing, in spite of the effect it'd had on Kenya. That was all before she'd made the split decision to leave for Raleigh. She wanted to get the baby away so they could spend some time together. At least, that's what she'd told him. Travis was now beginning to wonder why she wouldn't have told him about it sooner. She was already en route to Raleigh when he'd reached her. The possibility that Kenya wasn't able to handle this secret had crept into his mind on more than one occasion.

"What do you think, dog? She gonna cash in 'cause you used to sling dope?"

"Kenya's not used to dealing with people like me. She was one of those girls that had everything. She's never seen the things I've seen coming up. She probably can't understand how I used to be and the secrets that I've kept."

"The key words in all this are 'used to.' Get out of your own head for a minute. We all used to be something. You can't beat yourself up for something you used to be. I don't beat myself up about the past. Hell, dog, I'm proud of you. I know where you came from. Your shit should be celebrated. I wouldn't be here today if it wasn't for you getting me on. Shit, if it wasn't for a nigga like you, I wouldn't have gotten out the box and known there was a world out here for me."

The studio door opened and one of the production engineers stuck his head inside. "Man, it's snowing like hell out there."

"Chalk one up for the meteorologists," Bruce said. "They finally got one right, but it ain't gonna last."

Charlotte weather people were known for forecasting the big storms that never came. Big winter storms had snow accumulations of two inches. Bruce had developed a conspiracy theory that linked the local meteorologists to the local grocery stores. The meteorologist had income that was supplemented through bread and milk sales. It was a bunch of bull, but it sounded good.

"Are you serious?" Travis added, not believing his luck. He pulled out his cell phone and placed a call to Kenya's cell phone. An automated response came back with an "all circuits are busy" message. He got the same response when he tried his in-laws. "Bruce, I have to get to my house. I can't get an answer from my wife."

"I feel you. You want somebody to roll with you?"

"No."

"Take your time out there. You know Charlotte; if there's snow, there's bound to be some accidents."

"Fo' shizzle." Travis smiled as he tossed some slang with ease.

"Boy, you watch out. You keep that up and somebody's gonna know you from the hood." Bruce smirked at Travis, as he was on his way out. Bruce walked out with him and they said their good-byes. Once Travis left, Bruce went back to being all business. "All right, folks, it's time to get back to work. We got all night, too. Ain't nobody got nowhere to be tonight in this snow," Bruce joked. Some laughed, but they all knew they were going to be working hard this night.

The twenty-minute drive took Travis over an hour. He tried countless times to reach Kenya. The snowstorm that hit Charlotte had moved in from the Northeast. Not being able to contact her worried him. Travis had never let Kenya drive in the snow since she'd had an accident in a snowstorm a few years ago; nor did she want to drive in it either. If something happened to Kenya and Michael, he wouldn't be able to forgive himself. It was because of him that she was going through whatever changes she was experiencing.

As he approached his driveway, he knew Kenya hadn't arrived home. He held out hope that her SUV would be in the garage. It was only wishful thinking on his part. His stomach sank as the garage door opened to two empty spaces. The only thought on his mind was finding out that his wife and child were okay. He certainly didn't pay any attention to the cars that drove one way or the other through his neighborhood.

In the house, he noticed the answering machine's red light as it flashed in the kitchen. Travis moved to it as fast as he could to retrieve its messages. The indicator light flashed two messages. Travis hit rewind and waited impatiently, as the tape couldn't move fast enough for him. He pushed the play button as he heard the tape winding down. The first message was very faint; there was somebody holding the line but they weren't saying anything. There was a banging noise and a voice in the background that he couldn't understand. Travis feared the worst. His wife had been in an accident and she wasn't able to communicate on the phone. The call ended abruptly. Before Travis completely panicked, the next call began to play. It was Kenya's voice. His heart started to beat again. Kenya was in Raleigh, safe and sound. Her mother had taken her keys and made it clear to her that she wouldn't be going anywhere in this weather.

Travis breathed a deep sigh of relief. He picked up the cordless phone and called his in-laws again. He expected to get the circuit-busy message, but he was pleasantly surprised when the call went through.

"Hello?" Kenya answered.

"Hey K, you all right?" Travis was relieved at the sound of her voice. He wanted to say so much to her. He was sorry he'd told her of his past. He'd never meant to keep so much of his life from her for so long, and he certainly didn't want to be without her, but the words didn't come out.

"Yeah…are you? I couldn't reach you on your cell phone and you weren't at home." Kenya was worried herself.

"I made a couple of stops before I came home. I called there I don't know how many times and I couldn't get through. Are you coming back? I mean, not tonight, but ahh, I mean, is there more to this than... "

"No, why would you think that?"

"When you took Michael and left, I don't know, my mind started to wander. Then I couldn't get in touch with you."

"No, Travis. When I brought Michael up here, I intended to get back home tonight. I didn't count on this weather being like this."

Kenya and Travis continued the most positive conversation they'd shared in the last couple of weeks for another fifteen minutes. There was still some apprehension and, at times, the conversation seemed to dance around eggshells. They didn't talk about his secrets, but they would soon enough. Kenya vowed to get home tomorrow, even if she had to drive twenty miles per hour. Kenya promised to kiss their little man for him and they hung up by exchanging "I love you's."

Feeling good about his wife, Travis was content to call it a night. He rewound the tape again, then thought about that first call. Who was that? He punched play again and listened for any clues. He still couldn't make heads or tails of it. Must have been a wrong number, he surmised. He hit rewind again and went upstairs. He thought about his great wife, family and home. He was happy to finally be making peace with his past.

CHAPTER 21

Once the phone started working again, it didn't stop ringing. Then, there was the baby's activity added to the mix. Eddie paced in his bedroom because he couldn't find peace in his own house. Eddie had grown too accustomed to having the house alone to him and Lillian. Any overnight guest upset the rhythm of his home, even his only daughter and grandson.

There was a routine that Eddie followed every night prior to retiring for the evening. Tonight, Lillian had filled him in on the information she'd received concerning their son-in-law. To his credit, he'd handled the information with the same calm demeanor he'd always handled anything in his legal profession, but this had upset his usual routine.

Eddie was anxious to talk to his daughter. To hear Lillian explain it, Travis practically had a poppy field behind the house. He wanted to hear his daughter's take on the situation, himself. If Kenya took Lillian's reaction to heart, then he would have to get her to see the situation logically.

Kenya was finishing a conversation on the phone as Eddie walked into the kitchen. Their eyes met and they exchanged a smile. Eddie opened the refrigerator and pulled out a half-gallon jug of skim milk and placed it on the counter. Then, he went to the pantry and took out the fresh pack of Oreo double-stuffed cookies. Kenya fell right in line. She went to the cabinet, retrieved two glasses and placed them on the counter.

"Set 'em up, barkeep," Eddie said. This wasn't part of his current routine, but it was a ritual he'd started with his daughter when she was in elementary school.

"You got it," Kenya replied. She knew it wouldn't be long before she and her father would be discussing Travis. At every crossroads that Kenya came to in her life, she'd talk to her mother, and then she would run into milk, Oreo cookies and her father. "What's with the skim milk?"

Eddie looked at her with the shame of a drunk who'd fallen off the wagon and returned to his favorite watering hole. "I can't take the whole milk anymore." He and his daughter laughed.

"That is so sad, Daddy."

"I'd give anything for a glass of whole milk. Actually, I can drink it; it's your mama who can't take the after-effects it has on me. Believe me, she catches hell." Eddie smiled.

"Eeeww," Kenya said, with her fingers pinching her nose. Again, they laughed. Kenya poured the milk and Eddie opened the cookies. "Milk and cookies, huh?"

"Yep, so you know we have something pretty heavy on the plate."

"Mama already told you, right?"

"Of course she did. You know your mother; she has a flare for the dramatic. I wanted to hear what you have to say about it. So, what do you think?" Eddie dipped a cookie into his glass of milk. "Have you talked to Travis?"

"That was him on the phone." *Let the inquisition begin*, Kenya thought. "He sends his best to everyone."

Kenya then proceeded to give her father every detail she could recall from the previous evening. This time the story was peppered with various opinions that her mother had to offer. Eddie recognized them when Kenya presented them. Eddie listened, asked a few prodding questions and he could hear her pain. He was taking a mental deposition from his daughter. For himself, he was putting to rest any suspicions he had about Travis and the idea that he could be involved in any illegal activity.

Eddie had consumed eight cookies when Kenya finished her recap of the Travis Moore story, complete with Lillian's editorial comments. Eddie knew that his wife's concerns were weighing heavily on his daughter's mind.

"So, what do you think?" Kenya interrupted her father's thoughts.

Eddie thought about the son-in-law with whom he'd become very close. He'd gone to college basketball and football games with him. He'd spent a lot of time with him and never talked at length with Travis about his childhood. It wasn't Eddie's place to initiate that conversation. Eddie based his opinion on Travis by the character that he displayed, and he thought very highly of Travis.

Travis was the son that he and Lillian were supposed to have. Kenya never knew that her parents had had a baby before she was born, a son. Lillian had lost him during her third trimester. Kenya was their miracle baby. When Travis had come into their daughter's life, they both had taken to him.

"It's something to think about." Eddie stalled. His opinion had already been formed. "Let's go down to the wood shop. I think better down there."

"I'm not going down there with all that dust."

"Humor your old man. Get something to throw on from your mom and meet me down there." Eddie left the kitchen for the basement. Their conversation would continue downstairs.

Woodworking was a hobby that was quickly becoming an obsession for Eddie. He'd invested more than forty-thousand dollars on his soundproof shop and equipment. Gone were the pool and ping-pong tables. Their place had been filled by band saws, assembly tools, finishing supplies and wood.

His first major project was an armoire. It was a bold attempt that had gone awry. The armoire didn't make it into the bedroom like he had envisioned. Lillian wouldn't allow the hideous creation in the house. It sat in a corner of the forty-five-by-sixty-foot basement. It leaned slightly to the left, the two drawers at the bottom didn't close completely, and the doors were always ajar due to the way they sat on the hinges. Regardless of what the end product was, Eddie was proud of what he'd accomplished with his own hands.

Eddie's next project was going to be a little less ambitious. He was building a double-paddle canoe. Small craft boat-building was supposed to be relatively easy, he'd heard, as long as you had a solid time commitment. Semi-retirement had allowed him that time commitment. He began pulling out sheets of plywood.

"So, this is it?" Kenya asked as she approached her father.

"Yep, this is it." Eddie was proud of what he'd put together.

"What are you doing?"

"I'm preparing to build a canoe. I'm going to take your mother out on Jordan Lake in it. We'll paddle out on it and splash around for a while, then camp out for the night."

"Sounds like you have a plan. Have you told Mom?"

"Sure."

Kenya waited for more details. "And? What did she say?"

Eddie looked at his wood, then to his daughter and finally to his armoire. "She hoped it would float," he said flatly.

"Better wear a lifejacket and stay close to shore. What were you doing down here earlier?"

"Prepping the plywood. In boat-building, with big pieces of plywood, you minimize your cuts. Most of the connections are at right angles or mitered joints. You have to use a variety of fastenings. It's hard to make something that's water tight, but it takes time. This is going to be a floating work of art."

Kenya didn't know what the hell her father had said, but she could see his passion for it. "How long will it take you to finish it?"

"Couple of weeks."

"Have you worked on anything else?"

Eddie nodded with pride, then he pointed to the armoire in the corner. "My first masterpiece."

Kenya looked at his work that had a lean to it. She tilted her head to the left. "I sure hope the boat floats." She tried to mumble but Eddie heard her.

"You and your mama don't understand good craftsmanship," Eddie tried to say with a straight face. "That took me over two months to build. By the time I realized my angles weren't right, it was too late. That thing was getting made as is."

"It's not bad for a first project."

"I learned a lot from it. Patience, not to overcomplicate things before I'm ready to deal with them. It was a good first project. That's why I'm doing the boat next. It's something that I'm ready for."

"I'm sure it will stay afloat."

"I hope so." Eddie loaded a sheet of plywood onto the table saw. "Building a boat teaches more patience. You don't rush to make things happen. Each step requires time. That's what I needed with that armoire." Eddie watched his daughter as she nodded. "Sometimes people need it. Look at that tree stump," Eddie said as he pointed to the corner opposite the armoire. "You look at it and it's a big piece of wood. It's raw. That's how it starts. You trim away the rough edges, chip away at the bark, then start to shape and mold it. It could become a cabinet, a chair, anything. Paint it, varnish it and it becomes a thing of beauty."

"Okay." Kenya knew her father. His stories went around town to get across the street, but she listened intently.

"Travis was that raw piece of wood. He relied on himself to shape his image into the reality that he is today. He is a hard-working, respected, family man. He is in love with his wife and his heart is touched at the sight of his son. I know because I see it in him. You asked me what I thought, and that is my gut reaction based on what I know about Travis. Now, as far as him being involved in anything illegal today, based on what you've told me, I would find it hard to believe that he could be in that lifestyle anymore. Things are possible, but I doubt it. For his sake, I hope that life is through with him. It's taken some time for him to get to this point. His boat is coming together; he confided in you to help him fasten everything together."

"Thank you, Daddy." Somehow Kenya was able to make sense of her father's rambling. Her once-clouded thoughts were beginning to see rays of sun.

"You said thank you like you're done down here. We have some work to do." He laughed as his daughter's jaw dropped.

Eddie showed his daughter how to cut plywood and sand down the edges. They took their time, showed patience and began the process of creating a two-paddle canoe for Eddie and Lillian to set sail on Jordan Lake.

CHAPTER 22

Ballantyne Country Club area was amazing to Baby Jar. The houses were the kind he only saw on television, not in Charlotte. His world was confined to his public housing project and the streets of the Westside. His school, the streets he hustled in, even the time he'd spent in rehab, didn't get him out of the Westside. He couldn't imagine people living like this in Charlotte.

Bone knew the young, naïve and impressionable Jarquis "Baby Jar" Love was in awe. Jar's silence and bulging eyes told him as much. They passed house after house and each one was more impressive than the previous one. Bone drove slowly because of the snow and slick roads. That allowed them more time to view each house. The inclement weather couldn't hide their beauty and luxury.

One of these homes belonged to Travis. Thanks to the information from Lisa and Rick, Bone had the exact address. Bone had traveled the community on two occasions and wasn't sure which house belonged to Travis. He'd circled the neighborhood twice and was approaching Travis' house for the third time.

"We already saw these, didn't we?" Jar's trance was broken by the familiar surroundings.

"Fo' sho."

"Why are we looking at these again?" The question came out before Jar realized to whom he was talking.

The nerve of this little punk, Bone thought. He could end Jar's life without a moment's notice and never think about him again. He would put up with it, though; there was a greater purpose here. The time would eventually come when it would be necessary to dispose of Jar, but not now. He had the opportunity to continue his manipulation.

"That house, right there, I really like the way it looks." Bone pointed toward the Moore house.

"I didn't know they made houses like this around here."

"What ya mean?"

"I ain't never seen anything like it. Not live anyway. Must be a bunch of rich white people that live out here."

"Not everybody that lives out here is white. They might have some change, but that don't make them rich. I got more loot than most of these folks out here. They got some of everybody out in this joint, even niggas."

"Only niggas that could live out here are rappers and ball players," Jar said with the wealth of knowledge that a sixteen-year-old who had never been anywhere possessed.

"That so? Well, I'm a drug dealer, the slickest one in this town, and I'm getting ready to move out here."

"What?" Jar didn't think he'd heard that right.

"That's right. I got a crib under construction up in this joint."

Jar wasn't sure how to take it. Bone hadn't steered him wrong so far, but could he be buying a house in a neighborhood like this? Did Bone really have that kind of paper behind him? "Where's it at?"

"Not far from here. These ma'fuckers 'bout to get them a new neighbor. A real nigga's about to set up camp. I'ma turn all these fools out. This gonna be my new hood."

"These people ain't gonna let that happen." He didn't know everything, but he knew people in this part of town wouldn't take a drug dealer running his game out of here.

"Why not? It's already happening. I know most of these fools, or their type. Half these snooty-ass people out here is crooks. If they ain't, they daddies were. They might speak it a little different out here, but game is still game, no matter what field it's played on."

Jar contemplated Bone's words. The game was so much bigger than his hood, bigger than the Westside. It was bigger than he'd ever imagined.

Bone pulled up to a lot that was under construction. The footers and the foundation were in place. Construction crews had also completed the framing. Although it wasn't anywhere near complete, the skeleton was impressive. There was going to be a basement and two stories above it. Bone pointed the headlights toward the house.

"Come on, check it out." Bone turned the car off and left the headlights on.

As the snow fell, Bone and Jar got out the car. The single-family home that was under construction was larger than eight of Jar's project units combined. They walked into what would soon be the foyer of the home.

Bone measured Jar's response as he looked from right to left. Jar turned his head slowly, taking in everything in.

"This is yours?" Jar asked incredulously.

"It will be. All three hundred and ninety-thousand dollars of it, paid for in cash." Bone moved further into the house to give Jar a tour of the skeleton of his house.

"Cash?" Jar was stunned. Buying this house was one thing; paying three-nintey in cash was something else altogether. His mind was paralyzed by the thought that he was in such close company with someone that had the ends to buy something like this.

"Hell yeah, and that's just the tip of the iceberg." Bone didn't hesitate to brag on the fruits of his ill-gotten gains.

"You got that kind of loot?" Jar couldn't help asking; he had to know.

"I don't even feel this," he assured Jar.

"For real?" Jar was thinking that, if he hustled right, he could get from the street corners in Park Slope to here. If the game had done this for Bone, surely it would give him the same honor. For some reason, Bone had taken to him and he was glad. He would listen to his wisdom of the streets and grow wise from it. He would understand the game and take full advantage of it, as Bone had.

"This is real." Bone opened his arms wide in a gesture toward the spacious house. "You do what you got to do, to get what you want to get. When I hit them with this cheddar, can't nobody take mine away from me."

"What happens when you get caught?"

"You don't get caught. You keep everything on the low. You don't put yourself out there. That's a lesson I had to learn the hard way. Because I went that route, I can drop some knowledge on you. I'm gonna raise you up in this right." Bone paused to let his words settle with Jar. The boy was ripe for a big push. "When this house is finished, if you need somewhere to go, this is it. It don't matter if it's one night, a week or a year. Whatever amount of time you'd need, it's here for you."

The boy with nowhere to go, who saw little in the way of options for his life, finally had someone to cling to. Whether the man he saw in front of him was just or unjust, it was someone who was concerned about him. A little more than an hour ago, Jar was trying to convince his crackhead mother to spend some time with him. She had chosen the streets over him. He'd tried to contact Travis and had gotten his answering machine. The hell with Travis; Travis never reached out to him. Bone had taken him under his wing and showed him that he cared. That's all he was searching for, someone to care. On the cold snowy night, the thug that had welcomed him into his new home had warmed Jar's heart. Tears welled in Jar's eyes.

Sensing that Jar's emotions were moved, Bone played the moment before speaking. "I'm gonna let you marinate on that one for a minute, 'cause this is me and you, here. This is a circle that you don't break, and nobody comes between it. This little thing I laid on you, it got to you and it's cool, between you and me. Always remember, you can't show nobody you're soft, especially me."

"Yes, sir," Jar said, pulling it together. "Can't show them you're soft."

"That's my boy." Bone looked at the frame of the house again. "You don't tell anybody about this. You hear me?" Bone waited as Jar nodded his compliance. "Else you'll be kicked out before you get in." His tone was lighter.

"I ain't saying a word."

"Good. You my soldier out here on the streets. Off these streets, when it's you and me, you can come to me with anything."

"For real?"

"That's on the strength, dog. And, when I need you, you got to be there for me."

"I will be." There was no doubt in Jar's mind about where his loyalties would be placed.

"Let's get out of this weather."

"More work to put in?"

Bone looked up at the falling snow. "Yeah, but not on the street."

As they walked back to the car, Bone's cell phone vibrated. He motioned Jar toward the car as he stopped to answer the phone. "Crank up the car. I got to answer this call." Bone waited until there was some distance between him and Jar before he answered. "What's up?"

"Everything's cool," Flake said. "Rick said Griffen turned straight bitch on him."

"Nothing like free 'caine. You make the pickup yet?"

"In a few minutes. Sound like you outside. Where you at?"

"Out enjoying the weather, brother." He watched Jar as he got in the car and started it. "Yes, sir, I'm enjoying the night. I'm lining up the last couple of pieces to my puzzle."

"I don't get it."

"You will. Do you remember when you were sixteen?" Bone looked at Jar in the car and turned his back to him.

"What?" Flake didn't know what Bone was talking about.

"There is a wide-eyed innocence that some of these kids have about them. I never had it. I was running my own shit when I was sixteen. These niggas nowadays is easy to flip. They so eager to have somebody in them, that they'll believe anything that you shoot at them. I got his little punk ass now."

The car had heat and it had music. That's all Jar needed at the moment. He had no idea of how badly he'd been fooled. He was already thinking of things to put in a room for him. Bone didn't own this house, nor did he have any intentions of buying one in this neighborhood.

Jar's world would be shattered if he knew he would never see the completion of this house. Bone was using this as a tool to deepen Jar's trust and loyalty. The sixteen-year-old who was looking for somebody to care about him had no idea that he would be disposed of by Bone when his usefulness was no longer an issue.

When Bone finished on the phone, he motioned for Jar to move to the passenger side. The kid crawled over the seats of his custom-restored 280ZX. It was his classic and the dumb-ass kid had no respect for it. Bone damn near bit a hole in his lip to keep himself from going off on the kid when he got in the car.

"Looks like it's gonna be a slow night tonight. Flake's got to take care of a few things and I'll get up with him in a couple of hours. It's your world, dog. What you want to do?"

"You think Lolly's home?"

"She will be if I tell her to be there, but that ain't what you need. You don't need to get too familiar with one broad. You got to move on to some new guts. You start feelin' one broad and that weakens you in your game. Do you see me with a regular?"

"No."

"That's how you got to keep it, playa." Bone smiled at the kid. "I got something that you're gonna like better than Lolly."

CHAPTER 23

In the shadows of the darkness, Travis could see the face clearly. He'd been following him for hours on that early summer night. He'd waited for the right moment to confront the man that had killed his mother. But the tables were turned on him and now he was running for his life. Travis couldn't see where he was going. He was going nowhere in darkness. The man lurched from the shadows, wielding a knife. He came straight at Travis. The blade shined as the moonlight caught it. Travis' eyes bulged at the sight of it.

"Shit!!" Travis yelled as he woke up and reached over to his left for Kenya. His wife wasn't there. He was sweating heavily and breathing hard when he realized he was in his own bed.

Travis always slept on his right side and on the right side of the bed. His dreams were pleasant enough when the night had started. His head was able to rest easy after he'd spoken with Kenya. She was safe in Raleigh. Somewhere between the sweet slumber at night and the early morning hours, those sweet dreams had turned into nightmares of the past.

He rolled onto his back and tried to get control of himself. He looked up at the ceiling.

"It was only a dream," he told himself. Travis was waiting for his breathing to return to normal and he was glad Kenya wasn't present to witness. The last time he could remember having a dream like that, he was a junior in college. The face came back to Travis clear as it had always been. Big O, Otis Reader, was another part of his past, the part that haunted him the most. Why was that coming back to him now?

When he'd confided in Kenya, he felt like the weight of his past was finally off him. It wasn't. Maybe it was spending so much time with Bruce yesterday that had prompted the nightmare. The conversation about the incident didn't go very far, but it must have been enough to provoke other thoughts. That was it. That incident had bothered Travis, but he felt justified in his actions. Whenever Travis was bothered by the incident with Big O, he had remembered what had led to his actions, and he would be fine.

Too much time alone can cause the mind to wander. Travis turned on the radio to get a voice inside his head other than his own. The forecast for the day was being broadcast on 101.9. Travis shook his head when the broadcaster stated today would be sunny with a high of fifty-two degrees. The Charlotte weather could turn on a dime. Travis turned the radio down and listened. He could hear the sounds of water dripping. The snow and ice were already melting.

Kenya would be home soon. His mind would be able to focus on other things. Travis could not figure out why he was lying there revisiting the past. He'd come as clean as he needed to with his wife. It was their anniversary, and Big O and Kwame Brown weren't going to ruin it. It was time to celebrate. Travis hopped out of bed with a rejuvenated spirit. If Kenya wasn't going to get out in that weather, then he would go to Raleigh to get her.

Kenya was awakened by the familiar sunlight that usually met her whenever she slept in her old bedroom. It was a welcomed reprieve in comparison to waking to Michael's cries or one of his arms or legs lodged into a part of her body.

She went to the window, opened the blinds and soaked in the sunlight. Looking out, she could see what the dusting of snow left behind. Kenya closed her eyes and inhaled deeply. That's when she caught a whiff of the pancakes and sausage. She followed the scent to the kitchen.

Michael was having the time of his life. He was eating breakfast with his fingers. Michael was only two, but he knew better. He was showing out and Lillian was letting him. There was syrup on his face and a piece of pancake in his hair.

"Michael, what are you doing?"

Michael's eyes almost popped out his head. He recognized that tone of voice. He only heard it when he was in trouble. He looked to his mother and his eyes began to fill with water.

"Child, you leave my grandbaby alone," Lillian said, coming between Kenya and Michael. "He's just being a boy."

Kenya turned around to look for her mother because the woman standing in front of her couldn't possibly be her.

"What are you doing?"

"I was looking for the woman that would pinch me on my ear if she caught me playing with my food like that."

"He's a boy. He needs to express himself."

"If I had expressed myself like that, you would have put hand to hip. You know, you could go to jail for some of the stuff you used to do around here," Kenya teased.

"Oh, please." Lillian laughed. "Let me fix you a plate...and you leave that boy alone."

Kenya took a seat and watched Michael as he bounced his eyes from his mother to his grandmother. Kenya could see his little mind trying to comprehend what had transpired between them.

"I see the snow didn't hold up. Guess you'll be going home?" The phone started ringing. Lillian didn't move.

"Yes, ma'am, I'll be back on Sunday. Aren't you going to get the phone?"

"Your father will get it. So, you're sure about this?" Lillian turned back to her cooking.

"I was always sure about it. I needed some time to clear my head. That's why I drove home. The only reason I stayed was the snow. It's gone for the most part, and in an hour, I will be, too."

Kenya looked at her mother and waited for the next round of verbal assaults to begin. It didn't happen. Instead, she flipped a pancake.

"I have one child, one baby. That's you." Lillian didn't make eye contact. "All I want, all I've ever wanted was what was best for you. Until yesterday, I believed Travis was part of that. After you told me about how he grew up and what he did, it scared me. My maternal instincts kicked in and the only thing I wanted, and want, to do is protect my baby." She finally turned toward Kenya. "Your father told me about the talk you had last night."

"I thought he would." Kenya shook her head.

"He seems to be convinced by you. He stayed up half the night trying to convince me that I shouldn't be in such a haste to change my opinion of Travis."

Eddie walked into the kitchen. The cordless telephone was held to his head as he listened intently. Lillian stopped talking to look at him, but only for a second.

"Your father was right for the most part." She rolled her eyes. "I'm just afraid that one of those people from his past could come back after him."

"It went through my mind, too. But I'm not going to let it stop me from loving him."

"Why don't you tell her yourself?" Eddie said into the phone. "Phone, Lil."

"Who is it?"

"Travis." Eddie held the phone out for her.

Lillian reached out slowly to take it. "Hello," she said with caution.

"Hi. I…was talking with Eddie." Travis struggled to find the words. "He told me that you two had talked to Kenya. I'm, al… can't tell you how sorry I am…for…not being totally honest about my past. I felt like it needed to stay a secret because you would think less of me, but I needed to tell my wife. She is my rock and she is my world. I need her. I would…"

"Stop right there," Lillian said stone-faced. "Kenya, get this phone. And after you're finished on it, eat your food, get dressed and get your butt home before this boy makes me cry."

Lillian handed the phone to her daughter. The hard stance that she had taken was now demolished. Eddie and Kenya had been picking away at her guard; Travis had pushed her over. She realized in that brief conversation that her concerns weren't really about Travis as much as they were about his former life. Perhaps, it was the paranoia that comes from being a criminal defense attorney's wife. She'd heard so many of Eddie's stories about defendants having to come face to face with their pasts. But Travis wasn't on trial, he wasn't a defendant and he was coming to reality with his past.

"He's a good man, Lil," Eddie said.

"I know."

"And he's the best thing that's happened for Kenya. Look at the way she's smiling."

"I see." She glanced at her daughter.

"Where you start doesn't have to dictate where you end up. God knows I know that. I was a fourteen-year-old boy growing up in the rural South who couldn't read or write. Now, I'm a semi-retired partner from one of the most prestigious law firms in the Research Triangle area. Somebody believed in me and helped me along. Travis believed in himself and helped himself along. That tells me a lot about the man that he's made of himself."

Lillian had to agree with that point. As much as she hated to admit it, Eddie was right. She remembered their humble beginnings. Her mama had said, "Don't you marry that boy. He's as dumb as a box of rocks." She and Eddie had made out fine, and so would Kenya, as long as Travis' past stayed in the past.

CHAPTER 24

When the phone rang, Travis thought it might be Kenya calling him. She'd promised to give him a call before she left Raleigh. She assured him that the roads were passable. The snow that had hit Raleigh wasn't as bad as the snow that had blown through Charlotte.

"Hello?" Travis answered the phone, smiling from ear to ear.

"Hi, Travis." Lisa was surprised to hear Travis on the phone. "Is Kenya home?"

"No, she's not," Travis responded dryly. "Is there a message?" Travis wanted to get her off the phone.

Lisa had been over to their house too many times to count, and Travis was tempted to kick her out on each occasion. He wasn't a big fan of Lisa. She always had to know too much and she had a bigger knack for talking. Lisa wouldn't hesitate to expound on subjects she knew absolutely nothing about. That irritated Travis to no end.

"Good, she's on her way to the gym."

Who did she think she was fooling? She didn't have a clue where Kenya was and she was snooping again, when it would have been much easier to ask the question. "I doubt it." Travis hoped that would be the end of the conversation. If Lisa wanted to find Kenya, she could do it without help from him.

"So, where is she, or do you know?"

Travis paused for a minute to contemplate the correct terminology that should be used to address Lisa. Back in the day when he was in the street, he didn't hesitate to call a woman out of her name.

"Excuse me, Lisa?" He used and emphasized her name, but he was thinking "trifling ass."

"Where is she now, or do you know?" Lisa said each word slowly and emphasized each syllable as if she were talking to a child. She hoped to bait him into some verbal sparring.

"Yes, I do." Travis paused to let Lisa know that he wouldn't tell her. "Is there anything else I can do to help you?"

"No, there isn't a thing you can do to help me. Kenya told me all about you."

Travis was caught off guard. Kenya never told him that she had talked to Lisa about him. Of all people, she was the worst person to talk to. She would tell anyone who stopped for five seconds all about him and his drug dealing.

"So, where were you Wednesday night?" Lisa paused as if she had a right to know. "What's the matter? You forgot which lie you told?"

Wednesday night? Travis wondered what the hell she was implying. He was at the rehab center catching up on Baby Jar.

"Kenya said you were supposed to be at some rehab thing. I don't believe it. I got some ears out there and I'm going to find out about you. When I do, I'm going to tell Kenya everything I know about you. I can always tell when a man is running around on a woman."

She didn't have a clue about what was going on with them, Travis was sure of it. He was growing tired of her gum flapping. She sure didn't know anything about his past. If she did, she would have been running about it. It was time to have fun with her.

"You should know if a man is running around. From what I understand, you've had pretty much every game run on you."

Travis wanted to push her to see if she did know anything. Lisa couldn't hold anything back after she'd received such a low blow.

"Oh, you ain't shit." Lisa didn't have a comeback.

"And if you could get to that level, you'd triple your value." *She brought a slingshot to a gunfight*, Travis thought. "Always good to talk to you, Lisa. I have to go, I'll let Kenya know you called." Travis hung up the phone before she could get another word in.

"Whew." Travis was glad to have gotten rid of her so quickly. He was actually relieved that her questioning concerned cheap gossip and infidelity. He could deal with that, because there was none to be had. If the conversation had turned to his past, he would have been deeply concerned. Lisa was not someone he would want to have knowledge of his past. Sharing those private details of his life with Kenya had taken almost eight years. This was not something that he wanted spread around to the other people that they knew.

The phone rang again and Travis was sure it was Lisa. *She must have finally come up with a snappy comeback*, he thought. If she wanted to go back and forth with a pro, he was up for it.

"Yeah?" Travis was already loading up.

"Travis?" the familiar voice asked.

It was another woman, but it wasn't Lisa. "Emily?" Travis didn't expect to hear from her on his day off.

"You won't believe what's happening here." Emily spoke in a hushed tone.

From one gossiping person to the next, he surmised. At work and at home, he had people around him who couldn't wait to find out something or tell something.

"Emily, I'm on vacation and…"

"Tom Miller threatened Brad Johnson with a gun. They were in Walter Hill's office."

"What?!"

"From what I was told, it got a little loud. Mister Hill got everything under control. He really put his foot down. Security had to come in and talk those two down, too."

"I don't believe it."

"Tom was saying that Brad was trying to expose him. It had something to do with Patricia and Brad's wife..."

"Brad's wife?"

"Evidently, Tom had slept with Brad's wife in the past." Emily was in hog heaven. She had fresh gossip, hot off the presses, to dish out.

Travis shook his head in disbelief. *Holy shit*, he thought. *So that's what Brad's beef came down to*. Tom had slept with Brad's wife, and Tom was sleeping with Patricia, and she was screwing up Brad's department.

"I'll stop by there." Travis didn't wait for a goodbye; he simply hung up the phone.

Travis wasted no time getting out the house. The streets were already clearing. There were some remnants of snow. Old Man Winter had made its presence felt; it was now moving away. Yesterday, they were having what was supposed to be the snow of the year. Today, it was sunny and the temperature was supposed to get up into the fifties. Most, if not all, the snow would be gone by the time Kenya got back home.

Office drama was beginning to become the norm. If trying to cover up embezzlement for the sake of the bottom line wasn't enough, now they had one executive waving a gun at another one. It would be interesting to see how Walter wanted to play this latest debacle. For the first time, Travis was concerned about his stake in the company and his future riches. The vibration of his cell phone interrupted his thoughts.

"Hello?"

"Hey, baby, where are you?" Kenya asked.

"I'm running by the office. Are you on the road yet?"

"Not yet. I wanted to make sure the roads were safe before I left. How's it looking there?" Kenya wasn't ready to throw caution to the wind.

"They're fine and getting better. It looks like it snowed a week ago instead of yesterday."

"Really? I was watching the news this morning and they reported there were more than thirty accidents in the area last night."

"Baby, Charlotte has ten wrecks with a good rain. If it snows, you can pretty much triple that number. Now, you know I'll come get you, if you say the word."

"That won't be necessary."

"Well, hurry home. I missed you last night."

"I was only gone for the night." Kenya blushed.

"It might as well have been a month. I can't wait to spend some time with you. I got a couple of surprises for you."

"I'll be there as soon as I can."

Travis could hear the smile and blush in her voice. "I love you."

"I love you, too. I'll talk to you in a little bit."

"Bye, K." Travis hung up the phone. He was satisfied that she was feeling him again. His stop at the office would be a short one. Bottom line, the only reason why he was going was to be nosy. How prophetic was that? He was turning into Lisa and Emily.

Rick had been waiting for his opportunity to make his move. He was parked in a security alarm service van parked at the golf course clubhouse. Rick wore coveralls with the name of the security company on the left and a nametag that read "Scott" on the right. He started rummaging through the back of the van as the black Volvo approached him. He kept an eye on it as it passed. Rick picked up a hand-held monitor and turned it on. The hand-held marked the area where he was parked. He watched as the red light flashed and moved away from him. The tracking device that he had planted on the black Volvo was working. He smiled as he thought about what a great actor he could have been.

Rick had Travis completely fooled. It wasn't by chance that he'd run up on him the other night; it was by design. Rick had to tip his hat to Bone on that one. Bone's plan had worked like a charm and Travis was none the wiser for it.

He watched his monitor until Travis had been in motion for twelve minutes. It would take him four minutes and eighteen seconds to do what he needed to do at the house. Two minutes, forty seconds to get to the house and six minutes for any incidental contact with neighbors. This was down to a science for him. The only unknown was whether Kenya was there. He'd done a number of drive-bys and was confident that she wasn't home. It was time to make his move.

He drove casually toward the house and pulled into the driveway as if he had an appointment. Rick angled the van to hide as much of the front door as possible. He checked his monitor one more time before exiting the van. Travis was moving further away from the house. He saw some kids playing nearby in what was left of the snow. He concealed the small drill in his hand as he went to the door. He rang the bell twice and waited twenty seconds; plenty of time for someone to acknowledge the ring. He then rang the bell one more time and waited fifteen seconds. Once he was satisfied that the coast was clear, he began to drill and he quickly removed the doorknob. He slipped it into his pocket and went back to the van.

Rick pulled out a clipboard to appear as if he were checking for an appointment. He removed the doorknob from his pocket and freed the key cylinder from it. He replaced it with a generic cylinder. The tumblers would fall into place with the first key that entered it. He got back out the van and went to the front door again. He put the doorknob back in place. He rang the bell again and waited for someone to answer, for the last time. If anybody was watching him, he'd given another credible performance.

As he backed out the driveway, he smiled again. Smooth as clockwork. Do a couple of quick jobs for Bone and pick up an easy three grand here, five grand there, steal a little cocaine from Bone, nothing to it.

Bone had a locksmith that could duplicate a key from the cylinder. Bone wanted to have access to Travis' house and Rick knew he could help Bone for a nominal fee. This man who'd sworn to uphold the law was for sale to the highest bidder, and right now that was Bone. He'd deliver the cylinder to Bone and what he did beyond that point was Bone's business. It didn't have a damn thing to do with him.

CHAPTER 25

As the pounding and banging grew louder, Baby Jar realized it was time to get up and see who was trying to wake him this time. He tried to open his eyes, but the pounding seemed to get louder and louder. It intensified to the point of causing him pain. It paralyzed him and he could feel some type of weight all around him. He struggled to say something, but the only sound he was able to emit was a groan.

He concentrated on getting his eyes opened. Jar succeeded in cracking his eyelids and wished he hadn't as soon as they caught a ray of sunlight. It felt as if he'd scorched his retinas. What in the hell had happened to him? It took a few seconds for the pain in his eyes to subside, but that relentless pounding continued. He turned his head left and right, trying to escape the noise, but it followed him everywhere he turned. The noise wasn't coming from outside his head; it was inside. Jar struggled to move his arms. Something was pinning them down, but he eventually got them loose. He put both of his hands on each side of his head; the pounding began to subside, but the pain still lingered.

Slowly, he made another attempt at opening his eyes. Again, the daylight burned them, but he was able to tolerate it this time. Jar lay motionless in the bed with his eyes on the ceiling, trying to gain focus. He couldn't find that familiar crack in the ceiling in his bedroom. It was a much larger, cleaner ceiling. Jar didn't know where he was, but he knew he sure as hell wasn't at home.

Holding his head was working for him, things were quieting

down. He realized he was lying in a bed that was much more comfortable than his own. As he began to stir in the bed, he realized that he wasn't alone. There were bodies on both sides of him. He didn't look at them; he didn't dare. What had Bone gotten him in to now? His mind raced to recall what had happened the night before. He felt his bare skin as it met with the sheets under and on top of his body. He cautiously looked to his right, hoping he hadn't been taken advantage of. The body facing him was female. Jar breathed a sigh of relief. When he looked to his left, he discovered another female. Looking at the two women that he was sandwiched between told him something; he was the shit.

Last night, instead of working the streets, Bone had told him they were going to have a good time. Jar was introduced to cognac last night. It had a lot more kick to it than the cheap wines his mother drank. Bone let him have two drinks and that was more than enough to get his head tight. That yac, cognac, was going to be his drink from now on.

The night was coming back to him. When they had arrived at this apartment, there were eight women waiting for them. The music was blasting and the wood was blazing. The women had rolled some of the fattest blunts he'd ever seen, and they were guzzling Private Stock forties like it was water. Jar had felt good after drinking that yac. He had jumped right into the middle of the action, smoking and drinking right along with them. Bone had encouraged him to enjoy himself; Jar did and then some. The two women he was smack dab in the middle of were a testament to that.

What happened with them when he got into the room or who they were, didn't matter. He couldn't wait to brag about his latest exploits to Evan. In his youthful exuberance, he sat up way too quickly. The pounding in his head started again. This time, he fought the pain because his hormones overruled his head. Jar wanted to see if these ladies were as naked as he was. He tried to steady himself as he sat up. Jar used his feet to ease the sheets and comforter off their bodies. He peered at the beautiful women through his bloodshot eyes. His vision was blurred, he was high as a kite and hung over, but damn if these women weren't flawless.

"Pull the covers back up. It's cold," the woman on his left spoke, keeping her back to him.

"Okay." Jar started to hop to it, but then he realized he was in control here. Bone's tutelage told him so.

He pulled the covers up all right, and then scooted close behind her. Jar waited to see if she would reject his advance. She didn't. He wanted her to feel his manhood. Without missing a beat, she led him where he was anxious to go. They stayed on their sides, never once looking at each other face to face. It was faceless, harmless, casual sex. Their activity woke the other woman up. Apparently, she enjoyed what was going down because she started to kiss Jar on the nape of his neck.

"Save some for me," she whispered and gently nibbled at his ear.

His hormones had completely eliminated his throbbing head and those sexy words really lit his fire. Jar spent the next hour-and-a-half doing everything he could possibly imagine with the two women. It pleased him to no end that they had a few ideas of their own to share with him.

Exhausted, whipped and in need of a bathroom, Jar slid on his pants and went in search of a place to refresh himself. He spotted Bone as he opened the bedroom door. Bone was sitting back in a chair with his feet resting on an ottoman. He was freshly showered and the clothes he had on weren't the ones he was wearing when they had arrived last night.

"Been at it a while, huh?" Bone had a sly, knowing smile on his face.

"Those freaks are off the chain." Jar was still on unstable legs. The combination of last night's partying, which he couldn't remember much of, and this morning's tag team sexual endurance challenge, had taken its toll, but he was loving it.

"That's the life, Jar. These are the rewards for your work in the game. I call them perks." Bone wasn't going to miss any opportunity to emphasize how great the game was.

"Yeah, I'm feeling them perks." Jar no longer watched how he said every word to Bone. He was comfortable now. He was free to do and say anything he wanted around Bone. "Do you know where a bathroom is up in this piece?"

"Do I know? Shit, I better. I pay the mortgage for this ma'fuckin' condo."

"This is yours?"

"Hell yeah, it's mine. I got this girl who's got her name on it." The quizzical look on Jar's face humored Bone. "Don't worry. I'll school you on that later. Keep walkin' straight ahead. The bathroom is the second door on the right. Take a shower while you're in there. You smell like sex. There are some towels and a change of clothes in there." Bone had him set up.

Jar hurried into the bathroom. He wasted little time in getting the water running. Within minutes, the two women came out the bedroom that Jar was in. They apparently wasted very little time in getting dressed.

"You two served him up right this morning, didn't you?" Bone's tone was almost a congratulatory one.

"Fuck that small talk, Bone. Get up off that loot," the shorter of the two women said.

"Five hundred each," the other one chimed in.

"It's like that?" Bone shook his head. "Here's your four hundred dollars." Bone pulled out a wad of money and peeled off four one hundred-dollar bills. He held them up. "You must have misunderstood our terms?"

"You said five hundred! Each."

"Keep fuckin' with me and it'll be down to three hundred."

"That ain't right, Bone." The tall one was getting pissed. This was not the place to look for an argument.

"So? Who you gonna tell? You better take this four hundred and put a damn smile on your face." His voice was deathly sinister. "Run your mouth and somebody will be gettin' your body out a ditch." He continued to hold the money out for them. When they didn't move, he started to take one of the hundreds away.

The shorter woman walked over and grabbed the money before they lost another hundred dollars. She had obviously been down this road with Bone a time or two before. She snatched the other woman by the arm and dragged her to the door. Jar stuck his head out the bathroom in time to see them leave.

"You'll ain't leaving, are ya?" Jar called after them.

The women didn't acknowledge him. The door slammed behind them as they stormed out the condo.

Bone listened to the door slam. He slowly blinked his eyes as he prepared to speak. "Leave them..." Bone didn't have time for the drama.

"Bitches where they at." Jar completed the sentence for Bone. He was on his way to being on top of the game.

Bone smiled. His protégé was learning to play the game his way. The kid was ripe to do anything he wanted. Why wouldn't he be? He was sixteen with money in his pocket that Bone had put there, and grown women were serving him. Bone was the provider of that also. "There you go. That's how I like to hear you talk that shit!" Bone knew that was blowing his head up.

"It was fun, but it's time to move on," Jar added.

"My nigga. Sho' you right. That's how real players play."

"Fo' sho'." Jar bit Bone's favorite line. Jar nodded his head, then stuck it back into the bathroom.

"Yes, my nigga!" Bone hollered out. *Too bad*, he thought, *if the kid wasn't part of my plan, I might have actually liked him.*

Seconds later, the doorbell rang. Bone turned his head in the direction of the door. If those women had the audacity to come back and demand more money, he was going to put his foot in their asses. He took his time in getting up and going to the door. He walked quietly, extended his hand toward it and didn't bother looking through the peephole.

"What the hell ya'll want?" Bone barked as he snatched the door open. He intended to strike fear in their hearts.

"Ease up, player. Let a brother in," Rick said.

Bone moved to the side to let Rick in. "Come in here! I thought you were those hoes!" Bone yelled out the door in case they were still within earshot.

"What did you do to those women? They were mad as hell. That tall broad almost ran me over."

"They was tag teaming my little protégé. They a little ticked off because they left here a little lighter in they pockets than they thought they should be."

"You still shorten tricks like that."

"Hell yeah. My name is still Bone, ain't it?"

"Them was some bad-ass women, dog. Any more up in here?" Rick's head was on a swivel as he ventured in; he was like a bloodhound on a trail.

"Like I said, my name's Bone, ain't it? There's a few more layin' around in here."

Bone shut the door and joined Rick who was already making himself comfortable. He had the refrigerator door opened, looking for something to drink. After shuffling a couple of forties out the way, he got his hands on a Coke.

"So, you got it, right?"

Rick reached into his pocket and took out the cylinder that belonged to Travis' front door. "When you send a man on a mission, a man is going to get the job done." Rick smiled, pleased with his handiwork. He placed the cylinder on the table.

"That's why I had somebody out there I could trust." Bone studied Rick's face for a few seconds. "I can trust you, right?"

"Always." Rick didn't blink an eye or hesitate for one second.

Bone watched his eyes. He realized Rick was lying. Rick was a dirty cop and they both knew it. If he would swerve the right side of the law, he would damn sure swerve the left. "Good," Bone said with a smile.

"Where's your man that's going to get inside that lock?"

"First door on the right."

"How much is he getting paid for this?"

"Paid?" Bone looked at Rick and then down the hall toward the room. "Shit, that nigga's getting paid in full right now."

"What do you have going on in there?"

"No need to be shy, dog. Go in there to see for yourself and send that cat out here so he can get to work on this. I need to have this shit, like yesterday."

"If you don't mind, I I might step in there for him. Keep the spirits up, so to speak. I just hate to see shit left undone."

"Good idea." Bone smiled at his boy, Rick. Rick didn't acknowledge Bone; he was already making a beeline for the room. *Stupid son of a bitch*, he thought. These grown-ass men were too easy to manipulate. Not a one of them was thinking with the right head. He could tolerate Jar falling into the trap; he was only a kid. But not those grown fools. He shook his head in disgust. Rick had let him down in more ways than one. So be it, none of them would outlive their usefulness to him.

It took five minutes for the lanky six-foot figure to wrestle himself free from the room. Myron Snead was commonly referred to as "Mantis." He weighed one hundred and fifty-five pounds, soaking wet. He had dark skin and big eyes that were always clear and white. The thick, black-framed glasses magnified his eyes behind them. Myron was sweating heavily and panting as he came closer to Bone.

"You about to fog them glasses up, ain't you?" Bone shook his head at the sight of Myron.

"Man, it's wild up in here! It's all good."

"Bump all that. You got some work to do. The cylinder is on the table. I need that key made quick, fast and in a hurry. You mess this up and I'll kill you."

Myron chuckled at what he thought was a joke. He looked at Bone. There was no humor to be found in Bone's face. The coldness in Bone's stare rattled him. Myron's normally steady hands shook. If there were any way he could have sweat more than he was, he would have.

"No pressure," Bone added with a smirk.

Myron tried to steady himself as he sat down next to the table in the living room. He wanted to get a good look at the cylinder. Bone watched his tentativeness and enjoyed it. Myron was relieved at the sight of the cylinder. All he had to do was open the cylinder and decode the lock. It would be simple enough for him to complete quickly, once his hands stopped trembling. Myron made some quick notes of the position of the tumblers, and then created a clay mold to use as a reference. Doing the work he was trained to do, helped to calm his nerves.

When Jar came out of the bathroom wrapped in a towel, Myron

was finishing up. All that was left for him was duplicating the key and cleaning up his mess.

"Who's the square?" Jar asked Bone as if he had the right to know. This other guy was on his turf.

Bone couldn't believe how this little knucklehead was overstepping his bounds. The kid was showing some spunk and he liked it.

"Who you calling a square?" Myron stood up. "I'll bust your little ass up."

Jar stood there half-naked and unfazed. Nothing about Myron instilled the least bit of fear in Jar.

"Myron, sit your narrow ass down!" Bone snapped. *Jar is coming along*, he thought. Bone watched as Myron complied and went back to cleaning up. "How long is it going to take you to finish up?"

"I have to go to my van and duplicate the key. Another ten minutes." Myron was fuming, but he didn't dare show it to Bone.

"Cool. Once you finish up, you can go back into the room or whatever you want. It's your day."

Myron and Bone both knew he wouldn't waste any time getting back into the room with Rick. There were four women willing to take care of anyone that came through their door. Unlike the two women who'd spent time with Jar, they had been paid handsomely for the work they were putting in. They made sure they got their money first before any favors were exchanged.

"I'll be right back," Myron said as he gathered his stuff and went out the door. He rolled his eyes at Jar as he looked back at him.

Jar looked Myron up and down as if he was sizing him up. Then Jar sucked his teeth at him. Myron started to say something, but when he saw Bone looking at him, he kept his thoughts to himself. He did the only thing he could do: He closed the door behind him.

"So, what's the insect doing?" Jar let his curiosity fly. He was totally comfortable in this environment.

"He's making me a spare key," Bone responded without the slightest trace of irritation. "Never know when I might need to let you have one."

It was a lie, but it was a convenient one. It was the key to Travis Moore's house but, if Jar thought it was for him, it would score Bone some more points with the kid. The manipulation of Baby Jar continued. Bone was sinking his hooks further and further into him. Bone was giving the kid what he wanted. The kid felt free and accepted. Bone sat back, closed his eyes and relaxed. There were so many puppets whose strings he was pulling. He would have to yank one of Rick's soon though. He'd already gotten the word on the kilos that Rick had pocketed for himself. Bone trusted that Rick would be greedy enough to cross him, and Bone would use Rick's greed to his advantage.

CHAPTER 26

Travis didn't know what to expect when he arrived at Home Supply. He hoped that some semblance of order had been restored by now.

Travis was a little surprised to find everything so calm as he pulled into the parking lot. It was only a third full; yesterday's snow was responsible for some of that. There were a number of people who probably used the snow to skip work on a Friday. He couldn't blame them, but it was just his luck to burn a vacation day on a snow day.

When Travis walked through the front door, he expected to be met with some signs of panic or chaos, maybe some police tape. However, it appeared to be business as usual.

"This is certainly a casual Friday for you, isn't it?" the attractive young receptionist said pleasantly. She'd never seen Travis in a pair of jeans. "Aren't you on vacation?"

"Yeah. How are you, Sarah?" Travis was surprised by her pleasantness. There was no tension or fear in her voice.

"Doing fine. What are you doing here?"

Travis looked around. Everything appeared to be fine. He rolled his eyes when it dawned on him who'd called him. Not once in his efforts to get there, or when he'd created a diversion for himself at the mall, did he once consider the source.

"Anything out of the ordinary happening here today?"

"No...Oh, wait a minute. There was a little commotion upstairs in Walter's office this morning."

"A little commotion?" *Odd choice of words*, Travis thought.

"Yeah, how'd you hear about it so fast?" She realized the answer as soon as she'd asked.

"Emily," they said in unison.

I'll be damned, Travis thought. "So let me guess, there was nobody in here waving a gun, was it?"

"No."

Travis shook his head. "Is Brad in? I'm going to stop by his office."

"He's around here somewhere."

Brad's door to his office was closed. Without any hesitation, Travis opened it. He was sitting at his desk. He immediately tensed as the door opened. Brad was ready to spring to his feet until he recognized Travis. The two men looked at each other. Brad started to laugh and that put Travis at ease as he laughed as well.

"What the hell are you doing, Travis?"

"I stopped by to check on you. You're a little jumpy, aren't you?"

"You would be too if you had the morning I've had. Then again, you probably already heard about my morning, haven't you? How's Emily?"

Everybody knew about Emily and her penchant for gossip. "I've heard from her and I'm sure that the information she's given me isn't accurate." Travis was pissed. Although he didn't get there as fast as he could have, he had taken time out of his day to come into the office. With the inclement weather, there was no telling what could have happened on his way there. Travis was creating more reasons to be ticked at Emily.

"So you decided to come to the source and get the real story." Brad nodded toward the chair in front of him and Travis sat. "It wasn't much to it. I was meeting with Walter this morning on an unrelated issue. Tom came busting into the office, not unlike you, demanding to know what was going on. He accused me of making him look like the bad guy in the Bradshaw mess. He said his wife was questioning him about the incident. Then, he accused me of leaking word to her. Apparently, his wife had received some pictures of him and Patricia that weren't very flattering to either one of them."

"All of this in front of Walter?"

"Yeah, and the idiot left the door wide open for anybody to hear him. His only saving grace is that we have a skeleton crew here today. But, there were enough ears to catch every word he said."

"Sounds like he really put himself out there," Travis said.

"On front street," Brad added. He watched Travis' reaction. "What? My kids listen to rap music."

"Was that the plan, to make him look bad?"

Brad thought about the question and pondered the politically correct answer. "I laid out the facts. It looks how it looks. Good, bad or indifferent, that's what I told him. He accused me of having a vendetta against him because my wife wanted to sleep with him. That's when I fed into the argument and Walter shut the door."

"Did you attack him?"

"Verbally. I told him that my wife wouldn't have his sweaty, overweight, sexually inept ass. Miller has been hitting on my wife for fifteen years. During that same time, he's been trying to reel me into something, anything that he could hold over my head. Instead, the opposite has happened. He's the one who has come up short."

"When did he pull the gun on you?" By now, Travis was sure that there was no gun involved.

"Who said there was a gun?"

"Give you one guess."

"Emily." Brad watched Travis nod. "There wasn't any gun. Miller did threaten to shoot my nuts off."

"So, I guess that's it? Nothing is going to happen to Walter's golden boy?"

"He's out of here. He communicated a threat to a fellow employee. That's cause for immediate dismissal. After the company goes public, he'll be terminated. They'll hold his profits from the sale of stock in escrow for a period of two years. If he causes any negative fallout from this, he'll have to forfeit his shares at the price he purchased them for."

"Can you hold him to that?"

"He's already signed the paperwork. He didn't have a choice. It was either accept that or get fired, cash out his stock now and nothing else to show for his service to the company. Walter told him that it was his only way to save face. He jumped right at it, though. It's strange, seems like there's something else going on with him."

"Why do you say that?"

"I don't know. I've never seen him lose it quite like that before."

"Well, money can do some strange things to people. It's going to be interesting around here on Monday morning."

"That, it will be." Brad knew the rumor mill would be hard at work.

"I'm going to see Emily. It's time she and I had a long talk."

"Hope it does her some good."

Travis didn't hold out a lot of optimism. He and Brad shot the breeze for a few minutes until Travis was ready to go tackle Emily.

Emily sat at her desk concentrating on the parking lot and the game of solitaire on her computer. She had long since stopped pretending to be hard at work. For some reason, the black Datsun 280ZX kept drawing her attention. Of all the room in the parking lot, its driver chose to park next to Travis Moore's Volvo.

Normally, she would have been looking for somebody to tell about it. She resisted the urge because she'd already jumped the gun once today when she'd called Travis. Emily watched the person in the car but couldn't tell what he or she was doing. The person got out the car briefly and she could tell it was a man. He stood there for a few seconds, and then got back in the 280ZX. Maybe it was somebody waiting for Travis; it was his day off. When the car pulled off, she disregarded it. The car was only there for a few minutes anyway. Emily went back to her computer and deeply engrossed herself in the game of solitaire.

Emily was up by over three hundred dollars when Travis snuck up behind her cubicle. Travis didn't announce himself; instead he decided to let her find him there. Emily was so intent with her game that she didn't notice him. By the time she started her third consecutive game, Travis' patience had worn thin.

"Hello, Emily!" Travis spoke in a rapid pace and barked his greeting to her. It had the effect that he wanted on her. She jumped and, in a reflex motion, snatched at the mouse while trying to click out the game she was playing.

"Travis? Hi." Emily smiled as she turned her head to greet him. She didn't meet a smile in return. She could already tell he wasn't happy to see her. "So, what brings you by?" She could almost kick herself for that. Nervousness was taking over. The only reason Travis was there was because of her. Emily could see the look on Travis' face intensify.

"You know full well why I'm here." Travis fought the urge to go off on her.

"I was going to call you back..."

"Save it, Emily," Travis said, cutting her off. "At what point did you see Tom Miller pull a gun on Brad?" He peeked around the cubicle to see if anyone else was around. It was clear to him that Emily didn't have an answer. By the time the news from upstairs had reached her, there was allegedly a gun being pointed at Brad; and he and Tom were arguing over Tom's wife. Emily couldn't wait to tell somebody what she'd heard. That somebody was Travis.

"Were you, at any point, a witness to anything that went on between those two?"

"Not exactly."

"What is 'not exactly'? Either you were or you weren't."

"No, I wasn't there."

"But you didn't hesitate to call me and tell me things that you didn't know were true. And this isn't the first we've had a conversation regarding this type of situation. You are more concerned with getting gossip flowing than doing your job. Now, other people may want to hear it. I don't."

"I assumed you'd want to know. Considering all that's gone on the last few days. Patricia Brad..."

"You can't help yourself, can you? A moment awake is a moment to gossip. Unless you have something to say to me regarding an audit or policy, I don't want to hear it. I damn near put my car in a ditch trying to get here." It was an exaggeration but it would help to stress his point. Her gossip could put other people at risk. "You need to be mindful of what you say."

"I understand. I apologize."

Travis contemplated a response, but he didn't want to continue the conversation. He didn't accept or reject her apology. He turned and walked away.

Emily wanted to say something about the man that had gotten out a car and stood near his Volvo. She opted to keep her mouth shut because that was what Travis wanted. She had no idea that this would have been a good time to go with her natural instinct to say something.

CHAPTER 27

Carolina Place Mall drew his attention as he traveled the 485 loop. After the weather last night and hanging out with Bruce, he hadn't picked up anything for Kenya. If their anniversary rolled around and he didn't have a gift, he'd be back in the doghouse even deeper than before.

The mall would be a nice diversion for him. Travis couldn't believe he was gullible enough to run out the house on Emily's word. The possibility of becoming a multimillionaire with Home Supply was more important to him than he'd previously thought. His future riches were being jeopardized by the instability of the company's chief financial officer.

Brad, to his credit, was craftier than Travis ever imagined. He had to take his hat off to him. He'd orchestrated Tom's demise. He'd used Travis, Patricia and Walter as puppets to cause everything to crumble around Tom. There were a lot of things that Walter could sweep under the rug, and apparently had over the years that Home Supply had been in existence. Brad had had enough of it and had decided to start yanking some strings.

Brad knew an intimate relationship existed between Tom and Patricia. Brad also wasn't foolish enough not to know that she was stealing from the company. Brad used Travis to cover his ploy and put on a show in front of Walter. In all likelihood, Brad would have sacrificed Travis if anything had backfired on him. It didn't, but it didn't quite get rid of Tom either. Instead, they all signed documents to ensure they kept everything hush-hush. That must have been when he pulled the trigger on plan B and went after Tom on the home front.

It made great sense to Travis. Brad chopped away at Tom's credibility at work, and then toppled him with an all-out assault at home. Travis was sure that, if photos were involved, Brad had something to do with it. He was destroying Tom's reputation from all angles. Brad built a case against Tom using Tom's own past against him. Once Tom blew up at work and threatened Brad, he had Tom. If Walter didn't do something about Tom, rest assured, Home Supply would've had a lawsuit coming. Not the kind of stuff you want happening when a company was about to go public. Travis liked the way Brad worked but he also knew he would have to keep an eye out for Brad.

Travis' head continued to spin with theories as he pulled into a parking space at Carolina Place. The heck with it, he figured. Home Supply and everyone in it would be fine. If he wasn't a millionaire in two weeks because of problems at work, it would be okay. He couldn't miss what he never had. "I'm supposed to be on vacation," Travis said as he looked at himself in the rear-view mirror. He put the car in park and got out.

Travis Moore's life was consumed with corporate America, making things right with his wife and living down his past. Things in his life had a way of falling into place, and this would, too. His comfort level in his present life had dulled the street IQ he once had in his past life. He was on his happy-go-lucky way to pick out the perfect gift for his wife, oblivious to the rest of the world that moved around him.

Flake had watched the Volvo as it pulled off the loop. There were six cars that separated them and Travis never paid him the least amount of attention anyway. There wasn't any need for him to keep following Travis. He already had what he needed from the Volvo. It was time for him to get over to Bone's condo.

When he parked in the parking lot, Flake didn't get out the car immediately. Instead, he looked at the two vans in the parking lot. One was from a security alarm company and the other one was a mobile locksmith. There must have been some connection between the locksmith and Bone calling and telling him to get the vehicle identification number off the Black Volvo. After mulling it over for a few minutes, Flake changed the last number on the VIN number.

As he was about to get out the car, he noticed the front door to the condo opening. It was someone dressed in a uniform from the alarm company. As the person walked closer to the van, Flake sank down in the driver's seat. He recognized the person in the uniform. It was Lite Brite, Rick Nixon, the state trooper. What in the hell was he doing wearing a security alarm uniform? Flake stayed as low as he could and watched Rick as he moved slowly. Flake was aware of how things had gone down in that condo. Flake snickered when he got a better look at Rick. He wasn't being careful. He was probably tired from getting his brains knocked out. He waited for the van to leave before he got out the car.

INSIDE THE CONDO, BONE WAS CHECKING THE KEY Myron had duplicated. He compared it to the mold Myron pulled from the cylinder that belonged to the Moores' house. Baby Jar was watching him with little interest. He wished there was another woman that he could get into a room. His ladies had already been paid and dismissed. As he sat there, his head was beginning to knock again. The doorbell rang and it was a welcomed interruption for Baby Jar.

"I'll get it."

Bone and Myron barely acknowledged him. They kept studying the imprint on the key to make sure it was a good match. Satisfied, Bone nodded his approval.

"Looks good." Bone waited for Jar to get closer to the door. "Make sure you know who it is before you open it."

Jar looked through the peephole and recognized Flake. This dope game could do a lot of things to a person, but he was determined not to be anybody's flunky. He tried to see if there was anybody else with Flake.

"Who is it?" Jar demanded as he deepened his voice and watched Flake through the peephole.

On the other side of the door, Flake didn't have a difficult time realizing that it was Jar playing games behind the door. That little punk was still running around in there. The kid came over with Bone last night. Flake was surprised by what he saw. Jar was downing forties and smoking weed like it was all-good. If Flake tried anything like that, Bone would have his ass for it. Now the kid was playing games at the door with him. Flake looked into the peephole and said nothing.

"Who is it?" Bone asked, looking up.

"It's Flake."

"Open the door and let him in," Bone said sternly. "This is business time now. You been fuckin' around here all morning. Playtime's over. This is serious work we're takin' care of. You got to have your mind in the right frame to maintain your flow." Bone paused as a stunned Jar stood at the door in silence. "I need me a soldier that understands the war."

"What the hell does that mean?" Myron laughed. It was the biggest crock of crap he'd heard in a long time.

For an instant, Myron didn't exist anymore. He'd heard his comment and he would deal with him later. Right now, he needed his soldier to commit to the war. "Are you that soldier?" Bone's piercing stare was drilling holes in Jar. "Are-you-that-soldier?"

Jar understood what was being asked. "Yes, I *am* that soldier," Jar affirmed.

"Man, why don't you salute that little nigga, since he your soldier and shit." Myron let loose with a gut-busting laugh. For some reason, he found the interaction between Bone and Jar as great entertainment.

Bone had no regard for what was going through Myron's mind. He was concerned with Jar. His soldier was in line and ready for duty when called. "Open the door."

Jar obliged him. He held the door open like he was the doorman at the Waldorf-Astoria. Flake stepped inside, but he didn't keep walking. Instead, he stopped and slowly turned his head toward the boy who'd taken his time to open the door for him. If Bone wasn't in the room, he'd jerk a knot in his young ass.

"I'm over here, Flake." Bone was aware of the obvious tension that was growing within Flake toward Jar. Bone felt like he was keeping two children apart. Flake would settle down once his total plan was revealed.

Reluctantly, Flake hedged past Jar to get to Bone. There were a lot of things he wanted to say to Jar but, at the moment, he was swallowing his pride. Based on prior conversations, Flake knew defying Bone would not be good for his health.

"You got that vehicle identification number?" Bone was all business.

"I got it."

"You can make a duplicate of this key using the VIN number?" Bone turned his attention to Myron. He didn't notice Flake's uneasiness.

"How many times you gonna keep doubting me?" Myron shot

the question to him like he was in control of the situation. "I make miracles happen."

"Uh-huh." Bone looked at the cocky little nerd. He'd had a good time with some attractive women and now he was another king of the world.

"I'ma just call in this VIN to the local Volvo dealer and I can pick the key up in no time."

"They won't say nothin' about it?"

"I'm the locksmith, nigga. They ain't gonna ask me jack."

Bone heard the man, but was he actually saying it to him? Maybe he bumped his head on a headboard? "You the locksmith." Bone gave a half-smile and a throwaway laugh. "Yo, when you get back with that key, I'ma have a little somethin' extra for you."

"For real, I'ma make that shit happen for you quick, fast and in a hurry." Myron didn't know if that meant more time in one of the rooms or lining his pocket with some of that paper. But he'd do what he had to do and get back there to find out.

Bone's statement meant something altogether different to Flake. He discreetly made eye contact with Bone, and Bone gave him the nod. There was no mistaking what was being communicated to him. Flake looked back to Myron, who was still contemplating what wonderful possibilities lay ahead for him. Flake knew what was in his very near future.

"Flake, walk that man to the door. Jar, get out of their way."

Myron left with one purpose in mind, getting back. Flake walked to the door behind him as he was instructed and Jar traded places with him. Flake shut the door behind Myron and locked it. He had preparations of his own to make, and he sure didn't want to be bothered with that kid.

Bone waited until he and Jar were alone in the room. Bone sat up straight as Jar took a seat on the floor beside him. It was time for the master to mete out knowledge to his young apprentice.

"You know why I called you out, do you?"

Jar was hesitant with an answer. He was back to measuring his thoughts and his statements. The drinking and partying clouded his judgment, perhaps causing him to overstep his bounds.

"There's a difference in how you play yourself when it's money time and clown time. You don't clown when it's money time. Don't matter whether you got beef with a nigga. Whether you like him or not, you don't put nothin' in front of this."

Jar took in what he'd said. He was trying hard to concentrate on Bone. Sitting on the floor was causing his head to start banging again. "I feel you," he said, as he began to massage his temples.

"Head's boomin', huh?"

Jar looked up at Bone and nodded.

"Figured it would. You was hittin' it pretty hard."

Jar agreed. He definitely had been hitting it hard. Sitting on the floor in front of Bone was causing his head to split. Now, he didn't have sex and hormones to block it out.

"Jar, son, you got to learn how to balance the party with the game. I'm going to take care of you until you know how to." Bone was pushing for loyalty from the kid with a mother on crack. "There's gonna come a time when I'ma need you to step up for me." Bone played the moment. "Are you my soldier?"

"I am." Jar was struggling with his head throbbing.

"Good. Jar, you need to get out of here, clear your head. Take the 280, get you some eats," Bone slipped him a hundred, "and go home. And Jar, if you wreck that car, I'll kill ya." Bone smiled at him.

Jar saw the smile, but he didn't take the comment as a joke. If he wrecked Bone's 280, he'd kill himself before Bone had a chance to do it.

Flake couldn't believe his eyes. He was watching Jar leave in the 280 by himself. Bone was on some weird kick again. The kid was wheelin' the 280, while he was getting vehicle identification numbers and he had no idea what was in Bone's head.

"Wake the fuck up. You over there daydreaming. You got something to handle."

Flake shut the door. Slowly, he walked toward Bone, still not sure what to make of the situation.

"Somethin' on your mind?"

Flake started to say something, but thought better of it. "No."

"Nigga, I know you. What you got to say?"

"Why Myron?"

"You know the answer to that. That ma'fucker talks too much. The fuck you care? Ain't like he's your buddy."

"But, he don't know nothin'. Shit, I don't know nothin'."

"It's not what he knows now; it's what he'll know when all this shakes out. Got to shore up some of these ends so they don't come back to haunt me. Got to keep this clean; no mess." *This nigga's getting soft and asking too many questions*, he thought.

"I'll be in the first room." Flake had already made the decision on how to handle this. Didn't matter what he said to Bone, it was going to go down the way that Bone wanted.

Once he got into the room, he stood beside the door and waited. How his life had reached this point, he wasn't sure. He knew he didn't care too much for himself. He mourned for Myron and his four kids by three different women. They wouldn't have much to remember, but it would be a loss nonetheless. Flake shed a few tears for them, Myron and for himself, the soul he'd lost in the dope game.

Time passed quickly for Flake as he stood there. It wasn't long before he heard the doorbell ring. Time began to slow down for him until everything was happening in slow motion.

The sound of the front door being opened broke the silence that surrounded him. Greetings between Bone and Myron were noisy echoes to his ears; it was like trying to hear someone speaking to you when your head is under water. Bits and pieces of the conversation seeped in and registered in his mind. The key had been copied. Luckily for Flake, the VIN he gave matched some other key. They didn't have the car to test it against, so he was safe for now.

The voices continued to be a muddled mass of noise until Bone's voice rang clear through the barrage of noise. "I got something for you in that room, dog. You gonna love that."

Flake knew it was time. Bone was sending Myron into the lion's den. Flake positioned himself to attack his prey. The passing seconds felt like hours. The footsteps that neared the door were slow and thunderous as each one landed. Flake's eyes were glued to the doorknob. He could see the knob as it began to turn, one millimeter at a time. Flake's massive body tensed as the door opened. His senses were heightened as death neared him.

Myron entered the room with a smile on his face, waiting for some loving to rain down on him. The smile began to fade when he didn't see anybody in the room. Before a word could be uttered, Flake's arms began to squeeze around his neck like a python. If there were any thoughts that something good was about to happen, they quickly disappeared as the oxygen supply was cut off to Myron's brain. Flake snatched him up like a rag doll and continued to squeeze the life out of him. He never heard the front door open and close. The body was limp and Flake rotated the head to the right until he heard it snap. Tears welled in Flake's eyes as he kept squeezing. He squeezed until all of the muscles in his body trembled from head to toe. Only then did he finally let the limp body slump to the floor. It was done; and as Bone wanted, there was no mess to be found.

Flake looked at the body of Myron. Just moments ago, it contained life, and he had snuffed it out with his bare hands. He was a monster that would kill if Bone demanded him to do so. That is what his life with Bone had made him.

CHAPTER 28

Everyone sat in the studio listening to the hot track that Soul had put down. Twenty-three hours in the studio and four tracks later, everyone was tired—except Bruce. He felt like going another twenty-three. Some people were already asleep, but even their heads were nodding, feeling the music and digging the voice of this young man. It was that smooth R&B sound that moved your head and touched your soul. As the track ended, the hoopla and the hype began around Soul. Guys gave him dap and the young women hugged and kissed any part of him they could touch.

"That's how you do it, boo," one girl said.

"Is he really real? Is he really real? Holla' back!" said another.

"My cousin's about to blow up!" Harold was already counting his piece of the Soul pie.

Soul laughed and smiled, enjoying the moment until he saw Bruce, who was at the control board watching him. Soul met eyes with him and began to settle down. One by one, everyone in the room picked up on what was going on between the two of them. It didn't take long for everybody to be as quiet as Soul.

"So, what do you think?" Soul was almost reluctant to ask.

Bruce sat back in his chair, took a deep breath to ponder the question. Everyone else held their breath with him and hinged on the words he would speak. Bruce nodded his head methodically and a smile crept across his face.

"Straight-up platinum, baby!"

Applause and the sounds of joy erupted in the studio. Bruce was a producer revered in the music industry. He was a Grammy Award nominee who'd worked with some of the best in the business. He'd been nominated on four different occasions; and he'd vouched for Soul. Bruce watched as the group enjoyed themselves.

"Yo!" Bruce yelled to get the attention of the group. "We ain't done. We got a lot more work to do. Ya'll sound like you're ready to roll with it. Let's get ready to get back in on this."

That helped quiet the crowd. Once they realized that the longer they stayed there, more work would come their way, the crowd didn't waste any time in dispersing. The hangers-on had already endured twenty-three hours of relentless work. They didn't want another eighteen.

Soul, Harold, Bruce and a sound engineer were the only ones remaining when the crowd had left.

"You gonna be ready to go again tonight, Soul?"

"No doubt. What time?" Soul was eager to get back in the studio to pick up where he'd left off.

"I'm here at eight."

"Eight?" Harold was already calculating how much sleep he would get in the next five hours. Between eating, sleeping and washing his behind, it didn't leave much.

"I'll be here at eight. Soul has to be here at ten," Bruce said, which relieved Harold.

"So that means if I'm not here by nine-thirty, I'm late."

"Boy, you pick up quick." *This kid is really good*, he thought. Just had to keep him that way. "Soul, the stuff is good, real good, but we've got a long way to go. We ain't dropping nothing that's going to be for the minute. That voice has got a couple of decades in it. You got to take care of it like you know that."

Soul let the words wash over him before he drank them in.

Bruce wasn't trying to make a hit with him; he was attempting to build a career with him. Soul nodded his head and smiled.

"I feel you." Soul popped his cousin on the shoulder. "Let's bounce. I got to get back here at eight." If Bruce was going to be on it, Soul was going to be right beside him.

Harold rolled his eyes as they prepared to leave. Soul having to be back at eight meant seven-thirty for them which, in turn, meant that Harold had to be back here at seven-thirty. Shit rolled downhill. Harold sulked all the way out the door.

"That's why you don't mix business with family out of convenience," the sound engineer commented after watching Harold leave with Soul.

"He'll adjust. Once Soul is making loot, he'll adjust to whatever Soul's doing quite nicely. That kid's a gold mine." Bruce was a little more excited with everybody gone.

"It's like that?"

"You heard the kid. What do you think?"

"You're right, maybe more."

"It's a trip, you know. You never know how things are going to come to you."

"What are you talking about?"

"Soul. This cat I backed away from about twelve years ago brings this kid to me. I mean, I've seen the brother from time to time. I speak, but we don't get down like we used to. He put me up on Soul three months ago. Go figure."

"It's all good in the end, if you winning. You and this brother, ya'll straight now, right?"

Bruce hesitated to respond. He wasn't sure what kind of relationship he had with his cousin. "I'll let you know after I get this cheese," he joked. The vibration from his cell phone interrupted him. It was a welcome one until he checked the digital display.

Speak of the devil and he will show himself, he thought. "Excuse me, while I take this." Bruce waited while the sound engineer got out his way. "This is Bruce." Bruce answered as if he didn't know who was on the other end.

"What up, cuz?" The voice was happy and full of life.

"Working." Bruce was short and to the point. He was guarded in any conversation with him. It was Bruce's way of protecting himself.

"You makin' anything happen with that kid I brought to you?"

"The kid's got pipes. We gonna make something happen. We're laying some work down now."

"So, I can look for my piece of the pie, right?"

"That's between you and the kid, and whatever you got worked out with him."

"Get off the defense, B. Everything's cool. I'm just fuckin' with you."

"And you know I'm going to look out for family." There was a moment of silence. Bruce knew where the conversation was headed and didn't feel like doing a dance until they got to it. "So, what do you want?"

"B, can't a homey, a cousin, just holler at you? Me and you go all the way back." He waited for an answer. It didn't come. "What? Family can't get no love on that?"

"What do you want?"

"You find out anything on that stuff I put in your ear a few months back?"

"I don't have time for that, man. You need to put that down. All that shit that went down was in the past. I don't have any beef with it. You need to let that go, too. To answer your question, no, I haven't found out anything."

"I'll let it go, I'm gonna let it go real soon."

Bruce made a living reading people. That last statement had an ominous tone to it. There was something dark and dangerous lurking in that man's mind.

"What's up, Bone?" For the first time during the conversation, Bruce called his cousin's name.

"You might want to lay down behind that nigga, but I ain't. I been closing in on that bitch for the last six months. I got his ass surrounded now, and I'm about to close the show. This is your backstage pass. Ain't nobody seen the kind of shit I seen behind his ass..."

Bone continued to rant and Bruce had to put some distance between him and the cell phone to protect his eardrums. This brother was unstable. One second he was calm and rational, the next he was losing it. This caught Bruce off guard.

"What are you talking about, man?!!" Bruce tried to snap him back to reality.

"You know what I'm talking about. I'm talking about P. Mo. He got people around here fooled, calling him Travis. I tapped into a few people that know Travis. He laid down that P. Mo shit like that never existed. He got all these people fooled. Nigga running around town with a good job, fine-ass wife and don't none of them fools around him know a thing about him."

Bone was aware of what other people were thinking about him. In their eyes, the obsession with Travis and their past history was getting the better of him. He was in complete control and the time to expose him was drawing near.

"I got a little party coming up. Something special, you might call it a coming-out party for Perry 'P. Mo' Travis Moore. You might want to check it out. I know that nigga left you high and dry, too."

So, there it was. Bone was planning a coming-out party for Travis.

This was definitely something that Bruce needed to stay close to.

"Sounds like you're almost ready to make a move. You make sure I get put on the guest list. I don't want to miss a thing when it goes down."

Conversations between Bruce and Bone were of a cryptic nature by design. Neither one of them took for granted that there were no other ears listening. It was the paranoia that came with each of their chosen professions.

"Stay close by because it could be jumping off anytime. You know how my parties go down. Holla."

Bruce hung up his cell phone and knew that not much time would pass before Bone moved on his plans, whatever they were. Bruce could tell from his ranting that he was worked up over Travis Moore.

Bone was finishing his walk. As he neared his condo, his mood had become very pensive. Talking to Bruce usually left him that way. He had walked to a secluded wooded area that was about a mile from the condo to have the phone conversation. He wasn't ready to have too many ears in on his plan. The thirty-minute walk would also give Flake the time he needed to dispose of Myron's body. Bone had discreetly left the condo once Flake had Myron under control. Bone also had placed a number of calls before he'd called Bruce; he was establishing a timeline alibi in case anything came up with Myron. Bone expected complete loyalty from Flake, but there was no such thing as loyalty on Bone's part to anybody. He'd sell Flake out in a New York second if he needed to.

Bone opted to take a path that cut through woods to his condominium complex. He would be able to approach the condo from the rear and make sure the coast was clear before he returned to the unit. Bone strolled casually through the community. Although the walk appeared to be a leisurely one, it was not. It was meant to call attention to the black man walking along in the melting snow. Bone stopped on the street behind his garden-style end unit. The sight of the oversized rolling leather suitcase that Flake was pulling toward Myron's van stopped him in his tracks. The bag, three-by-two-by two, was more than enough room to host Myron's slender frame.

As Flake stood at the back of the van, he went about his business as if he weren't the least bit concerned with the life he'd just stolen. Inside, his heart still cried out for what he'd become. He opened the rear doors before hoisting the suitcase into the van. He handled it with relative ease. If anybody was watching Flake, they'd never have known he'd killed a hundred and fifty-five-pound man inside. Bone, on the other hand, kept his eyes on the van. The weight of what was in the luggage bag caused the van to shift slightly under the weight. It adjusted enough for Bone to know that the bag wasn't full of clothes.

The two men met as they walked toward the condo from different directions. Mentally, they were coming from two distinctive directions as well. Bone was aroused by the thought of his plan; the noose was squeezing tighter around Travis Moore. Flake, on the other hand, was void of any emotion. He was dying inside; it was a slow death that was gradually taking small pieces daily. It seemed lately that every time he set eyes on Bone, he was reminded of that.

"So, everything is taken care of?"

Flake looked over his shoulder to the van. He did not speak and walked inside with Bone.

"Good. I got a guy who is gonna take care of that van for me. It'll be a couple of hours before we head over there. He'll get rid of it." Bone took notice of Flake's inattentiveness. "Get right, nigga! It's almost showtime. You can't trip that. That brother served a purpose, but his mouth got too much use. We was just puttin' a muzzle on him. We coverin' ass; that's all."

"Yeah, you're right. We had to get rid of him." Flake concurred with Bone, but he didn't know where the "we" was when he'd strangled the life out of Myron. Or where "we" were when he was stuffing Myron's body into the oversized suitcase. "We" also didn't sweat or cry together. And what were "we" going to do when Flake was no longer of any use to Bone?

CHAPTER 29

Home sweet home. The return drive from Raleigh was much less hazardous than the one she'd made the previous day. Yesterday, she was thinking about getting Michael to her parents' house safely. Her mind was also swirling with thoughts about Travis. Although she was concerned with the roads, she was more concerned with getting away from everything for a little while.

Getting away for the night had done her more good than she could have ever imagined. She had spent some time with her mother and father. She'd also had the opportunity to get her thoughts out and bounce them off her parents. The apprehension on her mother's part was softening and her father was her saving grace. He was not only able to look at where Travis came from, but also what he'd pulled himself out of and where he was going.

Now that Kenya was anxious to get home, her nervousness about driving in inclement weather returned with a vengeance. Thankfully, the roads were clearing and the snow and slush that came so quickly was leaving in the same fashion. Still, it didn't keep the thoughts of the accident she'd had a few years ago from creeping back into her mind.

A sigh of relief snuck up on her as her house came into view. She was home. Kenya loosened the vise grip that she had on the steering wheel. As the garage door opened, she was elated at the sight of Travis' black Volvo. Once she pulled in, she fought the temptation to kiss the ground. The only reason why she resisted the urge was because she expected Travis to come running to the door to greet her. She didn't want to have to explain that. She waited for Travis, but he didn't rush the door.

Kenya thought it was a little odd when she stuck the key in the door and found it to be unlocked. That was not like Travis. Actually, he'd mentioned on a number of occasions the need to have a security alarm system installed. It was an idea that Kenya wasn't sold on. When Michael was older and able to get in and out of doors on his own, then they might need a system with door chimes that would let them know if Michael went out. She also didn't want to be like her father; a security alarm system and then security cameras. They didn't spend four hundred thousand on a house to feel like a prisoner in it.

She closed and locked the door behind her. She leaned against the door and listened for Travis. She didn't hear him stirring in the house.

"Travis?" She wondered what he was up to. "Travis?!" He still didn't answer. As she walked further into the house, Kenya began to notice how dim it was. All of the blinds and curtains had been drawn to prevent the sunlight from entering. Whenever Travis was home during the day, he'd try to get as much natural light as possible around him. Then, the aroma hit her and she smiled. It was a smell that once you know it, you never forget it. It was homemade spaghetti.

Travis could cook only one dish. It was his spaghetti. It damn sure wasn't Ragu or anything from a jar. His was made with fresh onions, bell pepper, tomato sauce and a pinch of garlic. If Travis had time, he'd make his own sauce from fresh tomatoes. That scent, mixed with that of garlic bread, wafted through the house and drew her toward the kitchen. You wouldn't want to touch much else that Travis cooked, but his spaghetti was to die for.

As she cracked the lid on the sauce, the pungent aroma and steam raced to her nostrils. The beef had already been added and it was simmering, begging to be tasted. Kenya wasn't going to resist this temptation. She grabbed a spoon and sampled it; and it was every bit as good as it smelled. Travis was going for broke; he knew Kenya loved his spaghetti. That old adage about the best way to a man's heart was through his stomach, worked for women as well.

She scooped up another helping before making her way slowly through the dimness to the staircase. Kenya moved as quietly as possible up the stairs. She had the added assistance of a relatively new house with steps that didn't give way to creaking. There was no noise to forewarn Travis of her presence. Halfway up the stairs, she met a new scent. The smell of coconut and pineapple whisked her away to the tropics. It was the fragrance of a new candle she had yet to burn. It brought back memories of the honeymoon cruise they had taken to the Bahamas. She had to give it to the brother; if he was trying to get back to square one with her, he was on his way.

Before she reached the top of the stairs, she could see the door to their bedroom was closed. Kenya was eager to find out what was waiting for her behind the door. Music could be heard drifting out of the room. Gerald Levert's *Love & Consequences* CD was playing. Quietly, she opened the door. Although it was dim, she could not miss the gift boxes that made a path toward the bathroom door. Her instincts were to go straight to the bathroom, but the boxes begged for her attention. There were four boxes that became smaller in size as they led to an envelope in front of the bathroom door. Kenya took a better look at each box and discovered orchids surrounded them. They were Bee Orchids; the same type he'd handpicked for her when they docked in

Freeport on their honeymoon. She was taken in by the fact that he had remembered.

Kenya wanted to know what was in the packages but was determined to find her husband first. He had to be in the bathroom. In an effort to be coy, Kenya knocked on the door and waited for an answer. Travis didn't respond.

"T-r-a-v?" Kenya called his nickname as she opened the door.

Sitting on the Roman tub with his body against the wall was Travis. His head was slumped forward into his chest. He was wearing a black silk robe with matching boxers. He did not move.

"Travis!"

Slowly, he lifted his head and smiled at her. "Welcome home." Travis scooted himself toward the edge of the tub to stand up. Kenya walked closer to meet him. "I am so glad that you are here." Travis spoke every word slowly.

"I could tell, you cooked. And, what are all the boxes about?"

"It's our anniversary. One thing led to another. Next thing you know, I came home with a few extra gifts."

"I only have one gift for you."

"You don't need that. You being here with me is the only gift I'll ever need."

Kenya's ears hung on to every word. Her lips quivered at the thought of being everything that he would ever need. She embraced him and held him tight.

"K, why don't you take some time to relax." Travis motioned to the tub. He'd run her a cucumber melon bath. There were also rose petals floating in the water. "You get in, I'll check on the food and I'll be back to bathe you." Travis started to let her go, but Kenya held him there.

"That's fine, but undress me first." There was no more getting back to square one. Travis was there. The thought of Travis Moore's pre-college life was the furthest thing from Kenya's mind.

Travis backed away again, but this time to give himself room to honor her request. He pulled away the jacket and let it fall to the floor. Slowly and seductively, he squatted in front of her to take off her shoes and socks. When he stood, he walked behind Kenya. Gently, he removed each layer of clothing until she stood in front of him wearing her underwear. As fate would have it, she was wearing a black bra and matching thong. Travis was mesmerized by the view of his wife as she stood there. He thanked God for being so fortunate. Reaching out his hands, he massaged his way from Kenya's shoulders to the middle of her back and unhooked her bra. Kenya helped him by sliding it off. Travis wrapped his arms around her waist and inched closer to her so she could feel what was on his mind. Kenya rocked her hips backward into him. It was all-good; she was thinking the same thing, too.

Feeling the need to slow things down, Travis took a step back to finish the job that Kenya had given him. He placed his thumbs inside her thong at the hips. He began sliding it down ever so slowly. As he bent down this time, he let his tongue trace her spine. Travis released the thong at her calves, placed his hands on her hips and licked his way back up. Kenya shuddered with anticipation. Travis swept her into his arms, walked her to the warm bath and eased her into the water.

"I want you to sit here and relax. Give your mom a call to let her know that you got home safely. I'm going to check on the food and be back to wash every inch of you."

"I'll be right here waiting for you," she said, maintaining her composure. There was no place that she would rather be.

Travis eased out the bathroom, trying to hide his excitement. Once out the bedroom, the cool bit went out the window. He dashed downstairs as fast as he could. He didn't want to leave his wife for too long. *Damn, she looked great in that thong*, he thought. The gym was paying huge dividends. He wondered where his eyes had been for the last couple of weeks—hell, the last couple of months.

Kenya was thrilled. She felt like she used to when they'd first started dating. She had to give Travis his props. The food was cooking, a bubble bath was waiting, the gifts—and she hadn't even seen those yet. The boy was definitely on point. She picked up the cordless to call her mother, leaned back in the tub and relaxed. She, too, reflected on her good fortune.

Travis took the garlic bread out the oven, turned off the noodles and the spaghetti sauce. He rushed back upstairs, taking them two and three at a time. At the top of the stairs, he stopped to catch his breath and get his cool flow back. Travis laughed at himself. He was sweating her like this was brand new, but he liked it. It was like starting all over again.

When he gathered his composure, he went back in to deal with his woman. He slowly opened the door to the bathroom. Kenya's eyes were closed. She was relaxed, reclined and beautiful. He watched as the water and bubbles danced over her body.

"I know you're not asleep."

"And miss out on this bathing I've got coming? I don't think so," she said, opening only her left eye.

Travis sat on the edge of the tub again. "Let me have one."

Kenya knew exactly what to do. She lifted her right foot out of the water and Travis began to massage it.

"Why don't you join me? There's more than enough room for you to wash me in here." Seeing that he needed a little more coaxing, she hit him with his favorite line: "You do me and I'll do you."

"Baby, come on. You can't steal my joint." Travis laughed, but there was no more hesitation on his part. He took off the robe and carefully pulled down his boxers for his own protection.

"Somebody is happy I'm home." Kenya smiled at him and she licked her lips slowly.

Travis stood proudly in front of her so she could get a good look at him. He hadn't worked out as much as he'd like to, but he was still in good shape. Deciding he'd given her more than an eyeful, he joined her in the tub. Travis started massaging her feet again, then worked his way up her legs.

True to his promise, Travis took pleasure in bathing every inch of Kenya's body. True to her word, she returned the favor. Both of them were driving each other crazy. By the time they started drying each other off, they were reduced to a fondling contest, testing each other, trying to see who would break down first and give in to their desires. This only heightened their sexual tension.

"Care to join me in the bedroom?" Travis knew he wouldn't be denied.

"Carry me."

Travis started to sweep her into his arms again. Before he could, Kenya wrapped her arms around his neck. She pulled up against his torso, and then she wrapped her thighs around his waist. Having no choice of what to do with his hands, he placed them on her cheeks and palmed her sweet onion. The heat inside of her raced out toward him. That broke Travis down; he could not resist penetrating her womanhood. Kenya welcomed all of him. His knees almost buckled, the pleasure landed a staggering blow. Travis, always up for the challenge, rebounded quickly and began walking into the bedroom. The motion sent waves through her body. They looked into each other's eyes. Her eyes fluttered as his opened wide. Kenya began to roll her hips. Travis squeezed his hands tighter, which caused her to roll those sweet hips even faster. Travis was frozen in ecstasy as Kenya continued to do what she intended to do, work him over. She released her pleasure as he stood still enjoying his. Kenya couldn't contain her scream as she reached her first climax and exploded. Travis wrapped his arms around her waist as Kenya arched her back and rode the waves of ecstasy in on him.

Travis avoided the gift boxes and carried her to the bed and they continued making love to one another. Each of them understood that the wall between them was coming down. Travis was finally able to open up about his past and Kenya had accepted him—not in spite of it, but because of it. Like her father had said, everything he'd gone through had made him the man he was today.

After they'd made love, Kenya held Travis in her arms as if he was her child. She was happy they'd found their way back to each other. In fact, she felt they had reached a deeper level of commitment.

Travis enjoyed being in his wife's arms. He was happy that she hadn't turned away from him, but there was so much more to tell her about his past. The door was opened and she would be willing to accept it.

"What are you thinking?"

"About how perfect this was. You are so full of surprises. Why? What are you thinking?"

Maybe this wasn't the best time to go back into the past. "About how much we needed each other. It's been too long since we've enjoyed ourselves like that."

"That's because we're usually trying not to wake Michael up."

"True. But, in all honesty, it's more because of me and how I've been."

"We're through that now. We move forward from here and leave whatever we have to behind us." Kenya glanced over toward the envelope and the boxes. "What's in there?"

"A little something for you. After we eat, I figured we could come back up here and you can take a look."

As much as Kenya wanted to tear into those boxes to see what Travis had for her, she agreed to wait. Kenya went into the bathroom to freshen up and came out wearing one of her heavier robes. Travis wanted no parts of a robe. He was keeping with the spirit of their honeymoon; he wasn't going to wear a thing. They had honeymooned for two weeks. The first week was spent in the Caribbean and the second at their townhouse. They never told anyone when they had returned and had spent a solid week with each other in the nude. They'd had the time of their lives. Travis was going to do whatever was necessary to recapture that free-spirited love.

CHAPTER 30

It took Jar a while before he figured out where he was going, but he eventually found his way home. As he did, he began to sense people paying attention to him. Never before had Jar seen so many heads turn their attention in his direction. It seemed that everybody in Park Hills had their eyes on the shiny black 280ZX that he was parking. The car got mad respect in the hood. People knew it belonged to Bone. The tint of the windows kept Jar hidden from the people he passed.

Bone wasn't around to tell him to keep the music down. So he let the Bose system knock while he bounced his head to the beat. The vibration of the music made the windows shake as the sound boomed the interior of the car. Jar was in his element and feeling it. He was rolling through his hood like he was the "Big Willie." There was one hand on the steering wheel and one on the gear-shift. He was pushing the 280 like it was his own.

He rode past his house a number of times. Jar was waiting for enough of a crowd to gather so he could make an entrance. He wanted to make sure that the word got out that Baby Jar was a baller, running right up under Bone.

It was the fifth trip past the house when he saw Evan. He was walking with three girls and Jar was eager to know how he had pulled that off. After taking a closer look, he determined that two of them weren't worth the time of day. They were probably gaming Evan. A couple of weeks ago, Jar would have been sweating them. After running with Bone, Jar now considered them hoodrats.

Qwanda Jackson was the third girl in Evan's party. What was Qwanda doing with a punk like Evan? This was a girl that had it going on. She was a seventeen-year-old senior and everything about her was tight. She had the face, the body and the brain. Jar had had a crush on her since he was nine and she was ten.

Mrs. Jackson threw parties every Saturday night for the kids during the summers. On one particular Saturday night, they were celebrating Qwanda's eleventh birthday. Jar and Evan were lucky enough to get invited. Jar was the biggest beneficiary that night; he was able to get a slow dance with Qwanda. She'd just had a falling-out with the thirteen-year-old boy she had a crush on. To make the boy jealous, Qwanda agreed to dance with Jar on a fast song. When the fast song ended, a slow one followed. Jar was nervous and started to go back to the sidelines, but Qwanda put her arms abound his neck and pulled him to her. He got such a rise in his pants that he didn't think it would ever go down. The nine-year-old was on cloud nine. He didn't care about Evan teasing him about having blue balls.

Jar slowed down enough for the group to give him their undivided attention. He parked the car diagonally so that it took up two spaces. He cut the wheel so that the tires were in an angle opposite from the car. The sun was setting and it hit the car just right. The chrome rims caused a glare to be cast in the direction of Evan and his little entourage.

Once he had secured their attention, Jar slowly opened the door to get out the car. He watched the two hoodrats start to whisper to each other. As he stepped out, he took great delight in watching Evan's mouth drop. What he was really hoping for was some kind of reaction from Qwanda. Jar wasn't sure, but he thought her eyes widened slightly. She was a cool one.

"Ain't that Baby Jar?" asked the first hoodrat.

"I know that nigga don't think he somebody," said the other one.

"What's up, Jar?" Evan spoke over the two girls.

"Just rollin'. You know you need to holler at me, right?" Jar smiled with confidence.

"That's the car Bone drive, ain't it?" the first girl asked as she looked at the car. "That lil' nigga in trouble. I heard about Bone. You don't fool with his shit."

Evan had heard about Bone, too. That couldn't possibly be the person that Jar was talking about yesterday. Bone wasn't some okie-doke that was running dope; he was the man that nobody could touch. Everybody on the street knew about Bone, but the police couldn't get anywhere near him. Bone was the Teflon Don of the ghetto. Evan excused himself from the group and went closer to Jar.

"So, that's who you're rolling with?" There was fear in Evan's voice and Jar could sense it. Jar rolling with Bone stepped up Jar's game tenfold in Evan's eyes.

"I told you I was down with a real player, kid."

"You told me it was a playa, not *The Playa*."

"Would it have made a difference in whether you got down with me?"

Evan looked at the car that Jar was driving. For a second, he was giving serious consideration to the offer. Was this something he was willing to become?

"Don't answer that. It's all good." Jar peeked over Evan's shoulder at the crowd he had with him. "How'd you end up with that crew?"

"Those girls are from the Slope. They're Qwanda's cousins."

"Come on, man. Ain't no way them chickenheads can be related to Qwanda."

"For real."

"No shit." Jar took another look at Qwanda. "Qwanda looking good, ain't she?"

"Yeah, that's always."

"So, you up on her or what?"

"You kidding?" Evan knew he wasn't in her league. "She missed calculus homework the other day. I was getting her the info on it."

"Calculus. College prep, huh? That's good." If this was another life or another time that might have been an option for Jar. Before too much self-pity set in, he took another look at Qwanda. "Can you calculate how long it's going to take me to hit that?"

"That's not even in your league."

"That's you. Brother, if you could have seen what I was working with last night and this morning, you'd know that nothing was out of my league anymore; believe that." Jar looked back over Evan's shoulder to watch Qwanda. Her eyes bounced between the car and Jar. He smiled at her as he caught her glance. Qwanda returned the smile. "Yes, sir, everybody loves the up man." He kept smiling at Qwanda but spoke so only Evan could hear him.

"What?" Evan was lost.

"She's feeling me. Diggin' on the ride. I'm all up in her head right now. Why don't you take the cousins to get something to eat?" Jar reached into his pocket for some money. He pulled out two twenties and handed them to Evan. "You play your cards right, you might get lucky."

Evan pocketed the forty dollars and went to talk to the girls. After some spirited conversation on the part of Qwanda's cousins, Evan was able to convince them to get something to eat with him.

Qwanda stayed her distance from Jar, even after her cousins had left with Evan. Jar waited for her to come to him. He wasn't going to step to her; he didn't have to. He was the one riding and she was the one walking. When he noticed the look of frustration on Qwanda's face, he figured that he'd better make a move. He didn't want to blow his chance; this was a girl that he'd had a crush on for seven years.

"So, how ya been?" he asked only loud enough to draw her to him.

"What?" Qwanda walked closer to hear him. She was about to turn and leave if he didn't say something. She didn't have time to fool around with this little sixteen-year-old. That's what she told herself, but she was the one who was walking closer to him. She knew she was feeding his ego, but there was something else on Qwanda's mind.

"I asked how you been, with your fine self?"

Blushing, she said, "Fine, and yourse?lf?" She continued to get closer to the car.

"Trying to make it." He smiled back. He could see Qwanda still eying the car. "You want to go for a ride?"

"Sure."

This was too easy, Jar thought. Qwanda was the kind of girl that wouldn't give him the time of day a month ago. A flashy ride and the girl could be had. To his knowledge, Qwanda wasn't into the dope game, couldn't be if she was preparing for college. Jar was seeing things differently with Bone's tutelage; any broad could be turned out. Qwanda wasn't any exception.

Jar got into his side of the 280 and waited for Qwanda to hop in. Qwanda expected Jar to open the door for her. Again, she debated ditching Jar but, against her better judgment, she got in. It wasn't like he was a date or anything close to it. He was a kid from around the way that she'd known since she was ten years old.

"Took you long enough," Jar said as if his patience were wearing thin.

Oh, no he didn't! Qwanda thought. No matter how much she liked the car, she wasn't going to take that off Baby Jar. Qwanda opened the door quickly.

"Where are you going?"

"I'm getting out of here. I'm not that desperate to ride in a car." True to her word, Qwanda stepped out.

Jar hurried out also. "Come on, Qwanda. I was joking."

"I'm not to be played with." Qwanda looked at Baby Jar. He wasn't the same as she once knew. He was such a good kid when he was younger. There was a lot of potential in him. She knew about his mom, his rehab and from the looks of it, what he was back into.

Evan had filled her in on Jar. Evan was concerned about his friend and he didn't want him in trouble. Problem was, Evan didn't have any influence over Jar at this point. Evan was well aware of the crush that Jar had on Qwanda; he hoped that she might be able to bring him around.

"What are you doing?' Qwanda was no longer playing the role of somebody that was taken with his material trappings. "What do you think you're trying to prove?"

"I am what I am. I ain't trying to prove a damn thing. Come on and get in this car with me."

"The only reason why I was willing to get in that car was to try to talk some sense into you. For some reason, Evan thought you might listen to me."

Evan had put Qwanda up to talking some "sense" into him. Evan was his boy and Qwanda was here because she wanted to get down with a playa, didn't she? Hell no, they weren't trying to play him? "Who the hell are you? What makes you think I'ma listen to you?"

"You probably won't and that's too bad. I don't know why I considered trying to talk to you."

"'Cause you know I'm the man and you want to get with me."

"That junior mack bullshit might work on them crack hoes, but you don't have a thing to offer me. It's a shame, too. You don't have to do this. You were always as smart as Evan, maybe smarter. You could offer the world a lot more than drugs. The only thing you're working on is becoming a statistic."

Qwanda launched those words at him like they were bombs. They struck with pinpoint accuracy. Jar stood there as the words fell on his ears. The lingering fog from that barrage seemed to leave him confused. Qwanda had done what Evan and rehab couldn't. She'd reached him.

Jar nodded his head. He looked down at the ground, then back up to Qwanda. He gave her a half-smile as he prepared to respond to the bombs she had laid on him.

"So, I take it you ain't gonna give me the pus yet?" Jar almost laughed when he posed the question to Qwanda. The look on her face was worth the asking.

"Stupid son of a bitch!" Qwanda couldn't believe him. "You don't get it. You think this is all a game. Six months, a year maybe, this path you're walking is going to have you dead by then." She washed her hands of him and walked away.

"I ain't the one who's gonna have a problem in a year. I'm playin' the game at a level street niggas can't begin to understand. Don't bring your ass around here looking for me then!" Jar let her have it as she left him. The words rang in his head: "You don't put nothing in front of this game."

She didn't understand what he was becoming. He didn't have to sweat some high school girl, even if it was Qwanda Jackson. He couldn't believe that she had the nerve to try to game him. Jar had convinced himself that he was laying it down with grown women. She was lucky that he had offered her a piece of him. One thing did bother him, though. Evan had put his business in Qwanda's ear. Jar couldn't figure out what Evan thought he would achieve by that. The people around him were slow to recognize that he was carrying mad weight on the street, but they would eventually.

With nothing else to do, nobody to impress and having been beat out of forty dollars, Jar decided to go into his house and shut it down for a while. It was Friday, the streets would be hopping tonight and the rest would do him good.

There was something different about the apartment. Jar noticed the coldness of the place as soon as he walked in. Jar shook his head in disappointment; he'd been here a number of times before. This was the first time since he'd returned home, though. As he reached for the light switch, he hoped his intuition was betraying him. He flipped the switch, nothing. "Shit!" The contempt for his mother was multiplying with each day that passed.

"I know you ain't cussing in my house!" Ladonna's muffled voice came from the living room.

Jar walked inside the door and slammed it shut behind him. This woman had let the power get clipped again. He went into the living room but didn't see her.

"Don't you slam my fucking door." Ladonna's voice was coming from a pile of blankets on the couch. She waited for Jar to say something, but he kept quiet.

Instead, Jar stared at the pile of dirty, wrinkled blankets. Under it lay the woman who was supposed to take care of him. They were in an apartment with no lights and no heat. The odor that he picked up as he neared the couch assured him that she hadn't washed her ass since running the streets the previous night. She had huddled up on the couch and said the hell with it.

"You don't have nothing to say about slamming that door?" Ladonna kept herself covered under the blankets.

"Why are you hiding under those blankets?" Jar stepped closer to her. His stomach began to turn from the stench.

"Ain't nobody hiding in no blankets."

Jar was as close as he was going to get to her. He reached out and pulled the blankets away. A stunned, bruised and battered Ladonna Love sat up on the couch. Her left eye was purple and swollen shut, obviously the result of a right cross. Her lower lip was puffy and cut. There was also a laceration on her right cheek. She must have met with somebody that was good with both hands.

"What are you looking at?" Ladonna snatched the covers back. She attempted to cover as much of her face as possible.

"No lights?" Jar didn't want or need to know the story behind her face.

"What?"

"Last week, I gave you money to pay the light bill. Now there ain't no lights. What happened to the money?"

"I paid that bill. They made a mistake."

"What happened to the money?" Jar watched as she tried to shrink further under the blankets. "You spent that money, didn't you? You smoked it up, didn't you? Mom!"

Shame or embarrassment wouldn't allow her to answer. Her silence answered the question from her son. Jar shook his head.

"Don't shake your head at me. Them fuckers ain't supposed to clip you if the weather's bad."

"Guess it wasn't too bad. So, you just shit on my money like that?"

"That wasn't your money; it was my money." Ladonna's crack theories and crack logic were in control of her. "It was your fault anyway. I wouldn't have done that if you took care of me."

"If I took care…You the damn parent!" The nerve of her; Jar was already giving her bill money.

"I told you about cussing in my house! You better respect it. I know what you doing out there."

"How you gonna force me to respect this place when you don't. We don't have no heat or lights." Jar paused. The last part of what she'd said registered with him. "What do you mean, you know what I'm doing?"

"Niggas already know you up in Bone's ass. You run around all that shit and you ain't taking care of me. You could pinch me off a little bit, keep me straight in here. Selfish motherfucker. I'm out here selling my ass and getting my head knocked. I done took care of you; you need to be takin' care of me."

Jar couldn't believe what he was hearing. This woman, his mother, was calling him selfish for not supplying her crack addiction. She was taking care of him? He looked around the dirty apartment with no heat, no food and no future for him. She was taking care of him all right.

"So, do you think you can hook your mamma up?" Gone were Ladonna's harsh words. She was trying to appeal to something sensitive in her son. "Mommy needs your help."

Jar was taken by her plea. His mother needed him. What was he supposed to do? It was only his mother and him. Maybe that would be the way for him to keep her at home. As much as he tried to fool himself, he knew that wasn't the answer. She would continue to take from him until he had nothing left to give. Then, she would be out on those streets again; rehab had taught him that. She was an addict. Then, he remembered what Bone had taught him, nobody came between him and his shit, not even his own mother.

"Can't do it. I can't help you like that," Jar said.

"Jar, I'm your mamma! You got to help me. I'll do anything. I'll suck your…"

"Shut up!!" Jar stopped her before she totally degraded herself.

Crack addiction had left Ladonna Love willing to do anything to get her next fix. Being told to shut up like she was a child, by her child, stopped her in her tracks. She was helpless, hopeless and confused. But she wasn't ready to stop hurting.

"You ain't shit anyway," Ladonna lashed out. "If you can't help a nigga, then you can get the fuck out of my house!"

Jar was overcome with rage. He grabbed his mother by the throat. He wanted to choke the life out of her, to shut her up, but he wouldn't. Jar managed to pull himself away from her. Anger continued to boil in him as he stepped backward slowly. If she said anything, it would have been wrong, and he would be back on her again. Ladonna sensed that he was looking for any reason to come after her again. Fear and shame stifled any comment that she wanted to make. Jar backed up until he'd lost eye contact with his mother. He turned and reached for the door.

"Don't come back to my house," Ladonna said, feeling that she was redeeming herself.

"I don't intend to." He snatched the door open and slammed it shut behind him.

Those last words uttered by his mother, as cowardly as they were, stuck in the pit of Jar's stomach. A mule couldn't have kicked him any harder. One day ago, he would have done anything to get her to stay with him. Today, he could not care less if he ever saw her again. The anger and rage gave way to tears. The sixteen-year-old man-child had no mother to wipe his eyes and tell him that everything would be okay. The hell with Ladonna Love, Qwanda and Evan; he wiped his own eyes. There was a better place for him than this. It was with Kwame Brown. Jar was now under Kwame's wing. *Leave them where they're at*, he thought. He looked at Bone's car; he was the one privileged to drive it. He tapped the money in his pocket; Bone had put it there. Although he was filled with rage at the moment, he knew that brighter days were ahead of him as long as he stayed close to Bone.

CHAPTER 31

Lisa sat at the bar of the crowded Outback Steakhouse. She was sipping on her second glass of Cabernet. In spite of the bad weather they'd had, the restaurant was popping with people, mostly couples. Young couples on first dates; married couples that had gotten away from the teenagers for the night, all looking to have a great time. Lisa was all too aware of the couples. Here she was, on a Friday evening, drinking wine by herself and waiting for Jasmine to join her. She'd hoped to hear from Keith, but he never called. She had begged Jasmine to have dinner with her and she had agreed. As she looked at her watch, she saw that Jasmine was now fifty minutes late. What a night; even Jasmine had stood her up.

The vibration from the beeper that the restaurant issued her momentarily snapped her out of her self-pity party. She would have a good dinner and enjoy her own company.

"Walker, party of two. Walker, party of two. Please," the announcement came over the PA system.

Lisa was sent back to her thoughts of self-pity; not much of a party for two. She shook her head and stood. She left the bar for the hostess; she would shake the stares off as well. As Lisa faced the front door, she caught sight of Jasmine busting her way through the crowd.

"Excuse me. Pardon me," Jasmine said as she bumped into one patron. She hit him so hard that she caused his toupee to jump. "Oooh, I am so sorry." Jasmine couldn't help but stare at it.

Lisa almost cracked up at the sight of those two. She was relieved to see Jasmine show up. Thank goodness she wouldn't be eating alone. "Jasmine, over here." Lisa was waving her hand to pull Jasmine's attention away from the gentleman's hairpiece.

"Hey, girl. Is the table ready?" Jasmine asked as she walked toward Lisa.

"They just called my name. Another ten minutes and it would have been a table for one."

"You know you don't want to eat by yourself. You sounded pitiful on the phone when you called."

Lisa sucked her teeth. That wasn't the pick-me-up she was looking for. "What are you talking about?" She didn't wait for an answer. Instead, she addressed the hostess. "Walker, table for two."

"Right this way." The hostess picked up two menus and led the way to their table.

The hostess sat them at their table and gave them menus. As soon as she disappeared, the waitress showed up and gave them a quick rundown of the specials for the day. After getting their drink orders, she excused herself to give them some time to look over the menus.

Jasmine buried her head in the menu even though she already knew what she was going to order. She pored over every item on the menu as if it were her first time at Outback. She could feel Lisa's eyes on her. She raised her eyes from the menu to meet Lisa's. Jasmine didn't say a word; it was a matter of time before Lisa started to talk.

"So?" Lisa broke the silence right on cue.

"So what?" Jasmine looked at her with a blank expression.

"You gonna leave me hanging here and not offer an explanation."

"I was right on time. Hell, you knew I was coming. Tell the truth, how many times did you call my house tonight?"

"You need to get a cell phone," Lisa mumbled as she looked down at the menu.

"So I could hear you all the way over here? I don't think so."

"I guess your man wouldn't let you out the house, huh?"

"You say that like it's a bad thing. Yes, my husband did want to spend some time with me."

"I don't have time for all that."

"Yeah, right. Why are you so down? Where's Mister Keith?"

"I haven't heard from him, haven't even thought about him."

Jasmine sat back in the chair. "Now you know, you ain't convincing anybody of that. Hadn't thought about him. I'm here to take your mind off him."

"I think I'm gonna have me a big ol' juicy steak." Lisa wanted to change the subject.

"What happened yesterday when ya'll left the gym?"

"What are you gonna have?" Lisa was staring at the menu.

Jasmine didn't respond. Instead, she waited on an answer to her question. Again, she knew Lisa would cave into the pressure. This time she waited until Lisa lifted her eyes.

"We went to the mall."

"And?"

"And, what?" Lisa waited for Jasmine to speak, but she didn't. "Okay, so he bought me some stuff."

"Oh, really. Where was Kenya?"

"She was there for a little while, then she left."

"She left? She rode with you, didn't she?"

"Yeah, but she got tired and caught a cab."

"Uh-huh. What else did you do with the two men you were left with?"

"Don't go there. Keith and I just talked. Fred hung around with us. He said he'd call and we would get together, but I haven't heard from him."

"Hmm." Jasmine thought for a second. "How much did he spend on you?"

"It was a little under a thousand."

"And you let him. He was trying to see how much you'd let him spend. Did you give up the booty?" Jasmine chastised Lisa with her tone.

"No!" Lisa answered emphatically. Truth was, if Fred wasn't with Keith, she very well may have given up the booty. She felt like the thousand would have justified it.

"Well, good for you." Jasmine studied Lisa. "So, you talk to Kenya today?" Jasmine had a sneaky suspicion that Kenya didn't go home and leave Lisa there for no reason. At some point, Lisa probably put her foot in her mouth.

"No." Lisa's eyes began to wander around the room.

"Uh-huh." Jasmine's tone said it all. She was sure something had happened between Lisa and Kenya. Lisa was so simple to read. "So what happened? I know Kenya didn't leave you hanging."

"Then, you don't know Kenya. She left me hanging. You know she's uppity, thinking she's better than other people."

Jasmine let the words go in one ear and out the other. She flagged down the waitress. "Can we get some bread over here?" The waitress was off in search of bread.

"You're not even listening to me."

"Soon as you start talking, I'll start listening."

Lisa paused for a second to ponder Jasmine's statement. "Kenya and I kinda fell out yesterday."

"That would explain why you haven't talked to her today. What did you say?"

"What makes you think it was me? It could have been her." Lisa tried to convince Jasmine she wasn't at fault. Jasmine wasn't going for it. "I might have said the wrong thing." Lisa waited for Jasmine to jump all over her, but she didn't. "I told her to consider hooking up with Fred. I figured that since she was having trouble with her man, she might as well have some fun. I was just joking, but it ticked her off. Next thing I knew, she was ready to go. I wasn't, so I stayed."

"That suggestion was your idea of a joke?"

"Yeah. Shoot, if that was me and my man was tripping, that's what I would do."

"And how's that approach working out for you?" Jasmine asked the question, but they both knew the answer. Jasmine was keeping her company for the next couple of hours. "What makes you think there's trouble with her man?"

"I was talking to her the other night. She went on about Travis not being there and she'd cooked. He showed up when she started to get to the good stuff. I told her he was probably up to something."

"Based on what? He was probably working. Why do you have to be so negative?"

"I'm not negative. I'm keeping it real. Men are usually up to something. You asked me about Keith, about how much money he spent on me. I let him spend as much money as he wanted. You and I both know he wanted something. Hell, I wanted something, too. He was supposed to call me today but he didn't. He probably ran up on a better deal. The same rules apply to Travis. Men ain't shit." Lisa had been waiting to rag on men.

The waitress returned with the bread and two glasses of wine. "Compliments of a gentleman at the bar. He said he noticed you while you were over there."

"Men ain't shit," Jasmine repeated to Lisa as they accepted the wine.

"Are you two ready to order?"

Jasmine ordered first. As was her Friday night ritual, she ordered fish—fresh halibut with mixed vegetables. There wasn't a Friday night in the last decade that she could remember when she hadn't eaten fish. Lisa ordered the biggest steak that she could find on the menu. Once their orders were placed, Jasmine asked the waitress to thank the gentleman for the wine and to let him know they wanted to enjoy each other's company.

That didn't sit particularly well with Lisa. She was the only one sitting alone at the bar. Obviously, there was somebody in the restaurant that was checking her out. Her mind was already playing out different scenarios. He didn't approach her because he could see her waiting for someone; and when Jasmine arrived, he realized it was safe to make his move. Oh, yes, she had to find out who this suitor was.

"I got to go to the bathroom."

"Bullshit! You sit your little hot tail right there."

"Oh, come on. You're not curious?"

"Why would I be? I wasn't at the bar. You had me come all the way out here to meet you because you were going to be alone. I'll be damned if you're going to leave me sitting here. You move and I'm gone."

Lisa did want to go to the bar, but she wasn't willing to risk finishing dinner alone. Besides, it would be fun to have someone waiting for a change. "You win."

"Anyway, if it was important enough to send you some wine, whoever it is, they will stop by the table to speak."

Lisa listened to what she was told. Jasmine made an excellent point. Somebody would own up to the glasses of wine. Lisa sat back and smiled; even down in the dumps she was still able to pull. While the two of them enjoyed their meal together, Lisa's head would snap up to pay attention to any man that walked by. She wanted to be sure not to let the wine man get by her, but she began to get irritated as the meal progressed. She wasn't able to pick out anybody who could have sent the wine. The only person she'd made eye contact with was an attractive brother who was sitting opposite a beautiful fair-skinned sister.

Jasmine didn't touch her glass of wine. She'd long since sworn off alcohol. It was something that wasn't widely known, especially to Lisa. Jasmine was well equipped to mete out advice; she had a few years on Lisa and Kenya. She'd done some living in her younger days. Alcohol had gotten her into more than one predicament. Her marriage wasn't always the perfect, even keeled one it was perceived to be. Jasmine had been married for nineteen years. She and her husband had four children. The oldest was a seventeen-year-old honor student and not her husband's biological son. Alcohol, hurt and revenge had led to that result. Ultimately, Jasmine and her husband had survived that rocky start to get to the place they were at today.

"What are you going to do with that wine?" Lisa giggled as she asked. Her buzz was kicking in.

"I'm not going to touch it. You're more than welcome to it."

Lisa was feeling pretty good. The wine was working for her. The three glasses had helped to pick her up; the fourth would put her over the top. She shotgunned the glass of wine.

"Damn, girl, slow down."

"I'm gonna enjoy myself tonight. I have been sittin' here tryin' to figure out who sent these drinks over and ain't nobody owned up to it."

"Why are you so worried about it? Somebody did something nice; just enjoy it. You don't need to be in such a rush to make something happen. Sometimes, you need to let things unfold." Jasmine was hinting to Lisa discreetly that Lisa was making herself look desperate.

"That's easy for somebody with the perfect home life to kick out, but that's not my reality."

"That's not anybody's reality. Don't nobody have it perfect. I sure as hell don't. Shoot, there were some days when you would have never been able to tell me that I'd be where I am today. That's reality, that's marriage. Shoot, girl, that's life. Ain't nothing about marriage perfect. Earlier you were knocking Kenya and Travis. I may not be privy to what's going on with them, but I seriously doubt their problems stem from him running around. I haven't sensed that. But it is a marriage and there's bound to be some problems." Jasmine paused. Lisa wasn't paying attention to her. Lisa wasn't interested in the problem of married people. "If you put more energy into yourself, for you, instead of putting the energy into yourself in the hopes of attracting somebody to you, you'd be better off. People always want to be around somebody who is about something for themselves."

"Thanks for the advice, mother," Lisa said sarcastically.

Her attention was drawn to the handsome brother she'd spotted earlier. The woman he was having dinner with had gotten up and headed in the direction of the restroom. Lisa took the opportunity to get a better look at the brother. His head was cleanly shaven and he had a chiseled chin. She noticed that he was hurriedly writing something down. Once he stopped writing, he got up and made a beeline for their table.

"I trust you ladies enjoyed the wine." The brother with caramel-colored skin had a French accent. He placed a business card that he'd written on in front of Lisa. "I hope you ladies don't mind me interrupting, but I noticed you at the bar earlier and I was compelled to meet you."

Lisa quickly forgot about the woman that was with him. She smiled as she picked up the card. Jasmine quickly snatched it from her.

"Thank you for the wine. Now hurry back to your table before your date gets back and causes a scene for your fake French ass." Jasmine smiled.

Sufficiently embarrassed, the brother did as he was told. Jasmine watched him as he took his leave, shook her head, and then tore up his business card.

"Why did you tear that up?" Lisa looked as if she wanted to piece the card back together. "I was feeling that accent."

"Girl, please. You're worth much more than that. I saw that brother hawking our table a half-hour ago. If he's going to step to you like that when he's with somebody else and you respond to that, he's going to play you like you are second string from that point on."

Jasmine was right on point and Lisa knew it. If the shoe were on the other foot, she would be quick to give the same advice to someone else. Lisa's problem was that she was never quick to heed her own advice. It was always easier for Lisa to find fault in a picture; seldom did she see any faults in her reflection in the mirror.

"Lisa, trust me. I know all about playing yourself." Jasmine decided to let her in on some of her past. Giving a little bit of herself, letting Lisa know that she wasn't alone being down, might be what Lisa needed to help her get out her rut.

"How would you know about anything like that?"

"It takes going through some things to know. You know that I don't drink at all, right?"

"Yeah, so you're a little square. So what?" Lisa smiled to make sure that Jasmine knew that was intended to be a joke.

"There are reasons. It wasn't something that I just left alone." Jasmine was taking a solemn tone. Before she could get started with her story, the ringing of a cell phone interrupted her. Jasmine was prepared to bare her soul in hopes of Lisa hearing something that might have an influence on her life. There was no way she would pick up the call.

Lisa put up her index finger, signaling Jasmine to hold that thought. She reached into her purse and retrieved her cell phone. "Hello?"

Obviously smitten by whoever was on the other end, Lisa perked up immediately. Whatever Jasmine had to say wasn't more important than the caller. Lisa laughed and flirted for less than thirty seconds, then ended the call by saying, "I'll be there."

"Who was that?"

"That was that crazy Keith." Lisa was still smiling.

"Keith? Why did you tell him you'd be there?"

"I was just telling him something to get him off the phone. You know I'm hanging with my girl tonight."

Jasmine looked Lisa in the eyes and saw what she was looking for. "I don't believe it. I've been sitting here wasting my breath on you. You let this guy call you up on a Friday night at the last minute and you're going to drop everything for him. You just told him that no matter what you got going, it doesn't matter if he wants to get up with you."

"Yup." There was no shame in her voice.

"You are going to call that man back and set something up for another time and day."

"Why? When we leave here, you're going home to your husband. Where am I going to go? Home, by my damn self to nobody. Not tonight. I understand what you're saying, but that's not going to keep me company. Keith will. That's where I'm going to spend some time."

It was a losing battle. Jasmine realized that no amount of conversation from her would cause Lisa to change the way she approached life tonight. Lisa had to hit her bottom, wherever that might be. As much as Jasmine would've liked to help steer her direction, she would not have been able to break Lisa's fall. What that fall would be, she didn't know; and how big it would be remained to be seen.

CHAPTER 32

He sat there staring at the cell phone. The call ended after twenty-eight seconds—all it had taken for Kwame to convince the woman to meet him. The display light went out. There were a lot of lights that would be going out tonight. Lisa would have to be taken care of, an innocent victim of circumstance. *A pity, too*, he thought. If Bone had more time and tonight wasn't the night, he would have given serious consideration to tapping that ass for her.

Bone sat in the passenger's seat of Myron's van and contemplated sex with a woman he knew would die at his hands. It was simply another passing day in his life. He had little, if any, regard for Myron's body crammed into the oversized luggage or Flake as he drove to the salvage yard on Reames Road. That was where they would dispose of the van and all traces of Myron. Bone placed another call on his cell phone and, when the line picked up, his instructions were given with four simple words: "Get the place ready." He hung up as fast as he had called.

Flake drove the van in silence. He had listened to the brief conversations from Bone's end. He wasn't sure whom Bone had talked to and he'd fought the temptation to ask. If his guess was right, it had been Lisa. She was to meet him at the Bojangles' off Reames. Flake may have been a little slow, but it didn't sound to him as if he had a way back from the salvage yard. Something big was about to happen and he still was in the dark. It was time for him to start asking questions.

"How do I get back from the salvage yard?"

"Don't worry about it. I got you taken care of. I got everything taken care of."

Flake nodded, but he damn sure didn't like the sound of it. Bone was zoning out on him again. "Who were you talking to?" Flake was nervous enough as it was. He didn't need to have Bone tripping on him. Maybe Flake was developing too much of a conscience to stay in this line of work. There was a time, not too long ago, when he could kill a man and never give it a second thought. Although he was calm on the outside, what he'd done to Myron a few hours earlier was tearing him up inside.

"Some more work we got to take care of," Bone said with a sick smirk on his face. The thrill of a kill was more exciting than sex.

We? Flake thought. *We ain't gonna do shit. We ain't gonna get our hands dirty*. The dirty work would be left up to Flake.

"You know what it feels like to control so many people's lives. I feel like a god. I'm pulling all of the strings and watching these people dance. They don't have any idea about what's happening to them. I am their destiny. They will kneel at my feet and beg for my mercy!"

The ranting continued as Flake drove. He tuned out Bone's volume because he'd listened to it all before. This time he understood the words, though; he heard them for the first time. Bone was controlling and manipulating lives, especially Flake's. What would happen to him when he outlived his usefulness? Would he fall victim to the same reality that other people faced? Flake kept his mouth shut, acted like he was listening and did what he was told—drive.

Flake dimmed the lights as he neared Duke's Salvage. It was already dark and the heaps of damaged cars made the junkyard even darker. Former fine automobiles were reduced to scrap metal. Among this heap of abused metal was where Myron would be put to rest. Flake coasted to the gate until the van finally stopped.

Bone was the first one out the van. He pushed the buzzer on the gate twice, waited ten seconds, then pushed the buzzer two more times. Duke recognized the code and seconds later, the automatic gate began to pull back. Flake pulled up and Bone got into the van.

Duke's office was located to the right of the salvage yard, midway from the front and the back. No lights could be seen from the outside. Bone got out the van and Flake followed him. The door to the soundproof office was open. It was designed to keep out the noise of the salvage yard. Bone let himself into the dimly lit office. Again, Flake followed.

"Put a g on the Hawks over the Kings; I feel lucky." Duke smiled at Bone. The phone was pressed against his head. "Yeah, I'm good for it, nigga...put my damn bet down. Tell your mama I said, what up?" He hung up the phone. "I used to work that boy's mama. Shit, she was a worker, too. That ho could turn six tricks a night and not break a sweat."

"Still fuckin' around with them bets, huh?" Bone looked his steely eyes on him.

"Ballers always got to play ball."

Duke was in his fifties, but looked to be in his sixties. Back in the late '70s, he'd made his money on the backs of women in the pimp game. In the mid '80s the pimp game had started to fail him. Crack was an epidemic that had run roughshod over his inventory. He'd taken all the money he'd stashed off his women's work, bought into the salvage business, and hung all of his women out to dry. He didn't take long in running his partner out of the business and taking the joint over for himself. Nowadays, his favorite vice was gambling. He'd bet on anything; he'd even been known to bet on a nephew's Pop Warner football games.

"The van's out here?" Duke asked. Bone nodded. "You got something for me?" This wasn't the first job Duke had handled for Bone; there was little hesitation on his part.

Bone reached into his jacket and pulled out a thick white envelope. "It's all there." He laid it on Duke's desk.

"I trust you." Duke picked up the envelope and started counting.

"You sending that through tonight? That shit got to be handled with the quickness." Bone wasn't making a request.

Duke was an old baller and he didn't get that way by being a fool. He'd been around Bone enough to know that he didn't play with him. Even if they were cool, he knew Bone wouldn't hesitate to flip on him. Business between Duke and Bone was good; Duke damn sure wanted to keep it that way.

They moved quickly and quietly through the darkness. Flake drove the van to the back of the salvage yard where the van would be compacted. There were three other guys that met them at the compactor. They immediately went to work, dropping the gas tank. This had to be done to eliminate any possibility of a fire.

This situation was perfect for Bone. It wasn't unusual for work to be done after-hours at Duke's, so the noise wouldn't arouse any suspicion. The double fortune was that the previous day's snow seemed to limit what normal traffic would have been out.

In less than five minutes, the gas tank was dropped, fluids removed and the van was ready to be crushed. The three men completed their work and disappeared. Duke, Bone and Flake climbed the tower that overlooked the compactor. The van would enter on one end and come out the other end as a square metal box. The metal would be shipped off and melted into a liquid. That simple. Flake, who hadn't said a word since they'd arrived, remained silent. He was numb to the chill in the air as the temperature dropped fifteen degrees. Bone made small talk with Duke until he was sure everything was set. He checked with Bone to make sure there was nothing that needed to be removed from the van. Bone denied the need for anything from the van. Duke then grabbed the switch that hung from a cable. It had a green button and a red one.

"Would you like to do the honor?" Duke held out the control switch in an offer to Bone. Bone pushed the green button and the compactor started its job. "Usually we make sure the vehicle is dry of all fluids, remove the glass, but I'm trying to get you playas out of here..."

Duke's yapping continued, but Flake couldn't hear any of it. His eyes were fixed on Myron's van. The metal bent like an accordion. The glass popped and shattered, but the compactor kept moving, doing its job. Despite the noise of the metal and glass, Flake listened intently. He could almost swear he heard the sickening sound of bones crushing under the compactor's might. Myron's body was being crushed inside the van. His internal organs were escaping the body anywhere they could find an exit. The picture in Flake's mind made him nauseous. His mouth watered and he felt sweat on his chest in spite of the chill in the air. He climbed down from the tower to regain his composure. He took a deep breath to calm himself. His conscience was beating the hell out of him. It was not something he was accustomed to. Flake took another breath and pulled himself together.

Moments later, Bone and Duke climbed down from the tower. Bone was giving directions on his cell phone. He shot Flake a look of disdain as he walked by. Flake met his look and shrugged it off. It let Bone know that he was cool. He fell in step behind Bone as they followed Duke back to his office. Bone repeated the directions two more times as they walked.

Bone pulled Flake aside as they entered Duke's office. "Baby Jar's on his way over here to pick you up. Take him back over to the money house we used the other night." Bone's piercing eyes locked onto Flake. "You ready for this?" Bone sensed weakness. Flake nodded. "Tonight is a big night. I need you."

"I'm down for whatever." There was no hesitation on Flake's part.

"That's what I'm talking about. I'm walking up to that Bojangles'. I got twenty minutes until that bitch is supposed to meet me. You guys sit tight when you get there. I'll call Jar when it's time to make the next move. Watch the kid. He had something on his mind."

With his marching orders in hand, Bone dispatched Flake to join Duke in his office. Bone turned and walked out the door. Flake watched Bone as he disappeared into the night. The grown man was relegated to sitting in an office at a salvage yard, waiting for a sixteen-year-old kid to pick him up. He was Bone's stooge that would kill when ordered to, sit when he was commanded to, and do whatever his master desired.

As he opened the door to Duke's office, he tried to ignore the sinking feeling in his stomach. The three guys that had removed the gas tank from the van were sitting with Duke. It was Flake's first good look at them and they appeared to be in their early twenties. *Son of a bitch*, he thought. Bone had caught him slipping. He'd had thoughts about outliving Bone's usefulness. Flake had no idea that he'd already done so.

"Why don't you get yourself a seat there, playa?" Duke snickered at Flake's uneasiness. The other three nameless, damn near faceless men snickered as well.

"I prefer to stand," Flake answered with a coolness that showed no signs of fear. It was going to be interesting to see how this played out.

"Suit yourself." Duke nodded toward the door. One of his minions got up, closed it and went back to his seat. The quick obedience brought a smile to Duke's face. "Want to empty your pockets? We wouldn't want no accidents up in here."

"No need to empty my pockets. I don't pack." Flake lied. The words were polite enough, but the underlying tone suggested that they were more than welcome to check, if they dared to.

"Suit yourself." Fred and his minions kept their eyes on Flake and Flake kept his eyes on all four of them.

There were a number of calls that Bone needed to make during the twenty-minute walk. The first one was to Baby Jar, in which he re-routed Jar's directions. Instead of going to the salvage yard, he was to go to the house where he had counted money two days ago. Jar started to go into details about his mother, but Bone cut him off. He appeased Jar by assuring him that he had a place to live, but there was a price for him to pay. Tonight, Jar would have his opportunity to pay it in full. For now, he was to park the car in Park Slope four blocks away at the corner of Lagrand and Small, and wait for Bone to call him again.

Rick Nixon was next on his list. Bone's proposition to him was short and sweet. He knew Rick had robbed him out of six kilos of cocaine and he let Rick know that he was aware of it. In fact, Bone was quite happy. He pulled out a mini tape recorder and held it near the phone. Bone played a recording of the conversation in the car between Griffen and his plant when the car was being stopped. Rick's voice soon joined the conversation and the threats that the state trooper conveyed to the occupants in the car was quite clear. Bone also let Rick know that there was video that accompanied the tape. Rick was to meet him at Travis Moore's house. Rick was to go there immediately and to have the cocaine with him. Bone would be there within an hour.

Bone knew that Rick was a crooked cop. He'd used Rick on a number of occasions in the past for various things. Bone also knew that Rick had a beef with Travis years ago, but Bone was not sure if those factors were enough to push him over the top. He needed something to hold over Rick's head in order to force him to help kidnap Travis and his wife. Setting Rick up with the cocaine was Bone's insurance policy that would lock Rick into his side.

The third call went to Tom Miller. Their money had crossed paths on two occasions, but they had never met face-to-face. Tom and Bone wouldn't know each other if they passed each other on the street. The call came as an anonymous tip to Tom. Tom was told that the stash Griffen was supposed to deliver had come up short because of someone he knew and worked with, but who he didn't know at all. He was instructed to meet at Park Slope on Lagrand and Small, and park near a black Datsun 280ZX.

Bone could almost hear the car cranking; Tom was in such a hurry to get there. Tom would destroy Travis' reputation and good name at work in an effort to save his. Bone's pieces were falling into the puzzle nicely. In all of his plotting and planning to destroy Travis, he wasn't aware of the latest events at Home Supply.

Fourth on Bone's list was Bruce Bowen. There was music in the background when Bruce picked up the line. "Fuck what you're doing; it's showtime, cuz."

"Bone?" Bruce was caught off guard.

"I'm fucking Perry's world tonight. You got front row. The house Perry grew up in on Lagrand is where the party's at. Meet me there in two hours. It's payback time for what that nigga did to us. You gonna love this little ma'fucker I got doin' him." Bone hung up before Bruce could respond.

The last call went back to the salvage yard. The call would have been a difficult one to make for a man with a conscience. Bone wasn't a man with one. He took pleasure in the call. It was time to jettison some of the dead weight hanging around him.

THE SILENCE IN DUKE'S OFFICE WAS BROKEN when the phone rang. Duke had been awaiting the call with further instructions from Bone. He picked up on the third ring. The other four sets of eyes in the room watched intently as Duke picked up the call. Everyone in the room knew a man's fate hinged on what was being said on the other end of that line.

"Yeah?" Duke spoke with a low voice into the receiver.

Flake kept his eyes on the phone while the other eyes bounced between the phone and Flake. Flake had no fear of what was to come. If this was where it all ended, so be it. But, he'd be damned if these punk asses were going to sense any fear from him. He had sized these chumps up; they probably weighed around a hundred and sixty pounds apiece. Flake was sure that at least one, probably two, of these guys would be laying dead alongside him.

"The nigga's right here." Duke pulled the phone from his ear and held it out for Flake. Flake stayed in place. Realizing that Flake wasn't moving, he clicked over to the speakerphone. "I got you on speaker."

"What up, Flake?" Bone's voice came through the speaker.

"So, this is how it goes down, huh?" Flake finally responded.

"Damn, son, those were the wrong words." He paused. "You can't handle this no more. You got soft on me. It's time for you to move on. Duke, shake that nigga down, then handle him."

"Fifteen years, and it's like that," Flake interrupted.

"Ma'fucker, I told your ass, you don't question me. I pull the strings! I control this shit and your pass is revoked!" Bone hung up and the line went dead.

The sound of the dial tone filled the room. Duke clicked the phone off as two of his minions made a move to shake Flake down. The third one sat in his chair and pulled out a Glock. A few minutes ago, everything was fairly cool. The wrong word to Bone and his path was chosen. Flake had been around this game long enough to know that no matter what he said, it would have been the wrong words.

As the two men cautiously approached him in the cramped office, Flake saw himself in these kids, ten years ago—doing whatever it took to get on, trying to earn some respect in the streets. Ultimately, they would probably find themselves meeting with an end similar to his. But Flake wasn't ready for this to end. Not on Bone's terms.

"Let me help you," Flake said. Slowly, he reached behind him and pulled out his .45. He made sure he took his time so he wouldn't alarm anybody in the room. He held the gun by its handle with his thumb and index finger. He raised his left hand out to the side. He watched their attention go to the weapon. He tossed the gun to the kid that was still seated. It was just enough off center to force him to find it with his eyes and free hand. The other two guys tried to see it as well. It was more than enough of a distraction for Flake.

He grabbed the kid closest to him and rammed his head into the other kid. Both bodies went limp. Flake slung one kid at Duke's desk in the direction of the light that barely illuminated the room. He held up the other kid and used him as a human shield, hiding as much of his massive frame as possible. He pushed his shield in the direction of the kid sitting in the chair. Shots rang out in the dark. Flake recognized the sound of metal as it pierced flesh. Three struck the kid's body and four more whizzed by striking other objects.

Flake launched the body in the direction that the shots came from. The scream in the dark let him know exactly where the kid was. Flake thrust his palm forward with as much force that he could generate. When it landed, he knew he'd found his target. He could feel the nasal cavity crushing under his strength; he tried to shove it into the kid's brain. Quickly, he moved to the kid who lay sprawled across the desk. He reached over and snapped his neck with very little effort. He had saved these kids ten years of anguish.

"This is how it goes down, huh?" Flake put himself nose to nose with Duke. "Those kids are good on cars; they ain't shit for the streets." Flake sniffed the air and smiled. "You smell that? Smell's like death to me."

Duke sniveled like the gutless coward that he was. He'd prostituted and beaten women to get to where he was today. He was a dirty businessman and doing dirtier business on the side. Now, he was nothing more than a punk scared for his worthless life. Flake wouldn't find much of a fight here. Duke beat on women, but he didn't challenge men. Death would not come to Duke swift enough.

"I'm glad you got this soundproof room. Too bad you ain't sayin' much."

Flake straightened the light and checked the pulse on his three victims. All the while, he hoped he could get some type of rise out of Duke. There wasn't. Fear had him hamstrung. Flake found what he was looking for—his .45. The idea of shooting Duke appealed to Flake, but a good old-fashioned pistol whipping would deliver one final message to the former pimp. It would be retribution for all of the women he'd robbed and abused. He would be beaten and mangled as his journey in this life came to an end.

CHAPTER 33

"Are we gonna start that track again? Yo! Are we gonna start that track again?" Soul shouted into the microphone in the studio.

"Ah, yeah...yeah." Bruce had no idea what he was saying yes to. It was his response to whatever it was that had broken his trance.

"B, you all right?" his engineer asked. "You look like you've seen a ghost."

A nod of the head was all Bruce could muster. A ghost would have been a welcomed relief; instead, he'd heard the ominous sound of Bone's voice. Nothing could deter him from working when he was in the studio; Bone just did. Bruce had been frozen in his tracks for the last two minutes, It was the cell phone in his right hand near his ear and Bone's words ringing in his mind: "I'm fucking Perry's shit, you got front row and it was going down at Perry's old house. It was payback time." Bruce's mind was on autopilot again.

"B! What's up, man? We gonna do this or what?"

"Yeah...yeah. I was tripping. We gonna get this." Bruce shook off the distracting thoughts. "Give me that playback."

His sound engineer gave Bruce a once-over to make sure they were back on the same page before he made a move. Bruce gave him a wink and the engineer knew Bruce was ready to put behind him whatever had him tripped up. He turned to his mixing board and began to play back the last track that Soul had laid down.

Bruce tried to focus on the track as it was being played. He closed his eyes and listened hard. As hard as he tried, he couldn't hear the music. Again, they were blocked by Bone's words. He was tempted to go to Perry's old house, but he was going to force himself to stay in the studio and get this work done. Whatever was going down between Bone and Travis was between them. No matter what he had planned for years to do, he was going to sit tight tonight.

It was the law of the jungle, rules of the street. Bone had a beef with Travis and it had to come to a head. Bruce was caught in the middle. He knew both Kwame "Bone" Brown's story and Perry Travis Moore's secrets. He knew more about Travis than his wife did. Maybe Bone was justified in what he was doing.

"You feeling that?" The engineer nudged him. The non-response pissed him off. Bruce was as lost as he'd been a few minutes ago. "What the hell is up?"

Bruce turned on the microphone inside the studio. "Soul, something came up. I'm shutting down for the night. It's up to you guys to continue to work, if you want to. Studio time is paid for." Bruce clicked the microphone off. "You can handle this. I'll review the tracks tomorrow. I'm out."

"Where you goin'?"

"I got a party to attend." Bruce got up, knowing that no further questions would be asked.

Minutes later, Bruce was sitting in his Benz, debating his next step. Knowing that this day might come, he'd developed a plan for himself to show where his loyalties lied. Bone was his cousin and an extremely dangerous man. Right now, he was a loose cannon and siding with him was the easy thing to do. Before he made the trip to Park Slope, he would need to make a stop at his house in the University area.

Bone stood inside Bojangles' as he waited for Lisa. He needed to warm himself up after his little walk from Duke's Salvage. He was riding a high as he placed his calls to the people he wanted to have witness the fall of Perry Travis Moore. He also took great pleasure in ridding himself of Flake. Flake had been asking too many questions lately and not showing enough heart. A lot of the dirt Bone had done over the last fifteen years would be put away with him; he had to go. The kid would serve him well over the next five to ten years, providing that he stepped correctly tonight. If not, he had ten other numbnuts ready to step in.

The dropping temperature set in on Bone once he'd finished his calls. He was so eager to get things going when he'd left the condo, he'd forgotten his gloves. Another ten minutes in the cold would have given him a case of frostbite. He was in the restaurant, blowing into his hands when Lisa pulled up in her Honda. Bone smiled at her through the window when Lisa spotted him. Bone turned on the charm and reverted to his Keith persona.

Keith walked quickly to Lisa's car. He tried to spend as little time exposed to the elements as possible. Bone also wanted Lisa to think that he was in need of her help. He opened the passenger door and hurried in.

"Thank you so much for coming to pick me up."

"Not a problem. Are you going to get your car?"

"You wouldn't believe the day I've had. I was over here on this side of town taking care of some business and I got sidetracked. I meant to call you earlier. Anyway, my classic 280ZX broke down right after I talked to you. Matter of fact, you probably passed the tow truck." Bone took a second to gather his breath. He wanted to see if Lisa was buying his ranting bullcrap.

"No, I don't think I saw it." Lisa was looking toward the street as if she was trying to find the tow truck. Turning her head so quickly reminded her of the buzz she had.

Bone knew she was had. "Enough about me. I hope I didn't catch you in the middle of anything, but I wanted to spend some time with you."

"I was having something to eat. No big deal." Lisa smiled at the man she believed to be named Keith. "Where do you want to go?"

Bone smiled back at Lisa. She had no idea what she was about to get into. The thousand dollars he'd spent on her yesterday was going to cost her more than she could ever afford to pay. "Anywhere, as long as I'm with you."

"Let's ride and talk until we figure out what to do." Lisa put the car in gear. She was taken with the man.

This is like taking candy from a baby, Bone thought. Lisa was the perfect mark. She was looking for a man to make her complete. He had an eye for picking them. He gave Lisa another smile. His plan for Lisa was to dispose of her immediately. Tonight was a night of cutting his dead weight loose. Myron and Flake were taken care of. When Travis and his wife came up missing, Lisa would think back to all of the questions he'd asked her. He knew Lisa was a talker, and sooner or later she would be talking to somebody. Bone decided against getting rid of her too quickly. He would let her be a part of the show before her lights went out for good. In fact, she would be his driver for part of the evening.

Kenya and Travis both pushed away from the table at the same time. Both were stuffed. The spaghetti that Travis had made tonight was as delicious as the first pot of spaghetti he had made for her. They had talked and laughed more in the last hour than they'd laughed together over the last year.

Kenya was still wearing her robe. Even though Travis wanted to keep the spirit of their honeymoon alive, he had come to the realization that this wasn't the Caribbean in February. It was winter in Charlotte and a little nippy for nudity. "I see you're feeling the effects of winter." Kenya was peeking at a particular part of his anatomy as she made the assessment.

"No, girl...you know I was full and relaxed and you know...I'm just chilling out for right now." The line of bull wasn't working. "Okay, maybe I'm a little on the cold side. What do you say we go back upstairs and play around with each other?"

"I'm not playing with you anymore...until I open my gifts from you."

"I have no problem with that. Hey, if you play with me right, there could be more gifts in it for you."

"I don't need any more gifts to play with you."

Travis rose from the table, walked behind Kenya's chair and pulled it out for her. She stood next to her nude escort and took his arm. Together, they walked upstairs to their bedroom. Travis turned on the light for Kenya, and then took a seat on their bed. Kenya gazed at the packages surrounded by orchids.

"Where should I start? Big to small or small to big?" Kenya wondered aloud. Travis didn't offer her any suggestions, so Kenya opted to start at the bathroom and work her way toward the big box.

Kenya opened the envelope and found the tickets and the backstage passes to the Anthony Hamilton concert. Thoughts of what to wear to the show were already dancing through her mind. The second package contained a burgundy thong and a matching bra. Kenya blushed as she looked at her smiling husband on the bed. Whatever she wore, she knew what would be under it. In the third box, she found a light-brown, silk Donna Karan blouse. She remembered seeing the blouse at Neiman Marcus. She'd been eyeing it for two months. It was the perfect complement to the

Donna Karan pantsuit she'd also been watching. She looked at the dimensions of the next box.

"No, you didn't," Kenya said excitedly, guessing at the contents. She ripped into it and found the tan two-piece outfit she'd been wanting. Kenya had no idea that Travis had been paying attention to her when she'd talked about it.

"Yes, I did. You thought I wasn't hearing you?" Travis already knew what she was thinking. He was happy to see the glow on her face. He looked forward to the thanks he was going to get. "Open the last one."

Kenya started working on the box. In it, she found a three-quarter-length cashmere coat that blended with the blouse and pantsuit. There was no doubt left in her mind about what she would be wearing at the concert tomorrow night.

"We'll shop for the right pair of shoes for your ensemble tomorrow." Travis knew better than to try to buy her another pair of shoes without her being present. The last time Travis tried to buy a pair of shoes for Kenya was on their second anniversary. That pair of shoes was in their closet, in the original box, worn only one time that he could recall.

"Thank you, Travis. You don't mind if I try this on?" Kenya asked while already gathering her boxes.

"It's yours, baby. Do your thing. Big Daddy's going to be right here waiting for you." Travis lay back on the bed, resting his hands behind his head. He gave his wife a quick wink.

Kenya looked at her husband lying there in the nude and resisted the urge to join him. She would be back. With her arms full of boxes, she retired to the bathroom and closed the door behind her. *I'll definitely have to step up my game*, she thought. Travis was making one hell of an effort to win her heart again. Game over, he'd won it. The Perry Ellis sweater she'd bought him as an anniversary gift was going to need something else to go with it, for sure.

Kenya took off her robe and set it to the side. She started with the silk blouse, and loved the feel of it as the silk slowly slid over her arms and her body. Next were the pants and the jacket. She admired herself in the outfit. She made a number of poses in the mirror before topping off the ensemble with the cashmere coat. There was a pair of shoes in the closet that would set the outfit off. Once she had them on, she re-entered the bedroom to show Travis how fabulous she looked.

Kenya struck her first pose for Travis, then heard a familiar noise. Travis was out. He didn't doze off; he was sleeping with a full-blown snore. Kenya shook her head and smiled. She'd let him take a little nap while she went downstairs and cleaned up the kitchen. Kenya looked at her outfit and stopped herself. She damn sure wasn't doing any cleaning in these clothes. Kenya meticulously hung her ensemble in the closet, and then threw on a sweatsuit.

It would be a pleasure to clean up behind Travis after all of the trouble he'd gone to. As she passed through the room again, Travis was still flat on his back, hands behind his head, snoring. She also noticed that the blood flow had been restored to the other parts of his body. She grabbed the blanket that was at the foot of their bed and covered him. Kenya was delighted to see the makeshift tent that was created by his blessing as the blanket rested on top of him.

Washing the dishes and cleaning up right after dinner was like her mother. Turning into her wasn't the worst thing that could happen. She hoped that Travis would still be napping when she was finished down there. She would enjoy waking him up in a special way. By the time he realized what was happening to him in his sleep, he would be ready to explode. Kenya started her cleaning; having no idea that there was danger brewing for her and her husband.

Rick had done what he was told. In a stolen vehicle, he'd eased himself back into the neighborhood he'd visited earlier. Travis was at home and had been stationary for a while. The black Volvo was still being tracked. Rick couldn't believe he was parked near the pool waiting for Bone to tell him his next move. He'd snooped around the house undetected. He found Kenya downstairs cleaning by herself. From the looks of it, Rick surmised that Travis had gotten himself a nice piece of that ass.

Corruption and greed is what had gotten Rick here, snooping around Travis Moore's house, guessing at what Travis and his wife had been doing. His own greed and stupidity had led him to think he could stiff Bone on the cocaine that had been lifted off of Griffen. Now, he was at Bone's mercy, doing whatever he was told in an effort to try to protect his name. Fucking around with Bone used to be a harmless way to pocket some change. Now, there was no telling where this road would lead.

CHAPTER 34

Eleven miles separated Park Hills and Park Slope from Chestnut Grove in the University area. It was a secluded gated community with a golf course and country club. Bruce had been across the country and around the world to get those eleven miles of separation. With a series of phone calls, Bone had succeeded in closing the distance on what, at one time, was worlds apart.

Travis was part of the world in Bruce's life that his cousin Bone wasn't given access to. For fifteen years, he'd maintained contact with Travis without anyone's knowledge, particularly Bone. Bruce was not given full access to Travis' life, as Bone didn't have full access to his life. Even now, Bruce was a vague part of Travis' life. Bruce had never been to his house, met his wife or his child. Bruce knew the past they shared and accepted the friendship as it was. He understood that, sooner or later, he would be a part of Travis' new circle.

The distances between the two worlds were getting closer and closer. Bruce tried to maintain the distance with his cousin but, family being family, Bone would pop up every now and then. Bone would invite himself back into Bruce's life, and then drop back out. Usually, it was under the premise that Bone was about to go legit. One way or another, the streets would always pull him back in. Bruce could tell when he was about to go back to the streets because Bone would start having conversations about Travis. The reality was that Bone was never going to let the streets go. It had its grip on him.

Bruce thought this last time might be different. Maybe he was hoping that Bone was ready to be through with that life. Bone was the person who was responsible for bringing Soul to him. Bone had come across the real deal in Soul. Bruce started taking the steps to include Bone on a legit deal. Bruce was down for helping to pull Bone up from the streets, but the conversations about Travis were back again. Bone's obsession was as bad as it was when Travis had first left. Bruce suspected that Bone had finally discovered that Travis was back in town and the last couple of days had confirmed his suspicions.

For years, Bruce had been playing the middle between his cousin and a man that he believed was his close friend. Now, he was stuck in the middle. On the one hand was his family, his cousin, and his blood. On the other was a friend who'd given Bruce an opportunity at life. Looking at all that he'd accomplished, nobody could deny that he'd made the most of his chances.

Bruce pulled up to the guard shack, waited for the guard on duty to identify his car and open the gate. He threw his hand up to acknowledge the guard as he drove past him. There was little time to waste in getting to his house. He looked at his fifty-two-hundred–square-foot house as he neared it. The state-of-the-art home set Bruce back six hundred and seventy-five grand. He'd definitely made the most of the opportunity he'd been given. From the humblest of beginnings, he'd built a great life for himself and he didn't owe anybody for that.

Bruce had a mind full of thoughts as he entered his house. A glass of dark liquor was needed to accompany them. For too many years, he'd thought about what he would do if this day ever came. Now that it was here, he was no longer the decisive person that he'd been. Bruce had devised a plan to deal with the situation and now he wasn't sure that he could follow through with it.

The wet bar was his first stop en route to his basement studio. He poured himself a glass of brandy over some ice. He downed the two ounces of liquid and quickly poured himself another. He would let that one sit until he came back upstairs. Bruce only drank on special occasions; tonight was going to be a different kind of special.

Bruce kept everything he valued downstairs in his studio. He had a safe that was in a walk-in closet with a door that was always kept locked. Once he was downstairs, he unlocked the closet, turned on the lights and walked in. He manipulated the number to the combination and opened the safe. He scrambled past the watches and rings. Bruce dug to the back of the safe until his hands found what they were searching for. Inside the small black bag he held, wrapped in plastic, was the one item that bound Bruce to the biggest secret of Travis Moore's past: an old .38.

Bruce made two stops on his way out the house. The first was to shotgun the glass of liquor he'd left on the wet bar; the next was to get a good pair of gloves. Where he was headed, it would be really cold. He secured the .38 in the inside breast pocket of his coat. It was time to go visit the house that Perry Travis Moore had grown up in.

The master of manipulation was fidgeting with his cell phone and getting exactly what he wanted from Lisa. Lisa confided in Bone. She told him everything that had gone down between her and Kenya in the bathroom at the mall. Lisa let him know, in no uncertain terms, that she didn't have time for Kenya's trifling behind.

Bone, the man who'd just left his close friend for dead at the junkyard, talked to Lisa about the value of friendship and not letting something so petty come between her and Kenya. Bone felt that Lisa needed to offer Kenya a genuine apology and he'd be with her. She was sucked in by his earnest concern for their friendship. Before she knew it, she was driving toward Kenya's house. Lisa started to call Kenya, but Bone convinced her that the best approach was to go directly to her and not give Kenya a chance to deny her apology.

Finding a man with so much integrity like Keith was what Lisa had been searching for. Here was a man who had money; she could tell by the thousand he'd spent on her yesterday. But he valued people and friendships more than anything. Whether it was infatuation or love, she was falling for Keith. She would soon have her eyes opened to the man that he really was.

When they made the turn toward Ballantyne, Bone gave Lisa the impression that he'd never been in this neighborhood. Lisa was trying to remember her turns and she didn't pay any attention to Bone as he continued fumbling with his cell phone. She certainly didn't notice him hit the speed dial button that dialed Rick Nixon. Bone carried on with their conversation when he heard the phone pick up. He talked about how beautiful the houses were in the Ballantyne area. What he was saying wasn't as important as was his voice being heard through his cell phone by Rick. Bone spotted a car that he suspected was Rick's as they neared the pool house.

"Oh, they got a pool house, huh? This Honda would look good sitting up here by the pool." Bone knew Rick would have his eyes up looking for any sign of him approaching.

"You think so?" Lisa was beaming as she imagined herself there with Keith.

Bone continued to dominate the conversation with Lisa while looking toward the pool. Their car was the only one passing by the pool house. Rick spotted Bone in the passenger's seat.

"Yeah, I could sit tight right here during the summers." Bone's words were more for Rick than anything else. Bone didn't hang up. He kept the line open because he was playing this by ear. Rick was his only backup, and Rick had as much of a clue as to how this would play out as Bone did.

"Are you coming with me?" Lisa parked in the driveway and waited for his support.

"No, I think this is something you two should handle. I'll give you a few minutes and then I'll check on you."

Lisa was hesitant to get out the car and confront Kenya. What she should have been leery of was the man she would be leaving in her car. "I hope her husband isn't home." Lisa sounded as if she'd had enough of him. She turned off the headlights but left the motor running.

"Can't be that bad. You never know, we might all have a great time tonight."

Lisa nodded her head. Keith seemed to be the eternal optimist and he was right. She was going to have to look at the positives. She would get her friend to forgive her, and then maybe she and Keith could have a good time with Kenya and her husband. Lisa got out the car and walked to the door with a purpose. This was going to be a good night.

"That's one gullible bitch right there," Bone spoke toward his phone. Lisa rang the doorbell and a few seconds later the porch light came on. A few more seconds passed before the door finally opened. Bone could see that Kenya opened the door. "Rick?" he spoke into the cell phone.

"I'm here. What's the next move?" Rick was a little uneasy.

"We don't need those keys. The trick I'm with just got me instant access." The thought of Myron making those keys and losing his life as a consequence for making those keys was a non-factor to Bone. The only thing he could see clearly was getting to Travis. He looked to see if he could detect any sign of Travis. "You sure that nigga's there?"

"His car's been parked in the garage for a couple of hours. He should be. His old lady was around in the kitchen cleaning up, but he wasn't nowhere around. Travis is probably upstairs sawing some wood by now."

"That nigga's name is Perry." Bone watched Kenya and Lisa talk at the door. They looked in the direction of the car, but kept talking. "You got his number, don't you?"

"Yeah."

"Dial it, nigga." Bone hung up his phone. He watched the door intently. Suddenly, there was a rush in Kenya's movement away from the door. That was enough for Bone to believe that Travis must have been asleep if he was home.

Bone felt his moment approaching. There was no room for turning back and nothing was going to stop him. His breathing quickened and his once freezing hands were beginning to sweat. He started to rock in his seat when the cell phone rang.

"Yeah?" Bone continued to rock in the seat.

"He's sleeping. Whatever you're going to do, you better move fast."

"Get down here." Bone hung up.

Bone got out the car and approached the house. Lisa and Kenya saw him coming. Kenya opened the door as he approached and welcomed him into her home. Lisa looked at him with a smile, but noticed that his demeanor had changed.

"Well, hello, Keith," Kenya started. "Welco..."

Before she finished the sentence or before Lisa had a chance to ask the man she believed to be Keith what was wrong, he'd grabbed the muzzle end of his nickel-plated Glock. In a stunningly fast move, he swung it into Kenya's temple. Jasmine's warning flashed in her mind before she lost consciousness. Even faster still, he turned on Lisa. She'd never seen so much rage and hatred in a pair of eyes. Shock and terror stifled any words she could utter. Bone gave her an equal dosage of his brand of sleeping pills. He quickly turned off the porch light.

With his adrenaline pumping from his little conquest, Bone hoisted both women onto his shoulders, one woman on the left shoulder and the other on the right. He carried the limp bodies to the garage and wedged them through the door. A quick search of the garage turned up some duct tape, rags and some old ropes. He jammed the rags into their mouths and put duct tape over each woman's mouth. He taped their hands behind their backs, then their feet. Bone then taped each of their hands and feet together.

Kenya was placed in the backseat of her SUV on her stomach. Lisa was placed in the tailgate. This is how they would arrive to their next destination; hog tied and gagged.

Rick had made his way to the house. He closed the door behind him. He looked in all directions in search of Bone. There was no sign of him. Rick's thought was to leave right then, fuck what Bone was trying to pull. As he turned to leave, Bone re-entered from the garage.

"Where are the women?" Rick whispered as he caught sight of him. He was sure Bone didn't see him turning tail.

"Ready to ride. They comin' with us. Right now, I'm getting ready to get what I came for. You gonna help me get what I came for." Boned searched for any dissension. He already had that pig over a barrel. One wrong step and he'd find himself in the death line tonight, too. Instead, Rick nodded his approval. "Good, these niggas got a kid, too. We'll leave that one for dead, but we taking Perry out this fuckin' house."

Travis was still asleep under a blanket and in the nude. The ruckus downstairs hadn't awakened him. The opening and closing of the doors did not disturb him. If there was an alarm system in place, perhaps it would have alerted him. Travis did not have a clue in the world that there was something awry in his house. While he was enjoying a peaceful slumber upstairs, unrest had settled in his house downstairs. His snoring led Bone and Rick to his room.

Travis began having a dream of Bone and Rick entering his room, mocking him and his erection as his nude body lay on the bed, covered only by a blanket. What was causing this dream and why were Rick and Bone together? In reality, Travis was half-awake, half-asleep. With the pummeling that these two unleashed on him, it was better that he thought he was dreaming. The dream was complete with pain, and then suddenly the dream went black.

CHAPTER 35

Jar was growing tired of sitting in the running car on the corner of Lagrand and Small. The streets were busy with a flurry of activity. There was no snow falling tonight. It seemed as if the crackheads that were on the down low last night were trying to make up for lost time. The temperature was dropping, but it wasn't stopping these hard-core crackheads from chasing that next high. It wouldn't have surprised him to see his mother out there in the cold looking for that next one, too. *To hell with her*, he thought. She had kicked him out and, as far as he was concerned, he wasn't going back. This was his money out here. This was how he was going to get his.

Jar kept his eyes moving up and down the streets, like he had been taught. He had one hand on the cell phone and the other was on the radio. When he became bored with one station, he'd quickly switch to another one. He was leaning over to make his third station change in the last five minutes when a set of headlights caught his attention. The automobile that had turned onto Lagrand approached slowly. The slow approach of the vehicle rattled Jar. There was a sense of security that came with being in Bone's car. On the other hand, there was also the possibility of inheriting whatever problems he had on the street. He turned down the radio and picked up the pistol and waited.

The late-model, money-green Jaguar slowed to a virtual crawl as it neared the black 280ZX. Tom Miller saw what he was looking for, but didn't expect such a young kid to be behind the wheel.

This was a young man's game, he surmised. After all, it was the excitement and youth that had gotten him involved in the dope game, albeit on the fringes. Tom was trying to recapture his youth. In the last twenty-four hours, he'd lost his job, seventy-five thousand dollars, and somebody at Home Supply was on to him. He was out here to find out whom.

As Tom carelessly sought the answer, what he didn't know was that the young-looking kid had a pistol in his hand, waiting for him to make a wrong move. Tom crossed Small Street and parked opposite the 280ZX. Fortunately for him, that wasn't a wrong move.

Park Slope Community Housing Project wasn't the ideal place for a middle-aged white man driving a new Jaguar. Tom Miller was becoming increasingly more aware of that fact as he remained parked on Small Street. He'd been enticed one too many times into flirting with this lifestyle. He'd profited from it, but he'd never been this close. He could smell the danger in the air.

Two days ago, Tom's life was sugar. The chief financial officer for Home Supply stood to make millions, and thanks to the golden parachute given to him by Walter, he still would make the money. But he was finished at Home Supply as a result of his tirade this morning. The embezzlement scandal, he could have survived. The affair with Patricia would severely damage the image he'd created for himself; and surviving that would have been extremely difficult and painful, but it was doable. Drug trafficking would bury him. If word got out about his involvement with cocaine, he would be destroyed. He thanked God that nobody knew the true reasons why he'd blown up this morning, and he wanted to make sure that no one ever did. That's why he was willing to take the risk of coming to Park Slope, to protect the only person he truly cared about: himself.

Neither Jar nor Tom realized the protection that the black 280ZX was providing for them. This was Bone's yard and everybody knew it. They also knew his car as well as they knew him. Any car that was bold enough to be parked near his fell under its protection. The car and the people that occupied them were off limits, no matter who it was.

"THE FUCKING KEY DOESN'T WORK!" Bone was disgusted as he tried to start the car with the keys he had made. This was Flake's fault; he had screwed up an idiot-proof task. He wished he hadn't had him killed, because he would kill his dumb ass himself for this. "Go upstairs in that room and find his." This was wasted time that Bone couldn't afford.

Rick wanted to find the quickest way out this mess, but he was in too deep. He had no other choice but to obey Bone's command. He had transferred the six kilos of cocaine into the trunk of the Volvo. Next to the cocaine laid Travis' bound, gagged and nude body wrapped in a blanket. Kenya's SUV was outside and running, her spot in the garage was filled by Lisa's Honda. All the lights in the house were turned off. Rick and Bone were operating under the cloak of darkness. He hurried upstairs and found the keys. This was the time to leave Bone hanging if he was going to make his move. He didn't like the way he'd been strong-armed into the situation, but it was better to ride it out than to face Bone's repercussions.

Rick returned with the keys and tossed them to Bone. Bone cranked the car and backed out. Rick disengaged the garage door opener and lowered the garage door manually. He didn't want the light to come on automatically when the door went down and this allowed him to complete the task quietly.

As soon as he got into Kenya's vehicle, he heard mumbles behind him, which startled him. It was a reflex move that caused him to reach over the seat and take a crack at Kenya's head. It was a move that delighted him. She was either unconscious or she'd gotten the message, shut up or get fucked up. He listened to hear if any noise would come from Lisa. There was silence. He put the car in gear and followed Bone. They were at the pool house before they turned on their headlights.

Twenty minutes of driving had gotten them to Park Slope. As Bone came up on Lagrand and Small, he saw his car and the green Jaguar. To his surprise, Tom Miller had actually shown up. He pulled out his cell phone and dialed Jar. He slowed the car down as he passed them so Jar could get a good look at him.

"Hel..." Jar started to answer, but Bone cut him off.

"Fifteen minutes, you get that white dude and come to the count house. You be ready to handle business when you get there, son. I'm counting on you to step up for me. I need you."

"I'll be there." Jar spoke with conviction. He was the one that was needed. He wasn't willing to fail the only person that was concerned for him.

With their headlights turned off, Rick followed Bone to the rear of the abandoned building that they would be entering. The unwritten law in this concrete jungle was that this area belonged to Bone. It didn't matter that it was condemned by the city. The police didn't patrol it, Bone did. He ruled it. This was the part of town where the police showed up an hour after the shooting stopped.

The two unrecognized vehicles were spotted long before they had parked. Seconds later, four men emerged from the shadows and descended upon the vehicles, two to each car. They were intent on finding out who had entered their restricted area. The tension in their bodies relaxed as they discovered Bone was the driver of the Volvo.

Bone's conversation was brief. The four men were instructed to help Bone and Rick get the three unconscious bodies upstairs to what used to be apartment 3B. They were to take whatever measures were necessary to keep them unconscious if they made any noise. Once they were finished, three of them were to go to the corner of Lagrand and Small. The other one would stand guard outside the apartment. They were to watch out for Jar and the middle-aged white man on their way to the building.

The three guys were to make themselves scarce after completing their tasks. They could speculate all they wanted, but they didn't need to know what else was going on in apartment 3B. The question that begged to be asked was, "Where was Flake in all this?" If he wasn't by Bone's side, he was probably nearby. None of the yes-men dared to pose the question of his whereabouts. Bone didn't bother to offer up an explanation to these chumps.

The apartment was prepped the way that Bone wanted. Black tarp covered the windows so that no light could escape. Dozens of candles illuminated the apartment, but it was still freezing cold. This atmosphere would make a number of people think that a séance was about to begin. There were chairs placed in the main room as if contestants were lining up for a game show. The people who filled these rooms were either going to witness a murder first-hand, commit the murder, or become the victims themselves.

Travis, the guest of honor, was taken into one bedroom. It was the old bedroom that he'd grown up in. This was where his nude body, draped in a blanket, would be on display. He was the featured attraction. Kenya and Lisa were taken into the large bedroom that belonged to Travis' mother. They were re-taped to chairs facing the door. It was within earshot of the room Travis was in. They would hear everything as it unfolded.

The nude body of Perry Travis Moore was placed on a crude

makeshift crucifix. His arms and feet were bound to it with his own duct tape from his garage and some rope that Bone had waiting for him. His feet were six inches from the floor and his arms were stretched as far apart as they could be. The blanket that covered his body was draped over his head. Bone wanted Travis to be in as much agony as possible when he came to.

Bone could taste the fear and terror that would soon fill these rooms. His obsession with Travis had tallied two bodies so far. Myron and Flake were the first to go and three more would follow. The rush Bone got from the thoughts of watching this develop in front of him was intoxicating. What made it that much more special was what he would get to watch Jar do to him. A kid that Travis had tried to save from these streets would pull Travis back into them, and then remove him from the face of the earth. The mere thought of it excited him more than sex ever could.

Satisfied that everything was in place, Bone went into the main room and took a seat. He waited for the arrival of Jar and Tom Miller; their fifteen minutes would be up soon. He was still holding out hope that Bruce would be there as well. Bone sat in the one seat that faced all the others. In the warped mind of Kwame "Bone" Brown, he was the host entertaining at an exclusive party. Rick elected to stand; he was still tripping on everything that he was caught up in.

A few minutes later, the door opened. Through it walked Baby Jar, Tom Miller and Bruce Bowen; he'd joined the party just in time. Bruce was the first to take a seat. He didn't know what to expect, but he was slightly relieved when he didn't see Travis. It was not a feeling that would last for long. Tom was there to recover his cocaine and protect his name from whoever knew about his illegal activities. Jar entered knowing it was time to prove his allegiance to Bone and, no matter what it took, he was ready.

"Tonight, I get my life back, completely," Bone began. He was talking to no one in particular and everyone at the same time. Never mind that he didn't know Tom or that his audience had no clue what he was talking about. "And the nigga who stole part of that from me will pay me back by giving his. Tonight is a right of passage, of showing that you're ready to live this." Bone locked eyes with Jar. "It's an opportunity to see someone go down that left some jacked-up shit on your table." His attention turned to Bruce. Bruce was forced to run the dope game when Travis burned out on him years ago. "A time to come face to face with a ma'fucker you seen for years and you don't have no clue about who this nigga is. It's some shit you can take back to work with you and let everybody know exactly who that bitch is. We gonna set that bitch straight tonight and anybody else that is associated with 'em. Anybody got a problem with that can kiss they ass goodbye, too." Bone had begun rocking in his seat. "We all connected in this circle by one man and that piece of poison is why we're here."

Pieces of Bone's ranting applied to each of them but, as a whole, it left them all confused. They were certain of one thing: Somebody would die tonight. Kenya and Lisa were in the room with the door cracked and they were able to hear as well. Bone pulled out his nickel-plated Glock and motioned for Jar to come to him. "This is what you use. You shoot him right between the eyes." Bone had ice water running through his veins, but the boy that he mentored was fooled into believing that there was compassion in his heart. Bone stood up beside his protégé, put his arm around and guided him to the room where Travis hung.

Years of anticipating this moment never prepared Bruce for this. He thought he would be able to get Travis and Bone together and settle their differences peacefully. Of all the scenarios he'd imagined, he couldn't picture this. Why in the hell was Bone bringing a kid into something like this?

Bearing witness to a murder wasn't why Tom was here. Who had his cocaine and who was it from work that knew about it? Judging by the comments that were made by the loud mouth that headed up this party, he was down to two people: Patricia or Travis. He was leaning toward Travis after taking the present company into account. If Travis had to die—hell, if Patricia had to die—to preserve his name, so be it. As long as no dark clouds hung over his head, he was fine. The idea of being a witness to someone's fate being determined by a lunatic excited him.

A week ago, the sight of a nude man stretched out across a makeshift crucifix with a blanket draped over his head would have been a hell of a shock to Jar. Tonight, it didn't faze him. If this is what it took to put him over with Bone and get him under his roof, then this is what it would be. He entered the room undaunted by the task that laid in front of him.

Tom was a selfish rat who was eager to see who was in the room. He practically ran up their backs trying to follow behind them. Bruce lagged behind for fear of what he might see in that room. Rick preferred to use this opportunity to vacate the premises. He'd done all he was willing to do. It was more than enough for him to be the accomplice to murder, but he damn sure wasn't going to bloody his hands with a murder for Bone. He'd square up with Bone at another time and place. As he eased out the door, he never bothered to acknowledge the sentry Bone had standing by outside the door.

Bruce put his head down when he got a glimpse of the room. He couldn't bear the sight of Travis stretched out against the back wall. He was being treated like a farm animal being led to slaughter. He could hear Bone's ranting starting again. Bone was working the kid up with his incessant chatter. Tom and Jar proved to be a captive audience. Bruce wasn't. He could go no further than the doorframe. His own indecision paralyzed him. A muffled noise to his right grabbed his attention. As he turned to track the noise, he noticed the cracked door and quietly moved toward it.

Carefully, he nudged the door open. In the dimly lit room, he saw two pairs of eyes, full of tears. Two women were sitting in there, shivering from the cold. There were dried salt stains on their faces where tears had fallen. One woman looked vaguely familiar to Bruce. It took a few seconds to register with him, but he was sure it was Travis' wife. He saw fear in the eyes of both women. What else did his cousin have in mind? Bruce said nothing to them. He pulled the door, stepped away from it and did absolutely nothing.

CHAPTER 36

Escaping Park Slope undetected would not be a difficult task for Rick; he knew the area too well. He went to the back of the building to survey his best escape route. It was dark and abandoned. There were plenty of options to get out of the neighborhood he used to call home.

Leaving behind three people to die at the hands of a man who was hellbent on revenge was of little consequence to him. He walked out into the night doing what was best for him. What would be of importance to Rick Nixon was not making sure he was alone before he walked into the cold dark night. Rick should have kept walking; instead he went to the black Volvo. The six kilos of cocaine would serve as leverage against Bone.

Rick was a few feet away from the trunk of the Volvo when he heard the sound of a lead pipe smashing flesh and bone. Vaguely came the words, "dirty fucking cop." Pain accompanied the realization the he was the one who'd been struck in the head. The thought settled in as consciousness faded out. A flurry of blows with the lead pipe against his cranium followed. Rick Nixon's only good fortune on this night was that he did not know how brutally his life had been snatched from him.

The massive figure that had done the damage pulled the body back into the apartment building. The body that moments ago belonged to Rick Nixon was hidden in another abandoned apartment on the ground floor. Once the massive man completed that task, his sights were set on ascending to the third floor.

When you were knocked unconscious, there was a feeling you got when you were fading back into consciousness. Reality was just out of your grasp. It was like running desperately down a dark alley while a rabid dog was chasing you. You looked up and saw a ladder to a fire escape. If you could reach out and catch that bottom rung and pull yourself up, you were going to be all right. Travis' mind reached out for that bottom rung as he struggled to regain consciousness. Travis heard voices in echoes, but he couldn't decipher the words that were being spoken. He had to concentrate to open his eyes. Travis desperately needed to see what was going on. He had no idea of where in the hell he was.

As his eyes began to change the environment from shades of gray to color, Travis realized there was something covering his head and his body was extremely cold. His head moved from side to side, trying to see anything in the dimly lit room. Travis writhed as he felt the pain shooting through his arms. He jerked his head to see what was causing it. What he could not see through the blanket was that both of his arms were stretched out from his sides at a ninety-degree angle, pulled away from his nude body by ropes and duct tape. Travis struggled to look down to his feet that were also bound by rope and tape. He felt his body was strapped to something and suspended in air. Travis' attention was pulled back to the voices and he struggled to see something, anything through the blanket. He was able to make out silhouettes of people in the room. He was on display. He sensed the two figures as they came closer to him. Thoughts of what must have happened and how he had ended up like this ran amuck in his mind.

"This is the kind of shit that makes you a man." It came ominously from the voice in the shadows closest to Travis.

Travis knew that voice. It had been sixteen years since he'd heard that voice, but there was no mistaking it. It was the voice of Kwame "Bone" Brown.

"This is what it's all about, Baby Jar, protecting what's yours. Now, it's time for you to step up the game. Get right up on him, look into his eyes and let that ma'fucker see what you're about to do to him." Bone snatched the blanket off to reveal Travis to his audience. Tom Miller's suspicions were confirmed.

The nervous sixteen-year-old started to walk toward Travis, pointing a nickel-plated gun at him. He hadn't yet looked at the face of his victim. There was no mistaking that gun. It was the gun that Kwame had bought when he and Travis were fifteen years old. It shook in the hands of Baby Jar as he raised it.

"Welcome home, Perry Travis Moore. Bet you thought you'd never see this place again, did you, nigga?" Kwame was enjoying his position of power. "I guess it's true what they say, your past catches you."

The announcement of the name caused Baby Jar to look at his victim's face. His mouth dropped at the sight of Travis Moore. The weight of the gun felt like a hundred-pound dumbbell in his hand. Travis, with his mouth bound and gagged, could not say a word. His eyes, however, conveyed his surprise. Bone had this kid ready to kill for him.

The surroundings were now all too familiar to Travis. He knew exactly where he was. He was in the public housing community of Park Slope, back at the condemned apartment where he had grown up. It was the place that Travis had left behind fifteen years ago. Right now, being unconscious didn't seem so bad if his past had caught him. Judging by the position of his body, it had. He definitely wasn't all right.

"Do him! Do it, damn it!!" Bone waited for him to respond. "C'mon, son. Put it right between that nigga's eyes," he coaxed Jar.

The gun shook more noticeably in his hand now. Bone was losing his grip on him. Jar was ready to pull the trigger on anybody he didn't know; he wasn't prepared to pull it on someone he'd spent so much time with.

"Bone! What are you doing?" Bruce yelled at his cousin. He could tell that the kid was about to crack on him.

It was another voice that Travis recognized immediately. Bruce was here; he was looking out for him. Somehow or another, the keeper of his most hidden secret had found a way to him to help, even if it meant crossing the bloodline of his family.

"That kid can't handle this," Bruce pleaded with his cousin.

"Yes, he can!" Bone didn't look at his cousin; his piercing stare was locked on Jar. "This isn't the man you think he is. None of you!" Bone made sure his voice traveled to the other rooms.

Tom was on pins and needles, waiting for more details on Travis. This was the man who had investigated his connection to an embezzlement scandal and knew of his drug involvement. He desperately wanted to know how Travis was involved with these people and what dirty little stories existed about him.

"Bet he never told you he ran dope?" Bone was still locked on Jar, but he didn't wait for an answer. "I know that nigga was all up on you when you was in rehab. That nigga tell you that he started runnin' dope at fourteen, huh? He was tryin' to keep his crack-head mama off the streets. Keep her from ho'in' to get high. That slut woulda been a ho without the crack." Bone spit in Travis' direction. "I know about him 'cause I was runnin' the shit with 'em."

"Let it go, Bone," Bruce said.

"I ain't lettin' shit go. This nigga made me take the humble for the shit we was doin'. I was the one shipped to the detention center; and when I got back, that trick-ass nigga broke on me. I was on lockdown for thirteen months. Three big 'ma'fuckers did me while I was up in there. Hell nah, I ain't lettin' this go. I got an uncle who ain't never been heard from since that nigga left here. It's the same uncle that killed his ho-ass mama. Now, you back here like you the Big Willie." Bone looked at Tom. "Foolin' you crackers in the daytime, stealin' your coke in the nighttime. You still turnin' street profits, ain't you?"

Travis was there suspended in air, being accused of different things. Some were true and others he didn't know where they were coming from. Tom was in the room. Why was he here and why was Bone talking about cocaine and looking at Tom? The surprises kept coming. Travis wondered when Bruce was going to make his move to help him and stop pleading with Bone. *Make a move*, he wanted to say. Then, Travis realized that Bruce wasn't there to help him. Travis was in a bad way and, if Bruce was there to help him, he would have done something besides join the audience and observe the humiliation. Bruce was one of two living people that knew what had happened to Bone's uncle.

"You know what happened to my Uncle Otis, don't you?" Bone spoke directly to Travis.

Travis flashed his eyes around the room. Jar was still stunned by the sight of Travis. Tom was salivating, eager to see Travis take one between the eyes and let his secret die with Travis. Bruce gave him a dead stare that told him nothing; his allegiance was with Bone. No longer concerned with his secrets, Travis gave a half-nod.

"See, he nodded his head," Bone exclaimed. Whether it was a true admission or not, he was going to make it so.

Travis paid little attention to Bone; instead he thought of graduation night. All of the high school grads were out celebrating their new lease on life and looking forward to their future. Travis was looking for closure for his mother and Otis Reader. Otis, the Big O, was Bone's uncle, but he was of no relation to Bruce. He was a part-time pimp and a full-time heroin dealer. He was all of that, all of the time to Travis' mother. He was the one who had administered the fatal dose of heroin to his mother. Travis had hunted him down like a dog. He'd had the aid of Bruce Bowen. When they found him in an old housing project that was about to be demolished, he was high and apparently suffering no guilt from the death of Travis' mother. Bruce and Travis had beaten him, but there was no intent to kill him. Ray had pulled a .38 on them to protect himself, but he was the one who had fallen victim to it. All three of them had their hands on the gun when it had gone off. The blame between Travis and Bruce was never placed on one another. It was something they shared. That was until now; and gauging by Bruce's involvement with Bone, it looked to Travis that things had turned. Why else would Bone be placing that on him now?

Tom Miller was already piecing together a plot to work himself back into the good graces of Home Supply. A dead man can't deny any accusations made against him. He'd be a hero if he saved Home Supply the embarrassment of someone like Travis.

"You see what kind of man he is, Jar? He makes you think you got to live a certain way and he livin' foul. Don't believe me, you can check his car. He got six keys out there." Bone looked at Tom. "Your cocaine, Mister Miller."

AS THE IMPOSING FIGURE REACHED THE THIRD FLOOR, he smiled as he saw Bone's sentry standing guard. The sentry smiled and nodded his head as he recognized the figure in the hall. The smile was short-lived. When the figure was within striking distance, he whipped out his butterfly knife and slit the sentry's throat. He placed his hand across the sentry's mouth. As the sentry began to slump, the imposing figure twisted and jerked the sentry's head until he heard the snap of the neck. The limp body was guided to the floor with care. He paid little attention to the victim's blood as the warm fluid met with the cold air. It flowed from the body and some of it onto him. He continued to move forward into the abandoned apartment.

BABY JAR WAS NOT ABLE TO BRING HIMSELF TO PULL the trigger on Travis. He shamefully lowered the gun. It was a move that greatly disappointed Tom. He was betting on this kid to come through for him like a gambling junkie betting a grand on a forty-to-one longshot at the horse track. The move certainly didn't sit well with Bone.

"What the fuck are you doing!?" Bone snapped. "Shoot that man!!" Bone waited, but the kid didn't raise the gun back up. He didn't budge in the least. "You punk-ass, disloyal, bitch-made nigga. You don't kill 'em, I'm gonna kill you." He punched Jar square in the face with his bare hands. The blow sent Baby Jar sprawling to the floor, but he held onto Bone's pistol.

"Bone, leave the kid alone. This shit is between you and Travis. If you want him, you take him, cuz!" Bruce reached inside his jacket and pulled out the .38. He tossed it to his cousin. Bone caught it with his bare hands, and then turned it toward Perry Travis Moore. "Rick, bring his bitch in here. I want her to see this."

Bitch, Travis thought. *This sick bastard has my wife*, too. It was the first thoughts of Kenya since he'd regained consciousness. Bone stuck the gun between Perry's eyes and waited for Rick.

Travis recognized the .38 pointing at him; many years had passed since he'd last seen it. In those few seconds of waiting, Bone's demeanor changed. Travis could see Bone thinking. He also saw Bruce starting to make a move on Bone. Bruce was down for him, but he didn't make his move fast enough.

"You ma'fucker!" Bone turned the gun on Bruce. "Why you rollin' up on me, and why you call that nigga Travis?" He didn't bother waiting for Bruce to answer. Bone squeezed a round off into him. Bruce dropped instantly. The gun felt like it was falling apart after he'd shot it. Bone looked at the weapon. It was an old .38, similar to the one his uncle used to carry. Bone was willing to bet money that both Travis and Bruce had something to do with his uncle's disappearance. "Rick! Get both of them bitches in here." Bone looked at Travis. "You remember Rick Nixon, don't you?" There was no response from Rick. Bone turned to the door again. All he could see in his sight line was a terrified Tom Miller. Tom knew that a man who wouldn't hesitate to shoot his cousin, wouldn't have a problem shooting him.

Kenya and Lisa knew the imposing man that was standing in front of them, covered in blood. It was the man they knew as Fred. They also kept hearing the name Rick. In the other room, they could hear the names Bone, Kwame and Perry. Nobody was who they said they were. Fred nodded at them, then ducked behind Lisa and pushed her toward the bedroom.

Hearing the movement in the hall, Bone was satisfied that his orders were being adhered to, so he turned his attention back to the man he referred to as Perry. He started to rip the duct tape off Travis' face. Before he could, the voice behind him froze him in his tracks.

"Thought it was over with me, didn't you?" Flake said as he stood in the doorway, soaked in the blood of Bone's sentry, Rick,

Duke and his minions. Flake had had a busy night so far and he wasn't finished tallying his body count yet. Tom was scared out of his wits by this massive figure that reeked of death. He'd taken refuge in the corner of the room, cowering, hoping to be forgotten. He was curled up in a fetal position, praying this would all be over soon. Flake's presence didn't strike fear in only Tom. Bone, the man who feared no man, was rattled by the man he'd left for dead.

Bone turned quickly and attempted to fire a round at him. The old .38 misfired. Bone pulled the trigger again to no avail. Flake closed in on him like a lion cornering his prey; he didn't bat an eyelash as Bone attempted to fire at him. Flake was no longer at Bone's beck and call. He was no longer a sentry in Bone's army. He was a rebel, hellbent on reclaiming his manhood. Flake calmly closed the distance between them. Bone lashed out hopelessly at Flake in a fit of desperation. Bone hit him with the .38 and a number of punches. Flake never felt a single blow, never blinked his eyes. Nothing that Bone did to Flake could cause him pain.

"Let's see whose mama's got to get a black dress." Flake thrust his right hand into Bone's throat. It caused Bone to gasp for breath. He squeezed Bone's throat as if he were trying to turn coal into a diamond. He watched Bone's face twitch and contort in pain. He enjoyed every second as he watched Bone's body become weaker and weaker. Life was gradually leaving his body. When he was about to go, Flake released him. Flake leaned closer to Bone as he desperately tried to place some lifesaving oxygen back into his lungs. "Who's controlling your world now?" Flake asked after granting Bone a brief reprieve.

"You are," Bone desperately struggled to say, hoping that mercy would be given to his life.

"You got that right." Flake spared no mercy, and instead began squeezing again, harder than before. This time he would not relent until Bone's light was completely extinguished. Flake added the person who had ruled his life to his body count. Flake's life had ended a long time ago and owning up to his part in the last eight hours would be fine with him. He welcomed the opportunity to tell the police everything he could about Kwame "Bone" Brown; no matter what price he had to pay.

Baby Jar was staggering but standing. He'd witnessed the final stages of Bone's life. He raised the gun and pointed it at Flake. Flake didn't see the gun pointed at him, but sensed the danger. Slowly, he stood and turned to face his executioner. He looked at Jar, saw the confusion in his eyes and the unsteadiness of his hand. Flake shook his head slowly at Jar. He extended both of his hands, palms up, to Jar. Jar placed the nickel-plated Glock into Flake's hands.

There was an air of fear in the room as the massive beast held the weapon. He slid the weapon into his waistline. Flake's face was vaguely familiar to Travis. It was a face he associated with his hidden life and based on what Travis saw him do, it gave him reason for grave concern. Flake snatched Bone's coat off, walked over to the makeshift crucifix and draped it over the nude body of Travis. He also covered Travis with his blanket for added warmth. As brutal as he'd been moments ago, he was extremely gentle in freeing Travis; letting Travis know that he meant him no harm. The threat in the air subsided.

Bruce's movements drew their attention. Bruce gritted his teeth to fight through the pair. "I'm sorry, I couldn't stop..."

"Don't sweat it, you take it easy."

"I'm all right, go see about your wife. She was in your mom's room."

Travis didn't hesitate to get moving in that direction. Travis met eyes with Tom as he looked up from his fetal position. The former CFO for Home Supply was no longer excited by what was going on here. Laundering and fronting money for dope buys when nobody knew who he was thrilled him. But any thoughts that he may have had about being able to hang in the streets were squelched. Any hopes of hiding his secret life died when Travis survived. Travis walked past Tom, knowing he had nothing to fear from him. They were both men with secrets. Tom wasted little time getting out of there, but Travis knew they would be in touch with one another.

Kenya was still confined to her seat. She heard the gunshot and the scuffle that ensued. She thought she heard her husband's voice but wasn't sure. There was no way of knowing if he had been harmed. She breathed a sigh of relief when he walked into the bedroom.

"I'm sorry that I've brought all this on you," Travis said after he'd freed her arms and removed the tape from her mouth. Kenya said nothing. "You heard what he said?" Kenya nodded. She had heard Bone's accusations of murder. Travis hung his head in shame. Slowly, he started to back away from his wife. There was no way she'd want to have anything to do with him; no way she could accept that.

Instead of letting him pull away, Kenya grabbed him and pulled him to her. She pulled his head close to her womb and held him there. There was nothing left for him to hide. "Anything you have ever done or will ever do, I accept it in you." The words tore down walls and reached his soul. Travis wept quietly; he was at home in his wife's arms.

Bruce had been taken to the hospital by an ambulance. Before he left, he'd given the police his statement about his cousin and the attempt that Bone had made on his life. He also gave them the time of his cell phone conversation with Bone earlier that evening. He explained to the police that it was his intent to prevent this from happening but, instead, he had become a victim. The police chastised him for taking matters into his own hands and vowed to do a more in-depth investigation with him at the hospital.

The weapon Bruce was shot with was an old .38. Ballistics tests would be conducted on the gun. If he were lucky, the cops would trace it back to Bone's uncle; a man who hadn't been heard from in fifteen years.

Jar told the police his story of being coerced by Bone into a murder attempt. Travis, the target of the attempted murder, listened in borrowed clothes as Jar gave his statement. He heard the vulnerability of the man-child who was unwanted by his mother and manipulated by a man he had trusted. That was followed by Kenya and Lisa's recount of how they'd come to be there. As Travis listened to stories of chanced run-ins, he became acutely aware of how much of his life that Bone had gotten next to.

Flake filled in as many holes as he could about Bone to the police. He knew of the vendetta that Bone had against Travis and he gladly accepted responsibility for the work he'd done this evening. Bone's death was on his hands. The sentry who lay dead in the hallway was his, as was Rick Nixon in an apartment on the first floor, and the bodies at Duke's Salvage on Reames Road. Countless others were his, and he told the story to the police as if he were a father telling a bedtime story to a child.

Flake was taken into custody and this night would lead to an investigation of Bone and Travis. But, there was no doubt in Travis' mind that any investigation into him would turn up nothing on him. The only person who'd kept alive the thought of Perry Moore, the drug dealer, was Kwame "Bone" Brown; he was no longer among the living.

Tom Miller was among the living, but his threat to Travis was neutralized by what was hanging over his head. His testimony, if they got it, was nothing more than hearsay. Plus, he would be more concerned with protecting his golden parachute at Home Supply than cause any ripples that could jeopardize the windfall of cash he was looking for. Exposing Travis would expose him; that was more than enough motivation to guarantee his silence.

Tom was now a part of Travis' past. He would have to deal with him sooner or later. So much of his life that he'd kept hidden had come back to catch him. Because of it, he'd put a lot of other people in harm's way. Death had entered in the wake of his past. Travis had a choice to make. It was up to him to keep the shame of his past from haunting him again, or to keep running from it. Travis thought about his interpretation of insanity. It was repeating the same behavior and expecting a different result. Keeping more secrets would bring him similar results.

CHAPTER 37

This winter was shaping up to be one of the warmest ones on record in the last twenty-five years. One year to the day had passed since that cold February night when so many lives were in danger. In fact, so many lives had been changed. Kenya and Travis were expecting their second child in two months. Another child would fill the fourth bedroom in their house. The third bedroom was filled eight months ago when Kenya and Travis became legal guardians to Jarquis Love.

Travis had stayed in regular contact with Jar after that night in February. Four months later, Jar's mother was killed while trying to run a hustle on a drug dealer. Jar didn't get high and he didn't get drunk. He picked up a phone. Travis was the first person he called. Donna succumbed to the same life that had taken Travis' mother from him.

After getting the okay from Kenya, the Moores welcomed Jar into their home. The young man was flourishing; he was a sophomore with a 3.8 GPA. Jar was considering his options for college. A growth spurt prompted him to try out for the basketball team, where he was the backup point guard. He had recently picked up his one-year sobriety chip from Narcotics Anonymous, celebrating a complete year without the use of drugs, alcohol and, in his case, slinging dope.

This marked an interesting night of celebrations for a number of people. Travis was pacing the floor and looking at his watch. Tonight wasn't the night to be late. "Kenya, you're not ready yet?"

Travis yelled upstairs. "Bruce is going to be here any minute."

"Hold your horses," Kenya yelled back. "I don't move as fast as I used to."

Travis rolled his eyes and shook his head. There wasn't much else he could do. The next two months couldn't past fast enough. The one positive that he'd found was that at least this pregnancy wouldn't take them through the summer like Michael's.

"Your queen, sir," Jar said. His voice was happy and full of energy. It was apparent he was somewhere that he was wanted. Jar and Michael led Kenya down the stairway.

Kenya wore a long flowing black gown that complemented the black suit that Travis was wearing. Her face glowed as she descended the stairs with style and grace. If ever there was a woman who used pregnancy as a fashion statement, it was Kenya. She was beautiful.

"You take my breath away." Time didn't matter. Kenya was worth the wait. Travis wouldn't check his watch again.

"It's better than being out of breath," Kenya joked as she patted her stomach breathing a little heavier than normal.

They shared a laugh with each other. There was a sense of peace in their home. The dark clouds that once existed were completely removed. Travis had opened his past to anyone who needed to know about it and even to people that wanted to know. He no longer harbored who he used to be; he embraced it and used it to inspire others.

The investigation into his past drug activity lasted two months before it was officially dropped. Tracking information that was fifteen years old, on a man whom they never associated with drug activity, was not a task in which the police wanted to invest a lot of man-hours. That particular trail had gone cold a long time ago.

There was one secret that did remain, though. It was still kept between Travis and Bruce. The gun that Bruce was shot with belonged to Bone's uncle. Possession was nine-tenths of the law and Bone was the only person seen with the gun. Bruce and Travis had confirmed that. The disappearance of Bone's uncle was associated with Bone. Dead men don't talk and that's where the association would rest.

Bruce and Travis established an afterschool study program in the Park Slope Housing Community. It provided students, K-12, with access to computers, books and musical instruments. Home Supply was a primary benefactor to their program. The company could see firsthand what people from the Park Slope community could do when they knew there were other opportunities out there for them.

"What time is Bruce supposed to be here?" Kenya was starting to fan herself. The walk downstairs and the climate heated her up.

"Should be any minute." Out of habit, Travis started to check his watch but stopped himself.

"It's not too late to get a sitter," Kenya said to Jar. "You could go to the CD listening party with us?"

"That's all right. I'm going to hang out...at home with Michael. You'll have a good time. I got your cell number."

Travis smiled, glad that Jar was comfortable calling this home. Michael was glad to have him around for sure. He always followed Jar around, copying him. As much as Michael gained from having Jar around, Jar had gained so much more from Michael. Jar was able to be a kid again.

The rumblings in the driveway drew everyone's attention. It could be heard getting louder as it pulled closer to the house. Seconds later, the doorbell rang and Kenya answered it.

"Girl, you got to see the limo my man has got out here!" Lisa exclaimed.

Bruce had rented a stretch limousine to take them to the CD listening party for his hot new artist, burning up the charts—he was simply known as Soul. Bruce stood behind Lisa and winked his eye, then nodded his head in the direction of the white limo. They would definitely be arriving in style tonight.

Bruce was celebrating more than the CD release of his artist. It was also one year ago to the day that he'd met Lisa. They had been virtually inseparable ever since. That night, filled with all its dangers and close calls, had definitely changed a lot of people's lives. Lisa was a different person for it, and Bruce was in love with her.

Travis looked at the limo, the couple in front of him, his wife, and Jar. A brief moment of reflection left him with one thought: out of negative beginnings can come positive endings.

ABOUT THE AUTHOR

J. Leon Pridgen II is originally from Aberdeen, Maryland, but makes his home in North Carolina, with his wife and two children. His journey in life so far has taken him from the jungles of Panama with the 82nd Airborne Division, to Hollywood film sets starring opposite Halle Berry and Omar Epps in the college football film, *The Program*. He has performed in numerous theatrical productions. One of his best and most challenging experiences was working with Director Larry Leon Hamlin on the August Wilson play, *Fences*. Visit the author at facebook.com/jleon.pridgenii

DISCUSSION QUESTIONS

1. After reading *Hidden Secrets, Hidden Lives*, what is your feeling toward Travis Moore and the life he led in order to better himself?

2. Have you ever done the right thing for the wrong reason or the wrong thing for the right reason?

3. Did you find yourself understanding Kwame "Bone" Brown, maybe even sympathizing with his belief that Travis abandoned him?

4. Was it fair for Kenya to spend that many years with Travis and not completely know his life story or should Travis have informed her immediately about his past even though he believed it would never be part of the life they shared?

5. Do you think it is common for young men such as Jarquis Love or young women to be manipulated and enticed by the drug game?

6. Would you be able to keep your own secrets hidden from the people closest to you?

7. Could Travis ever have been able to make peace with his past by mentoring young men with similar backgrounds as his own or did he need Kwame to force him to confront his past?

8. Is it possible that the harder you try to keep something secret, the more you succeed at giving it power to cause you harm?

9. What kind of friendship do you think that Travis and Bruce will share going forward in their lives?

10. Have you or a family member fallen prey to this type of lifestyle and how were you or your family member able to pull out of that situation?

11. After reading *Hidden Secrets, Hidden Lives*—do the ends "sometimes" justify the means?